DAVID TO
SHOULDI
HUGE HA
SQUEEZED

For a moment Lisa thought he would shake her. "Lisa, we both know where the trouble lies. We both know who ordered the sabotage, who's behind the threats." David said the name, spitting it out, as though tasting something foul. "Victor Sun Chen."

Lisa let her breath hiss out. There had been a time when even the passing mention of Sun Chen's name had made her shudder with revulsion. *But I have come a long way since that time,* she thought. *I have kept David from suspecting how deeply run my feelings about Victor. How well I know his nature . . .*

"You're crying," she heard David say.

"No. I cannot be—" She touched her cheeks and found them wet. "I'm sorry."

"What's made you so sad?" David produced a silk handkerchief, and Lisa dried her eyes. She did not answer him. "Lisa—"

David moved close, following Lisa as she tried to back away. She pressed herself against the wall of a building. His breath was hot and sweet against her skin. He kissed her then, and Lisa returned the kiss before she realized what she was doing. By then it was too late, and she opened her mouth to his . . .

Books in the HAROLD ROBBINS PRESENTS™ Series

Blue Sky
  by Sam Stewart

At the Top
  by Michael Donovan

The White Knight
  by Carl F. Furst

High Stakes
  by John Fischer

Acres in the Sky
  by Adrien Lloyd

Superplane
  by Carl F. Furst

Fast Track
  by Michael Donovan

Published by POCKET BOOKS

Harold
Robbins
Presents:

Fast
Track

A Novel by
Michael Donovan

PUBLISHED BY POCKET BOOKS NEW YORK

Another *Original* publication of POCKET BOOKS

POCKET BOOKS, a division of Simon & Schuster, Inc.
1230 Avenue of the Americas, New York, N.Y. 10020

ISBN: 0-671-61871-7

First Pocket Books printing June 1987

10 9 8 7 6 5 4 3 2 1

POCKET and colophon are registered trademarks
of Simon & Schuster, Inc.

HAROLD ROBBINS PRESENTS is a trademark
of Harold Robbins.

Printed in the U.S.A.

For Donna and Pat O'Rourke:
Paperback Princess and Prince

From the diaries of
James Wellington

11 January 1981: The team has been installed in their fine new facility. New Mexico should agree with them. *"Clear air promotes clear thinking,"* Ernest Schliemann said to me before I departed. I hope he is right: we will all need clear heads as we embark upon this project.

And yet I feel no trepidation. Rather, there is a nearly palpable excitement at the thought of what we seek to create. A universal cure. A programmable agent ready to do combat with any disease we choose.

An end to illness! Change the world!

6 July 1982: Ellen Siebert called last night. They've cracked the molecular code and are hot on the trail of control over it. Designing the mutability that will enable us to program our little gene to eradicate viruses harmful to human life is the next step. Are we ready for it?

10 October 1982: I have resigned the presidency of Wellington Laboratories, in favor of David. My son will make a fine CEO. Monica is delighted. A year after our marriage she continues to thrill me, and tells me that she feels the same. The age difference does not matter to her and, in truth, I feel more virile than I have in years. Monica says she is looking forward to having me home more often now that I am no longer in the center seat.

I will, however, continue to manage the New Mexico

7

project, my devastating little secret. David and Monica agree that it should remain my baby.

21 October 1983: The climate in the country is not favorable toward genetic engineering, and I think there would be an angry distrust of engineering on such a scale as New Mexico promises. Particularly since we have come so far in secret, for all that our facility and procedures adhere to international regulations and constraints governing genetic experimentation.

My mind is made up. Our project must continue shrouded in absolute secrecy. We will deal with the public—and the government!—only when we must.

13 September 1984: I had a dream last night.

There was a battlefield, at once infinite and sharply proscribed. Fierce war was being waged there, with no quarter given by either combatant. Unambiguous war as well: the defenders were virtuous and deserved to live, the attackers malefic and unstoppable. The battle and the war, my dream made clear, belonged to the attacker.

And then a new combatant entered the field of combat. Devastatingly effective, this new weapon shredded the invaders effortlessly, even as it went about rebuilding the damage already done. The war ended swiftly. For once, goodness—health, well-being—emerged triumphant.

When I awoke I had a name for our advance: omnigene.

19 June 1985: Have I been open enough with David and Monica? Certainly I have kept them appraised of each step toward the realization of omnigene, nor have they been kept in the dark about my reasons for maintaining absolute secrecy around the project.

But my growing suspicion is that once omnigene is finished our problems will only be starting. There will be the usual endless rounds of review and delay by the *bureaucracy, complicated by what will undoubtedly be a large scandal over our hiding the research for so many years.*

23 January 1986: A wild wintry day here in my beloved North Carolina mountains. Monica and I lingered late in our bed, making lazy love. She delights me and my love for her remains as boundless as on the first day of our marriage. She still maintains that my age is of no importance to her, and when I look into her eyes I believe her. I do love her so.

9 May 1986: A conversation with Xiang Peng, and the most difficult decision I have yet made. Xiang now knows about omnigene, but I have not yet told David and Monica of his knowledge, or of the offer he has made. It is an offer that tempts me greatly, in truth, and an offer that would be of benefit to the world. I have given Xiang a letter to deliver to David in the event of my death.

17 May 1986: I am not feeling well, and am filled, suddenly, with strange forebodings. I'm very tired . . .

1

THE JETFOIL SPED westward through a splendid sunset, bound for Macau.

The last time I made this journey, David Wellington thought, *it was for pleasure. This time*—he wasn't sure. Two hours earlier he'd been relaxing in his suite at Hong Kong's Mandarin Hotel, catching his breath in preparation for a long evening's work. There remained a small mountain of memoranda pertaining to his just-completed purchase of the Malaysian pharmaceutical distribution firm. Nor did the demands of Wellington Laboratories' other operations diminish simply because the company's president was engaged in complex negotiations overseas. David Wellington planned a sequestered night, surrounded by nothing more exciting than briefcase, computer terminal, telephone. He'd drawn the drapes tight against the countless distractions Hong Kong offered after dark. If he got through enough work by ten, David promised himself a late snack in the hotel's Chinnery Bar. Otherwise—room service again.

Then a message arrived that changed all of his plans. *Join me for dinner tonight in Macau? It may be worth your while. Lisa Han.*

Business or pleasure? David wondered. *After all, she turned down every invitation I extended.* For the past ten days he'd been working closely with her, bringing to completion two months of hard research and tough bargaining. The final purchase price had not been cheap, but the deal was good business. With

Kwang Pharmaceuticals now a part of Wellington Laboratories, David's strength throughout Indonesia and free Southeast Asia was greatly enhanced. The Japanese pharmaceutical market alone was second only to the American and combined with the rest of Asia, there was a potential for profit in the region far beyond that in the West. *And we need that strength,* he thought. *We need an Asian success.*

Things were not dire—yet. But the Pacific Rim strategy that David had unveiled with such confidence three years earlier was proving costlier than anticipated. Over the past three years Wellington Labs had scored some points, made a few inroads here and there, but had yet to establish itself as a serious Asian competitor. *It's not enough to have the best products,* David thought. *We do. But to get the products to market you've got to fight government regulations, distrust of foreign medicines, graft, blackmail, and kickbacks.* Suddenly David grinned. *None of which is all that different from the way business is done elsewhere.* The grin faded quickly. David's cockiness had long been replaced with a grim resolve and an unshakable determination. *But the price gets higher and higher,* he thought.

There had been incidents of sabotage aimed at Wellington Laboratories property and personnel since the company's entry into Asian markets. Lately these incidents had become more frequent. In two cases they had been fatal. Wang Derui, the best salesman in Taiwan, killed by an explosive charge placed beneath the hood of the new Cadillac of which he was so proud. Just last week, Elizabeth Jonklaas, director of Sri Lankan operations, had been murdered at her desk in Colombo. She'd been working late, putting together a plan to capitalize on Wellington's growing market share in Sri Lanka, a growth that was largely her doing. David took a day off from negotiations with Lisa Han and flew to Colombo for Elizabeth's

11

funeral. He did what he could to boost morale in the office, but with Elizabeth gone it would be some time before the operation regained its momentum.

David thought of the long months he and Elizabeth had spent assembling an effective Sri Lankan organization. There had been no end to the licenses and certifications required by the government. For a while he had thought they would never succeed in establishing a manufacturing facility, as in essence he'd been forced to create his own labor market, bringing in a staff to train pharmaceutical technicians from scratch. Yet Elizabeth had negotiated the bureaucracy effortlessly, never complaining. The sales force had been little easier to launch, as David would not relax the Wellington Labs tradition of highly motivated, superbly prepared detail men and women. It was a point of pride with him that every member of Wellington's field sales force be able to answer, clearly and honestly, any question a physician or pharmacist might have about the products they represented.

Perseverance had paid off. Wellington Labs' manufacturing and office facilities on the outskirts of Colombo were models of modern efficiency. Computerized manufacturing processes were carefully overseen by technicians in sterile clothing. David thought that there were operations in the United States that could take a page from the quiet pride and competence with which his Sri Lankans went about their duties. He was proud of them—and even more proud of Elizabeth, who had made it all a reality. Her death hurt him more than he could say.

David turned to the window and for a moment watched Lantau Island recede, putting thoughts of business from his mind. The jetfoil would reach Macau within the hour, and there would be time enough then. Part of David hoped Lisa's motives were impure. The only thing as attractive as the deal Lisa Han brought him was its architect herself. David was two inches over six feet tall, but Lisa could look him directly in the eye. She wore her height gracefully, cloaking her lithe curves in businesslike but not severe silk suits, favoring light colors that handsomely set off her black hair and fine features. She cloaked those features as well, though, with a reserve and concentration as complete as any David had encountered. *Maybe Macau will be lucky for me,* he thought. *It has been before.*

He had not been to the peninsula in a year, but that last visit had initiated a relationship that had not yet ended. Frustrated over the poor projections from Wellington Labs' first year of Asian competition, David planned a month in the region to shake things up. Halfway through his stay, he'd stolen an evening for himself, and hopped a jetfoil for Macau. He was in the mood to gamble. *But I did not bet on encountering Hilary Bishop.*

He had not seen her approach the table. After an hour of shooting craps to outstanding effect, David had carried his luck to the roulette wheel. In this instance, at least, luck proved transferrable: his numbers never missed and the size of his winnings began to attract an audience. David ignored the crowd—his attention was focused fully on the spin of the wheel, the skitter and settle of the ball, the surge of excitement that accompanied each win. By the time he'd tripled the money taken from the craps table, he was ready to try his hand at cards. David signaled the croupier to convert his winnings into manageable denominations, tipped him handsomely, and turned from the roulette wheel.

"Hello, David," said Hilary Bishop softly. She stood facing him, poised and calm, a cool island in the midst of the clamor of Lisboa Casino.

For a moment David did not speak. Hilary's blond hair was swept back, held in place by a velvet ribbon. There was a slight flush evident at the line of her high cheekbones, and a chip of diamond glinted at the lobe of each ear. The lights of the casino were caught and cast back by the facets of the gold mesh camisole worn above a long, slitted skirt. A single pearl was suspended from a simple chain above the cleft of her full breasts. Hilary drew a long, slow breath, her tanned shoulders rising.

"Hilary," David said, surprised to hear a hoarseness in his voice.

Hilary waited for David to step forward, then offered her cheek for a quick kiss. "It's been a long time," she said.

"Yes."

She showed David a smile. "You seem to be having quite a streak tonight. Don't let me interrupt."

David shook his head. "Are you gambling?" he said. "Can you join me?"

Hilary studied David for a moment. David looked beyond her and noticed for the first time a tall young man whose eyes were fixed upon David and Hilary. A moment later Hilary turned and raised a dismissive hand. For a moment a pout clouded his features, and his lips pursed petulantly. Then he tugged the sleeves of his dinner jacket tight, spun and left the gaming room. Hilary turned back to face David. "I'd love to join you," she said, some hint of mockery in her voice.

David raised his eyebrows. "Your companion?"

"Nils?" Hilary's chuckle was deep. "A spoiled rich boy from Norway." Her eyes grew dreamy. "My Scandinavian diversion, nothing more."

David hesitated for only a second. "Then shall we?" he said, and offered his arm.

They adjourned from the Lisboa to the floating casino known as the Pirate Ship. David proved more than buccaneer enough for the croupiers. His luck held and he emerged from a two-hour duel with an implacable blackjack dealer damp with perspiration, but three thousand dollars wealthier. Throughout the game Hilary's arm brushed often against his, and more than once he felt the pressure of a breast. Her breath was warm when she leaned close to whisper encouragement. The one time she tried a hand of her own she lost on the third card. "Count me out," she said, and winked at David. "Besides, it's more fun to watch."

"Not everything," said David.

Hilary's eyes grew wide. "No," she said and caught her bottom lip between perfect teeth.

By midnight they were back at the Lisboa, sharing a secluded table for two at A Galera. Their attention was divided between a platter of succulent spiced prawns and each other's eyes. "How is Monica?" Hilary asked, giving voice to a question that had hung unspoken.

David smiled. "She's doing all right. She misses him a lot. When I talked to her the other day she said Tallpines was still empty. You ought to pay her a visit."

The corners of Hilary's full lips turned up. She nodded. "I will. Some weekend when you're in residence."

David felt a sudden surge of longing to be at the family estate in the North Carolina mountains. He'd virtually grown up at Tallpines, knowing and loving every inch of the Wellingtons' thousand acres. *But it's hard to go back since Dad died. It still hurts.*

"They had six years," Hilary said.

"Six good years." David raised his wine glass to his lips and sipped chilled Casal Mendes. "To everyone's surprise."

Hilary shook her head in disagreement. "I never disagreed. I thought from the first they were a perfect match."

"You were nearly alone." James Wellington's marriage to a woman forty years his junior—seven years younger than his son, in fact—had set more than one tongue to harsh gossip and comment. But Monica Davenport proved to be wonderful for James. The marriage grew even more successful after he, as a first anniversary present to his wife, announced his surprise retirement from the helm of Wellington Laboratories in favor of his only child. *Five years,* David thought. *So fast.*

Hilary lifted her fork, but grew thoughtful and put it down next to her plate. She looked into David's eyes. "How about you?" She reached across the table and fleetingly touched his wrist. "How are you doing?"

David did not answer immediately. It was a tough question. "I miss him," he said at last, slowly. "It's only been a few months. I'm learning."

"You're learning quickly," she said. "The whole industry's talking about you."

"Waiting for me to stumble," David said. He speared a prawn and chewed it slowly before continuing. "Dad still casts a long shadow."

Hilary would have none of it. "Don't be modest with *me,* David. You were standing on your own long before he died. He was terrifically pleased with what you're doing with the company. Monica *was* my roommate, after all. She told me all he talked about was you."

David changed the subject a bit; he did not want to talk about business—his own business at any rate. "I saw *your* father, not too long ago. He seemed . . . unchanged."

Hilary chortled and pressed a hand to her chest. *"Monroe? Change?* He's still doing business the way he started—trading companies now instead of horses." She winked at David. "The Bishop Group's not giving big old Wellington Laboratories any trouble, now, is it?"

Monroe Bishop had built quite a company on horsetrader's instincts and gambler's nerves. His reputation—well-deserved—was for a willingness to go for the jugular. He'd entered the pharmaceutical industry in the late sixties, and a joke quickly grew that Monroe Bishop needed no skeletons in his own closet—he had the bones of a dozen companies he'd stripped bare. David chose his words carefully. "We're feeling the effects of Monroe's way of doing business," he said. "Everybody is."

Hilary was amused by David's tact. "That's a nice way of putting it. You can't deny that he gets results."

"I wouldn't think of trying," said David Wellington.

"And just think. Someday it'll all be mine. That means you and I will be competitors."

David gave a genuine laugh. "Now, there's a prospect that could make Wellington shudder."

"I think I'd rather be friends," said Hilary.

"To that, then." David raised his glass and touched it to Hilary's.

After the toast, Hilary said, "Monroe keeps talking about retiring to the farm and raising horses. I think he wants to find himself a nice young wife and have the kind of life your father did."

"But there's only one Monica."

"Oh, yes. You're right about that."

David finished the last of the prawns. He was curious. "What about you, Hilary? What brings you to Macau?" He narrowed his eyes. "Nils?"

Hilary did not hide her laughter. "David, I thought that was clear. Nils was nice—but a diversion. And not quite so nice a diversion as *he* thinks. As for Macau—why, I'm looking for excitement."

David pushed his plate aside. The restaurant grew more warm. "And have you found it?"

Hilary took a moment longer with the last of her meal. "I'll let you know," she said.

Over Courvoisier their conversation became soft, almost whispered. "I was planning to return to Hong Kong tonight," David said when they left the table.

Hilary stared up at him. "Must you?"

"No."

"Are you going to?"

"No," he said with no hesitation at all.

"I have a suite at the Excelsior," Hilary said. "Walk me there?"

"Of course."

Hilary's suite offered a high, endless view, showing the Pearl River. The waters glowed beneath a full moon. David stood close to Hilary before the wide window. For a time neither spoke. Hilary stepped out of her shoes, then padded over to switch off the lights. The moon's glow flooded the room. Hilary became a shimmering, seductive wraith who approached soundlessly. David was taller than Hilary, and put his large hands on her shoulders, but she would not let him pull her into an embrace. "Wait," she whispered, her warm breath on his throat. She reached up and unknotted his tie, brushed his dinner jacket from his broad shoulders.

David let the jacket slip away, then took Hilary into his arms. She offered no resistance. David lowered his mouth to hers, began a gentle kiss that quickly became brutal. The kiss broke and David sought the steady, pounding pulse of Hilary's throat. Her long fingernails traced patterns on his back. Hilary said his name, her breath hot in David's ear. They discarded their clothing, one piece at a time, becoming more bold in their exploration of each other. The tips of Hilary's breasts scalded David's palms. When he entered her, she cried out as she rose with him, then sank back shivering in release.

It took us six months of occasional meetings just to find all the pleasures our bodies could give, David thought. The memory made him warm. He'd never known a lover as insistent and adventurous as Hilary Bishop. He'd returned in a groggy daze to Hong Kong after their first night together, and hadn't been worth a damn at the day's round of meetings and conferences. By the time he reached his hotel that night, he wanted nothing more than a long soak in a steaming tub and ten hours' sleep. Stretched out in the tub, a hot washcloth draped across his face, David had not heard Hilary enter the steam-filled room. He gave a startled jump when she said his name.

Hilary stood beside the tub, a light robe loosely belted at her waist. David stared at her for a moment before he found his voice. "How—"

"I bribed the concierge," she said with a smile and a shrug. "He knows me." She moved next to the tub. "Are you unhappy?"

"No," said David, not certain. "Of course not."

Hilary removed her robe and stood nude before him. David forgot his reservations and took her hand, drawing her gently into the hot water with him. He bathed Hilary, and she him. They took a long time drying each other with thick towels before making gentle love. David and Hilary fell into a deep sleep with their arms entwined.

And woke up and should have ended it there, David recalled with regret. His reverie faded and as he looked about the jetfoil, he grew more reflective. He had not wanted to have an affair with Hilary, and yet he had not fought against her pull. *Not enough to argue that I was busy—not with the kind of pain we have caused each other lately.* He gazed for a while through a spray-flecked port. He had not been paying attention then, seven months earlier, when Hilary had taken it upon herself to see that she and David were together first thing in the morning and last thing at night. It was easier just to go along with her, and David also admitted that she was wonderful company both in and out of bed. He said nothing when she moved a set of essentials into David's Atlanta townhouse, nor had he objected when he found a shaving brush and mug with his name on them occupying a central spot in the medicine cabinet of Hilary's Baltimore apartment. *We enjoyed each other's company, and I told myself that there was nothing more to it. And I was distracted.* David's business responsibilities, and the growing burdens Hilary handled for the Bishop Group, kept them separated most of the time. When they were together, it was like being on an island in the midst of a sea of schedules. *Neither of us used the word love,* David thought. *I because I did not feel it. And Hilary?* They met at Tallpines for a couple of long weekends. It was Monica Wellington who broached the subject at last, teasing them on New Year's Eve about the possibility of a spring wedding.

David shifted in his seat, glancing toward the bow where a deckhand was wheeling a refreshment cart, and signaled for a bottle of Kirin. *Monica had been delighted—her college roommate and her husband's son: too rich!* She was more animated than at any time since James's death. Jokes were made about the merger of the two pharmaceutical families, a union of David and Hilary doubtless presaging the union of their companies. The rest of the New Year's celebration was a charade. David did not speak up immediately. *It had already gone too far to be set straight easily.* And he admitted to himself that the relationship pleased him in many ways. Nor could he doubt that a combination of their companies would exert a powerful influence upon the pharmaceutical industry. Wellington Laboratories was nearly a century old, well-established, with healthy reserves of cash and a large, steady income from Pandrex and other products that were among the world's most frequently purchased and prescribed remedies. The Bishop Group was adventurous and ambitious, with an impressive record of luck and foresight. Monroe Bishop had gutted a dozen companies, but he'd also assembled a core selection of products that promised to be the foundation of a major pharmaceutical empire. *Between Hilary and myself, we could have remade the industry,* David thought.

The Kirin was cold. David took a long swallow of the Japanese beer, and then another. A spring wedding, he thought, annoyed with himself. It never should have gone that far. Before he was able to speak honestly with Hilary, he found himself standing beside her under a dreary February sky while her father was buried. The massive coronary that ended Monroe Bishop's life left Hilary in complete control of the Bishop Group. David gave Hilary what comfort he could, but she would not take the time to mourn. He thought he saw in her face an expression of his own. *She's had the reins of responsibility thrust on her,* he observed, *far more quickly than happened to me.* David understood now that James's unexpected death had left him feeling vulnerable for the first time in years. He'd taken Hilary into his bed and his life as a balm against the loneliness he felt. Seeing it clearly, he wanted to tell her, but he waited. It seemed too soon after Monroe's death.

For a while he hoped the confrontation would not be necessary. Suddenly Hilary had little time for him. It was clear before Monroe Bishop was ten days gone that his daughter intended to run his company her own way. She would not be a figurehead, not even close. A whirlwind of work swept Hilary away from David, and he did not object. For the first time in months he found himself going out with other women. His business time was filled with plans for his Hong Kong trip. He did not call Hilary, and was distant when she phoned him. David used his contacts to keep watch over Hilary's management of the Bishop Group. Hilary blossomed swiftly at business, completing a complex transaction and takeover that Monroe had started. It was the sort of maneuver that David disliked—with Hilary using pressure to force the target company into a corner, then swallowing it whole. She did not even wait a decent interval before dissolving those aspects of the company that did not interest her. *Like research, marginally profitable but vital medicines, many employees.* There were moments when David offered quiet thanks that he and Hilary were ended as an item. He threw himself into preparations for his trip.

This trip, David thought, *I nearly got away clean.*

David spent the weekend before departure at Tall-pines, hoping to collect his thoughts and gather his energies. He would need both—a grueling agenda was planned. It was with some dismay that David heard Hilary's voice calling him across the wide expanse of lawn late on the Saturday afternoon before he left.

It had been weeks since he'd seen her. Hilary had changed. The job of running the Bishop Group had taken the last hints of girlhood from her face. She stood taller, he thought, walked faster. Hilary talked fast, too, her conversation focused almost obsessively upon her accomplishments in the few months since the company became hers. "People are talking about the Bishop Group, David," she said, walking him back to the terrace. She held his arm and he could not shrug her away. "I like that. Get them scared and you're halfway home."

"You're certainly succeeding at that," said David carefully.

Evidently, he hadn't been careful enough. Hilary's eyes widened, her nostrils flared. "You disapprove," she said with disbelief. "Is that what I heard—disapproval?"

David shook his head and did not bother to watch his words. "That's just not for me. I disapprove of short-term strategies—if you want my opinion."

Hilary released his arm and took a step away from him. "I'm not sure I do," she said. "But of course I couldn't expect Wellington Laboratories to be impressed."

David said nothing, waited.

Hilary did not hide her contempt. "You run such a solid, stable business, David. Steady growth, steady profits, and dull, dull, *dull.*" She stared hard at him.

David spread his hands wide. If this was the opportunity he had, he would take it. "We're different people, Hilary. Maybe more different than we've noticed before."

She was paying no attention. "'Short-term,' you said. That's what you think I'm doing?"

"Yes. And it's dangerous."

"Kind of you to worry about me," Hilary snapped, almost sneering.

David did not speak until he'd drawn a long breath. "You like having people scared of you, Hilary. But one of these days, one of these *deals,* you're liable to run into someone who's even scarier than you. Someone who plays harder ball, for higher stakes. And then all your posturing and footwork won't be enough."

"Posturing!"

David did not stop. "My opinion? I think that good business is good business. Especially for us, especially for our industry. I know how much responsibility we carry. The better we live up to those responsibilities, the better our business will be. There are things to consider, Hilary, beyond how quickly you can absorb a company's assets and discard its . . . responsibilities."

"That's *enough!*" Hilary said. "I won't be lectured in business ethics by you. I don't need this." She looked at him and for just a second David thought he saw, deep in her eyes, a flash of the spirit that had attracted him to her in Macau. But just a flash, gone instantly, replaced by something fierce and hard. "And I don't need you, David. I'm going back to Baltimore."

Where, David supposed, she was now. Monica had been displeased by Hilary's abrupt departure from Tallpines. David overheard her urging Hilary to relax and accept this as just a lovers' tiff. "James and I had one two days before the wedding," she said. David himself had declined to discuss the matter with Monica, and left the mountain estate sooner than he planned.

The jetfoil shed speed preparatory to making dock in Macau. Lisa Han's secretary had informed David that he would be met at the dock. David leaned close to the window and scanned the busy pier that led to the passenger terminal. He realized suddenly how very much he wanted to see Lisa Han. Over the past ten days he'd grown aware of her in ways that had little to do with the business between them. *No business tonight,* he hoped. David glanced around the interior of the jetfoil. In the seat across the aisle from him sat an elderly Chinese man, rubbing his temple. He reached into his jacket and produced a packet of medicine, then signaled a deckhand for a glass of water. The bright yellow foil on the medicine packet was familiar, the ideogram on the wrapper accompanied by more familiar English lettering: *Pandrex.* Wellington Labs' most famous product, the company's analgesic annuity.

An omen, David thought, grinning. *But for good or bad?* There was no way to tell. As the jetfoil bumped against the pier, David's mind flashed once more through the night in Macau when he'd met Hilary. *Of course, the way things turned out maybe my luck was not all good that night.* He thought of Lisa Han, though, and found himself swept with a sudden surge of desire so sharp he could taste it.

2

DAVID DID NOT spot Lisa until he disembarked from the jetfoil, but once he caught sight of her he did not look away. Lisa was dressed less formally than usual for business, the padded shoulders and thigh-length tunic of her Caroline Herrera pants suit emphasizing her height and the richness of her figure. Lisa spotted David simultaneously, showed him a quick smile of recognition, and waved before walking swiftly toward him. Her black hair fell in open curls past her shoulders, bouncing in rhythm with her purposeful stride. Men on the docks paused when she passed. Lisa met David halfway—*as always,* he thought—her right hand extended. "David," she said warmly as they shook hands. "I'm so glad you came."

"I make it a point never to decline a cryptic invitation," David Wellington said. *Be careful,* he reminded himself. He'd learned during their dealings how easy it was to become lost in Lisa's dark eyes. He gave a gentle squeeze as Lisa withdrew her hand from his. He thought he saw a slight flush rise at her high cheeks.

"I apologize for being cryptic," Lisa said. "But I have no doubt that you will be glad you made the trip."

"I already am."

Passengers from the jetfoil pushed past them. "Come," she said, glancing at the Cartier watch on her left wrist. "We have some time before we eat, and a distance to go. Do you mind a long walk?"

"In Macau?" said David with a grin. "With you? Lead on."

Lisa set a brisk pace, guiding David from the jetfoil pier and past the crowded passenger terminal. They walked inland, David delighting as always in the peninsula's mingling of Oriental and Portuguese architecture. Four centuries of Portuguese rule—and despite its recent proclamation as a Chinese territory under Portuguese rule—suffused every aspect of Macau.

To David's right rose Guia Hill, the peninsula's highest point. Perched atop the hill stood the thick walls of Guia Fortress, and the oldest of all the lighthouses on the Chinese coast. Even in these days of satellite tracking and Loran, David noted with a smile, the keepers of Guia lighthouse continued to fly the traditional Chinese bamboo weather symbols, dangling them from a high yardarm to warn sailors. David squinted to see the symbol more clearly. "Good weather."

Lisa nodded. "For a time. We're quite fortunate this evening. The rainy season will be upon us soon." They stepped aside as a tourist-laden pedicab cycled by, its operator pedaling furiously while its occupants clicked their Nikons and Canons.

Once past the verdant park that surrounded Guia Fortress, David and Lisa took a course that let them skirt the busy center of Macau. The evening air was warm, and heady with the rich scent of spices. A gentle breeze bore the clatter of commerce and conversation through the streets.

"Do you know Macau?" Lisa asked.

David thought of Hilary, then pushed her from his mind. "I've visited." He glanced up and down the street until he spotted an apothecary's shop. "I do business here," he said, pointing to the shop.

"You're doing a great deal of business throughout this part of the world," Lisa said.

"More, now that *our* business has proved successful," David said.

"Kwang Pharmaceuticals should serve Wellington Laboratories admirably," Lisa said, her tone a bit distant. "It's a good match for you. And your resources will permit Kwang to develop the sort of firm that he could not on his own." She graced David with a smile. "Everyone wins."

"Even you?" he asked. She did not answer, and they walked for a time in silence. When David's shoulder brushed Lisa's at one point, she quickly put space between them.

"I'd like to get to know Macau better," David said, largely to get her talking again.

"It's a wonderful place, David. I'm very fond of it. The Macanese have done an outstanding job of maintaining their independence from the mainland, yet we are within a couple of miles of the border." Lisa glanced at David. "You must visit the Barrier Gate. The entranceway to China."

They turned left, down bustling Rua do Campo, one of Macau's busiest thoroughfares. "Perhaps you could show it to me," David suggested. "Will we have time to play tourist?"

Lisa looked away from him. They walked a few steps before she stopped and spoke. "David. Perhaps I should clarify something now. Before there is any misunderstanding."

"Yes?"

Lisa sighed, and put a hand for a moment to the single pearl that was suspended from the thin golden choker at her throat. "We have business to accomplish tonight. We're being joined for dinner, by someone who wishes to speak with you. Who has a business proposition to make."

"I see," said David. "Who?"

Lisa gave an almost imperceptible shake of her head. "I would prefer to wait until we are at the restaurant. I've reserved a private room at Henri's Gallery. Not too much farther."

David studied the Eurasian businesswoman. After all the hours of work and conversation they had shared, he still did not know her. "Being cryptic must be a hobby of yours."

That at least brought a sparkle of amusement to her eyes. "You will understand," she said, all steel and professionalism. "And then I think you will agree with the course I have selected." She looked at her Cartier again. "We must hurry."

David was not yet ready to move. "Answer something for me."

"All right," Lisa said impatiently. Her guard was unmistakably in place.

"Don't you ever break away and just enjoy yourself?"

This time there was no misreading the shake of her head. Her eyes became cold and unreadable, as though she had drawn shutters over them. "I take my pleasure from business, David," Lisa Han said, her voice free from emotion. "I'm certain you do as well—whatever frivolous activities you pursue in your free time." She locked eyes with him for a long moment. "We need to move along."

"Yes," said David. He had to step quickly to catch up with her, and their conversation did not resume.

Nightfall was complete by the time they reached Henri's Gallery. Beyond the banyan trees that lined the waterfront, the lights of boats and barges winked at them. David held the restaurant door for Lisa, and she granted him a quick smile. David was not fooled —as they neared the restaurant the flawless skin around Lisa's eyes had grown tight, and a nervousness had entered her step. *She's spooked. Who are we meeting?*

The maître d' greeted David and Lisa with a toothy smile, cocking an ear to catch Lisa's softly spoken instructions. They were escorted quickly through the restaurant. The maître d' closed the door behind him, leaving David and Lisa alone in a comfortable dining room. Lisa did not look at David. "Our guest will be here soon," she said.

"I'm intrigued," David said.

"An . . . appropriate choice of word," Lisa replied with a chuckle. This new smile seemed genuine, but it did not last. "May I try again to answer your earlier question? I feel that—" Lisa fumbled for words, but could not find them.

"You don't owe me explanations, Lisa. I was out of place to ask. We've done good business together, and I can leave it at that if you wish. But I won't deny that I find you . . . *intriguing.*" That earned another smile, one that lived a bit longer. David felt sudden warmth spread through his stomach. *She's lovely when she smiles.*

"Thank you."

David put on his best southern manners: "No need, ma'am." He had enough nerve to take a step toward her, holding her gaze with his own. "Maybe business isn't all we'd be good at. That's all I meant to suggest." He drew himself up to stand tall before her. For a moment he thought that she would come close.

Lisa broke eye contact. "David, I—"

A soft knock interrupted her words. The door swung open and the smiling maître d' ushered in a stout Chinese gentleman of advanced years. *Surprise, surprise,* said David to himself, and stepped forward to embrace one of the Wellington family's oldest and closest friends, Doctor Xiang Peng, molecular biologist extraordinaire, Director of the Institute of Biophysics of the People's Republic of China. "Peng," he said as the Chinese patted him on the back. "I might have known."

Peng released David finally, to step back and stare at him with bright eyes. "Surely, David, you did not think I could let you come so close and not have a good visit."

David shook his head. Not long after James Wellington's death, David had received a long and touching letter from Peng. James Wellington and Xiang Peng went back a long way, and Peng's letter had touched upon many wonderful memories. "It was good to hear from you after Dad died."

Peng brushed the thanks away. "I would have been at the funeral. But—"

"Dad wasn't a great believer in funerals, anyway."

"No," said Peng, his demeanor growing somber. Then he brightened. "But your father *was* a great believer in life. He did more with his than any four men I have known."

"Thank you, Peng," David said.

Peng nodded happily and spoke to Lisa Han. "And this one," he said, waving a hand at David. "He was full of life from the moment he was born. Would you believe that on more than one occasion I helped change this young man's diapers, and gave him his bottle while his father and I argued over research."

There had been no little friendly scientific rivalry mixed in with the friendship. James, scion of an already well-established southern pharmaceutical family, and Peng, an impoverished foreign student, had first met over a laboratory bench at Duke University, and the two jockeyed for top honors throughout their undergraduate years. Company responsibilities forced James to forgo advanced degrees, but he'd underwritten Peng's graduate training and the doctorate he earned with honors. Neither ever doubted that Xiang Peng would join Wellington Laboratories.

Then came the Long March, the revolution, the upheaval in China that finally called Peng home. I was still a toddler when he left, David recalled. He recalled as well how often his father spoke of Peng, the circuitous routes by which the two remained in touch during the years when their nations were estranged, and then the renewal of close ties that followed hard upon normalization of relations. James and Monica had made two trips to China together.

"You agreed more often than not," David said.

Peng nodded. "Of course we did. Early on we saw the promise that genetic medicine offered. And of course James funded as much basic research in the field of genetic engineering as anyone." His eyes clouded with reminiscence. "I think he was always happiest at a laboratory bench. Certainly he was never delighted with the burdens of running the company."

"For all that he did a wonderful job of it," David said, not without a trace of defensiveness.

Peng waved a stubby finger at David. "Of course, of course. But your father's first love was always his research. He could have been far wealthier had he not funded so much of it."

David smiled. "We've made money on a good deal of that research. Products have come from it."

"True," said Peng. "And much of the research supported by Wellington Laboratories has also been . . . pure research at the genetic level. Research whose benefits, when they arrive, might have potential for profits but would also be subject to . . . constraints."

What's he getting at? David wondered.

Peng went on. "And since your father's passing, David, Wellington Laboratories' commitment has continued undiminished."

"That's correct." David glanced at Lisa Han's impassive face.

Peng moved to the immaculately set table in the center of the dining room, pulled out a chair and sat down heavily. "Please," he said, indicating the other chairs. "Shall we sit? We have a long evening ahead."

David held a chair for Lisa. He buzzed for a waiter to take their drink orders, then took his own place. David and Lisa ordered martinis. "I would like a little *bourbon,*" said Peng, in a bad imitation of a southern drawl. He spoke to the American. "A taste I acquired at your father's elbow, David. Way down south when we both were young. A . . . *libation,* I believe he called it."

David grinned broadly. "Exactly right." He quoted his father: "'The perfect accompaniment to a long evening's conversation.'"

Peng's eyes were wide. "We shall toast his fine memory, then," he said when the drinks arrived. "To James Wellington." Peng raised his glass, touched its rim to Lisa's, then to David's. The waiter lingered long enough to take their orders. "I am quite fond of African chicken," Peng announced as the waiter departed. "Good food, drink, and companionship. This will indeed be a pleasant evening."

Until the meal was served, Peng talked about his long friendship with James Wellington. David found himself opening up as well, bragging to Lisa Han about his father's accomplishments. After his retirement, James Wellington, with Monica's assistance, had written three books. Each volume spoke eloquently and persuasively about the biological revolution that would transform the world, about the new generation of wonder drugs that would soon be available. The era was approaching, Wellington had argued, when both the most common and the most intransigent diseases would fall under medicine's control. James spoke frequently at commencement exercises, and had testified at more than one Congressional hearing about genetic engineering and the pharmaceutical industry.

"But not even all of James's persuasive powers could overcome all of the resistance to new methods. Isn't that correct, David?" Peng beamed at the platter of grilled chicken and chilis, a traditional Macanese specialty that sizzled before him.

David glanced at Lisa, whose face was a perfect mask. She hadn't spoken ten words in the last ten minutes. "I'm not sure I understand," he said to Peng.

Peng eyed the waiter, and said nothing until they were once more alone in the room. "Your nation—so bold in so many areas—errs often on the side of caution where the pharmaceutical industry is concerned. Wouldn't you agree?"

David watched Peng delightedly chew a morsel of spicy chicken. "Our industry is . . . monitored, yes," he said slowly, keeping his eyes on the scientist. "And it does seem sometimes as if the delays imposed upon the introduction of new medicines are excessive." David took a bite of chorizo. The hot sausage and Portuguese fried rice stung his palate with wonderful flavor. "Why do you ask?"

For a moment Peng did not speak. He carefully chewed another bite of chicken, then sipped the Portuguese Vinho Verde they'd ordered to accompany the meal. He drew a breath. "David, I must speak bluntly."

David put down his fork. "Go ahead."

"Wellington Laboratories, under your father's guidance, and for the past five years under your own, has used its resources to accomplish a great deal, much of it without prospect of immediate profit or even return on investment. Not the least of these accomplishments have occurred in the fields of pure biophysical research. Correct?" Peng waited impassively for David to answer.

"We believed early in the promise of genetic engineering," David said. "But you're aware of this, we've been over it."

"Yes, yes." The scientist scrutinized David. "You have your mother's eyes, you know." To Lisa he said, "David's mother was a strong, a beautiful and brilliant woman."

"Peng—" David prodded.

Peng shrugged. "Genetics," he said with a sigh. "Wellington Laboratories' investment in genetic engineering has not been . . . inconsequential?"

"Dammit, Peng," David said. "You know all this."

"You would agree that your government's restraints would make it exceedingly difficult for you quickly to perfect and then introduce new medicines which result from your research?"

David turned his attention to his food, buying time to find the right words. "I understand my nation's caution," he said at last, "however much I disagree with it. Genetic engineering is a controversial issue. No matter how promising the results, the subject frightens a large segment of the population." David said no more. *Where is Peng leading me?*

Peng nodded vigorously. "Precisely, David, precisely. And some of your research of late has been *quite* promising, has it not?"

A shiver skittered up David Wellington's spine. "It's time for you to make your meaning clear, Peng. What is this about?"

Peng pushed his empty platter aside before answering. He took the time to arrange his silverware neatly, fold his linen napkin and place it on the table. "When your father and I were able to communicate openly, after the normalization, we talked a great deal. He visited me, I visited him. As always, we argued over research." A smile crossed his face. "But in recent months we found ourselves in more and more agreement. The research that your people at Wellington and mine at the Institute pursued was toward similar ends." He breathed deeply. *"Revolutionary* ends, I might say." Peng made a temple of his fingers and pressed them to his lips, waiting.

David turned to Lisa Han, who said nothing. She sat without moving, as though carved from ice. David faced Peng. "Yes?"

Xiang Peng lowered his hands. *"Omnigene,"* he said in a voice that was nearly a whisper.

I should have guessed. "Where did you hear that word?" David asked.

"From your father, David." Peng reached into the jacket of his dark, well-tailored European suit, withdrew a cream-colored envelope, and handed it to David Wellington.

David, recognizing immediately his father's neat, small handwriting, noticed only after a moment that the name on the envelope was his own. He stared at it for a moment, then turned the envelope over, unsure of his own feelings at suddenly receiving a letter from his father. The envelope was sealed with green wax, imprinted with a crest consisting of a test tube and a microscope—one of James Wellington's favored affectations. As a boy David had been delighted and fascinated by his father's large collection of seals and signets. David placed the envelope face down upon the table. He reached into his jacket and produced his ivory-handled Gerber pocketknife, opened it, and carefully pried up the wax seal. David closed the knife, put it away, and without further ceremony opened the envelope. His throat tightened when he saw his father's careful handwriting and the salutation:

My dear son—
   I have not kept many things from you, but you will understand soon why I have held you in the dark on this.
   Xiang Peng will by now have told you of his awareness of omnigene. After you read this letter, he will make a proposal. My friendship with Peng should not be considered as an endorsement of what he has to offer. Hear him out and we will discuss it fully upon your return—

David looked away from the letter for a moment, sentiment thickening in his throat. When he began reading again it was with clear eyes.

You are the head of the company, son, a far better one than I ever was. Approval or rejection of Peng's proposal rests with you.

I don't know that I envy you that responsibility. It is not given to many men to remake the face of their world. Omnigene can do that, as you and I both know. I am glad the responsibility rests with you, who are so well-equipped to handle it.

I am proud of you. You have never shied away from risks. The stakes of this new risk are much higher than any we've ever known.

I look forward to talking with you, and I will support whatever decision you make.

Your Father

David read the letter again, taking his time. He looked up. Peng was watching him, as were Lisa Han's dark, unblinking eyes. "How much of this are you aware of?" he asked her.

Peng answered. "I have held that letter for nearly two years, David. There were things to attend to in China before I could contact you. When James gave me the letter—we were together when he wrote it—he told me to deliver it at my discretion. Wellington's presence in the Orient was growing even then, and we knew that opportunity for my path to cross yours would arise."

"And Lisa?" David said, unwilling to go further until he knew how she figured in this.

"As you will discover momentarily, I have a proposition to make which, if you accept it, will require the services of a skilled business negotiator and broker. One with ties to our region." Peng smiled at Lisa who bowed slightly to him. "As you have already discovered, Lisa Han more than meets the business requirements. And as I feel certain you know, she and her organization adhere to the highest standards of discretion and honesty."

"Agreed," David said. As Lisa would not look at him, he spoke to Peng. "Make your proposal."

Peng breathed heavily. "Several years ago, comparing notes, Wellington and I discovered that our research was pursuing similar tracks. I provided him with certain information which he in turn delivered to Wellington researchers. Understand: I am taking no credit for omnigene. What I shared with James saved time, but your people would have made their own breakthrough eventually." Peng looked at Lisa. "Omnigene appears to be the large advance that genetic tailoring has sought for so long. This . . . *marvel* is nothing less than a medicine which can be programmed to combat specific diseases. It is especially effective against previously invulnerable viruses. While the technology required to create omnigene is advanced, the medicine itself is surprisingly inexpensive to manufacture, the more so in relation to the great good it can accomplish." He leaned close to Lisa. "Perhaps more important is the evidence that omnigene can serve not only as a treatment but also as a vaccine, lending those inoculated an immunity against even the most mundane of diseases."

"Omnimmune," said David with a quick grin. "The cure for the common cold."

"Colds and infections," said Peng, "but not just those. Omnigene is proving surprisingly effective, and *permanently* effective, against cancers, against lupus, against many of man's old enemies."

Lisa sat still. *"Marvel* is certainly the appropriate description," she said in an even, low voice. "Is this breakthrough exclusively yours?"

David shrugged. "So far as we know. Of course, an hour ago, I thought that Monica and I, along with the researchers responsible for the project, were the only living people aware of it." He studied his hands for a moment. "We've kept very quiet, and broken a few rules in doing so." He gave Lisa a smile. "There are those in our industry, and our government, who would frown upon the amount of secret research Wellington Labs has undertaken."

"Your competitors would be overwhelmed," Lisa said.

"Perhaps. But Peng has not told you everything." David took a second to select his words. "We're confident that omnigene can be ready for clinical use within two years. But that assumes a reasonable schedule for testing and approval—which we don't have. The National Institute of Health, among others, and the FDA, are going to impose some serious slowdowns on us once they get wind of omnigene. People worry about monsters. Frankenstein fears," David said with a forced smile.

"How slow?" Lisa asked.

"Assuming a perfect product—and omnigene appears close—years at least." He shrugged once more. "More likely decades."

"These regulations," Peng interjected, "began as reasonable precautions. James Wellington worked hard helping to draft some of their early incarnations. Caution was reasonable when the processes and technologies were new."

"Caution is always reasonable."

Peng lowered his head, granting David the point. "You are your father's wise son," he said. "But your father also believed that the climate in your country has grown *too* cautious."

"Omnigene was his last baby," David said. "In many ways it was the culmination of his life's work."

"A fitting one," said Peng.

David had a suspicion where Peng's proposal would lead, and he pressed his hunch. "How is the climate in China?" he said, sitting back in his chair.

"We are a cautious people as well, David. But we are also . . . *eager.*" His round face grew grim. "It is not easy thing for China to go from Mao to marketing in the space of a few years, but we are managing. At the same time, we must keep our covenant with our citizens. Omnigene can be of great benefit to them."

"In more ways than just as medicine," David said rapidly. He worked to keep the excitement out of his voice. He was ahead of Peng, now, his thoughts gathering speed, the rational, conservative part of his mind boggled by what he suddenly foresaw. "You want Wellington to come to you," he said. "You want us to bring omnigene to China."

"We are prepared to negotiate," Peng said, holding up a hand to restrain David's enthusiasm. "If the negotiations go as I hope, and as I believe they *can,* we will be able to offer you a benevolent eye upon your project." His tone took on a note of warning. "Not without safeguards. Mind you, we will impose our own regulations and guarantees. But there will be a *reasonable* schedule for the testing and introduction of omnigene, with a more than generous potential for profit. After all, we can offer you over a billion people who are as eager to be rid of disease as anyone."

"Oh, come, Peng," said David with a trace of humor. "You know what else you're offering me."

Peng pretended innocence. "With Lisa's help we will route your company's entry into China through Hong Kong. Registered there, your firm will be able to take omnigene throughout Asia. More billions, David."

He nodded his agreement. "Complete the offer, Peng," he said. "Tell Lisa what else such a proposal can do."

"Why, David," said Peng, with a chuckle that became a laugh, "it can make you easily the most controversial man your industry has ever known."

3

AN HOUR LATER, when David Wellington asked Lisa to walk with him back to the passenger terminal and jetfoil pier, she almost refused. She had already informed him that she would not be returning to Hong Kong that evening. Peng departed the restaurant in a private car, accompanied by his personal bodyguard and chauffeur. "I'm not sure a walk would be wise, David," Lisa said.

The American stretched his arms wide, drew a deep breath of evening air. "After that meal?" He stepped to her side and spoke more softly. "My head's still swimming a little from all of this. Let's walk."

He tried to take her hand, but Lisa drew back. "David—"

"If you're so scared of the shadows, Lisa, you'll never get to enjoy the night. Come on," he said, nearly whispering. "Walk with me."

Lisa hesitated only another second. "You let me talk for a while," she said. "And *listen,* David, to what I say. Promise that, and I'll walk with you."

"Done," said David Wellington. He offered his arm, but Lisa shook her head. "On your terms, then."

She established a brisk pace, and did not pause before beginning her speech. "Do not grow so excited over Peng's offer that you overlook the very real dangers that accompany it."

"Well, the way I understood it, Lisa, as broker you stand to profit very handsomely from this arrangement yourself. *If* we take the offer."

Lisa kept her tone formal. "David, I think that

40

everyone profits from the arrangement Peng has proposed. For a time you will be in the hot seat—"

"To say the least!" David laughed, breaking his promise and interrupting her once more. Lisa said nothing as David counted off the problems that lay ahead. "My government's going to be after us for transferring advanced research and technology overseas, although we've kept such a tight lid on our work that the government's still not aware of a lot of it. Which, in itself, can get us scalded should word get out. And I don't imagine the National Institute of Health is going to be thrilled about our moving our 'dangerous' operation out of their jurisdiction.''

"Your own industry is liable to turn your partnership with the Chinese against you," Lisa said.

"Oh, there'll be people back home ready to string me up," David chortled.

Lisa stopped walking and took David's arm. She stared hard at him. "This is not a game, you know. So far you've done a wonderful job of establishing Wellington Labs here. For all the problems you've faced, and still face, you have come closer than any Western firm to cracking the hold of the regionals. And you see what's happened in recent months. The stronger Wellington Labs grows, the more overt and deadly the actions taken against it. Once word gets out that you're entertaining thoughts of joining the PRC in a venture, especially one so audacious as this, you're going to encounter—"

David took her shoulders in his huge hands and squeezed firmly. For a moment Lisa thought he would shake her. All of the humor was gone from his face, and his eyes were bright and unblinking. "Lisa, after just ten days you ought to know me better than that. I've buried two of my best people in the past few months. Elizabeth Jonklaas isn't even cold in her grave yet. There've been threats, acts of sabotage. But what do you do? Give headstones to the dead and scurry back home where it's safe? I won't." He released her, but her shoulders remained warm from his grip. Lisa waited for more, but he cut off his words with a headshake and stalked away.

Lisa's heart beat rapidly, as though she'd been running. "David! Wait!" she called after him. She hurried to him when he turned. "You must understand—"

He did not let her finish. "I understand." David showed a small, almost bashful grin. "And I *did* listen, for all that I didn't let you talk. I appreciate what you want to tell me."

"With Peng, though, and the PRC. The atmosphere will grow far more . . . deadly."

"No. I won't have that. I can't believe the other companies will tolerate it, either."

They resumed their walk, although more slowly. "Your regional competitors will grow fierce in their denunciations of you, should you proceed with Peng's proposal."

"But they're not terrorists, Lisa. We both know where the trouble lies. We both know who had Elizabeth killed, who ordered the sabotage, who's behind the threats."

Her voice was harsh. "Yes, we *know*. And that's enough. How many killers are required, after all?"

David took a moment before answering. "In other words, so long as Victor Sun Chen is willing to do the dirty work, all of my other . . . *colleagues* can avert their eyes. They can persuade themselves that their consciences are clear." David said the name again, spitting it out, as though tasting something foul. "Victor Sun Chen."

Lisa let her breath hiss out. There had been a time when even the passing mention of Sun Chen's name had made her shudder with revulsion. *But I have come a long way since that time,* she thought. Sun Chen had been a topic of conversation more than once as she helped David Wellington acquire Kwang Pharmaceuticals. *How could we not have talked of Sun*

Chen and his vile tactics? He is vulnerable, now, but he still dominates the industry in much of the region. Domination was a word that came easily to mind when thinking of Sun Chen. *I have kept David from suspecting how deeply run my feelings about Victor. How well I know him and his nature. Now—* Lisa did not rage, nor allow any emotion into her voice when she spoke. "Victor Sun Chen is a man who belongs dead."

"But we're *honorable* people," David Wellington said. There was no missing the bitterness in his voice. "We cannot condone such things."

Lisa did not reply. Over the years she had given too much thought to killing Sun Chen herself.

David went on speaking. "But we can ruin him. He's cash poor now, in a bind that grows tighter every day. We can take his business away from him. And I would say that Xiang Peng's offer would provide Wellington Laboratories with all the edge we need to do so. Wouldn't you agree?"

"It is still just an offer, David," said Lisa Han. She felt suddenly weary—so much lay ahead, and none of it would be simple. "For one thing, you must live long enough to make the deal a reality." She did not look at him.

"I'll live long enough." His determination was obvious. "Besides, there's more at stake here than just Wellington Laboratories or Sun Chen Chemical." David made a slashing gesture with his hands. "We can change the world."

"Not easily done." They turned a corner.

"Of course it's not easily done," David said. "Isn't that part of what makes it all worthwhile?"

Lisa sighed. Her legs felt as though they were made of lead. "What is it you so want to change, David?"

"Not much," he said with a dry laugh. "Only all of it. I want to do away with national boundaries where medicine is concerned. It's time. Medicines can't be restricted to a single country or group of countries.

Not when there are children suffering from disease. Not when we can make life less fearful for the aged, more productive for the young."

"Not to mention turning a profit for Wellington Laboratories," Lisa said.

"Oh, you can bet on that. But you know as well as I do that we can make safer profits, easier profits, less . . . dangerous profits than these."

"Then *why?*" Lisa demanded again. Her own bitterness rose within her. "Because it's there?"

The gentleness of David's answer surprised and soothed her. "Because I *can.* Because if *I* don't take this step . . . if *I* don't make omnigene available as safely and as quickly as I can, I won't have done my part."

"Your part?"

He nodded. "In fulfilling my responsibilities. Help the world, Lisa, and the world will help you," he said. "I believe that."

They fell into their own silences. Lisa's thoughts roiled. *Help the world.* She made her hands into fists, her long nails biting into the flesh of her palms. *And has the world ever helped me? Or anyone to whom I have grown close?* Lisa steadied her breathing, sought to make it rhythmic. It had no effect. Too many memories were crowding back. *Help the world.* David's world was so different. Lisa could still see all too clearly the slums of Taipei, still hear the raucous cries from the streets drowning out the softer whimpering of hungry children. *I have come so far,* she thought, *and it is as though I have come no distance at all.* She looked at David, lost in his own thoughts. She could almost picture the world he wanted to create, but only almost. Nothing would ever be so vivid for her as the memories of her childhood, or so painful. *But I have controlled my pain, and I will continue to keep it under control. That is what has lifted me this high.*

That, and the assistance of Victor Sun Chen.

Once, that name had been wonderful to Lisa. It was the name of a hero, a benefactor.

A father? she wondered as she had wondered before.

Lisa Han knew all about her real father—a British seaman in port for a few days, or a few hours. *A few minutes in a cheap hotel room with my mother was all that was required to create me. I do not even know his name or what he looked like, but I know all about him. He left Mama a few dollars and me a mixed genetic heritage—English cream complexion and Chinese eyes.* Lisa glanced surreptitiously at David, concerned that he might sense her turmoil, but he kept his eyes forward, his stride steady.

Among Lisa Han's earliest memories was an awareness of her own nature, of the difference between her and the other children. *How I hated mirrors!* Sometimes, still, her ears rang with the taunts directed at her by the children among whom she grew up, and even now she could feel her eyes begin to swell with tears. *But I have learned so many things, and chief among them is the ability to swallow my tears.*

The taunts that hurt so badly had spurred Lisa toward other differences. *Smarter. Harder working. More determined. Able to take care of myself better than anyone I knew. Able to read Chinese at two, English at three. Keeping my thoughts organized, shutting out anything and anyone who interfered with my learning. Not letting myself grow frightened alone in our room every night while Mama—*

Not even frightened the night her mother left and never returned.

Such determination! How could it not have brought me attention?

After her mother abandoned her, ten-year-old Lisa lived and learned for two years on her own. She would not abandon school. She moved easily through her work. *And was always clean, my clothes fresh, however ragged. I created the person I have become. I did it all*

45

myself after Mama left me alone. Even my name is my own creation. The little jobs she found here and there quickly gave the child an understanding of money, of its acquisition, of its overriding importance. *I paid my own rent, bought food, even saved.* Someday, she had promised herself, she would be able to buy her way out of the slums. She would buy herself a good education, a chance. *But Victor Sun Chen denied me that opportunity.*

It was raining the afternoon her teachers kept Lisa after school to tell her of the honor she had been awarded. She was twelve years old, her grades higher than those of any other student and among the highest in the history of the school. If she seldom made less than a perfect score, Lisa's features never made less than a perfect mask. *So few had ever seen me smile—until that afternoon.*

She remembered looking beyond her teachers to the windows where heavy raindrops gathered in a dark sky. *But oh how the sun came out when they told me of the scholarship! I vowed then that I would one day repay the kindness extended me by Victor Sun Chen.* Lisa hurried from the school and visited the library where she found, to her delight, that Victor Sun Chen was, like herself, of mixed ancestry.

New discoveries flowed quickly. Sun Chen's scholarship paid Lisa's tuition and room and board at Li Juan Academy for Young Women. *How I loved that school. The terraced grounds colorful with flowers we planted and tended ourselves. Delicious food, in quantities that seemed unbelievable. A room of my own, and a bed with crisp, starched sheets. Cotton blouse, navy wool skirt and blazer—how tall I felt in my uniform, how attractive, how poised and grown up. I wanted nothing so much as I wanted Victor Sun Chen to see me.* Lisa sent Sun Chen a snapshot of herself in the Academy's uniform, and took to writing a weekly note telling him of how much she had learned, how hard she was working, how appreciative she was of the opportunity he had made available to her. *But he never answered my notes.*

Some discoveries were not so pleasant. Most of the girls at the Academy came from wealthy families, and brought with them to the school a snobbishness that excluded Lisa from their cliques. Her mixed ancestry was no less a focus for derision from her schoolmates than it had been on the streets of Taipei's slums. *More veiled, more polite, more hidden—it would not do for the Headmistress to hear such cruelty—but no less hurtful. They guessed correctly about my mother, and tried to use that knowledge to make me miserable. Those spoiled, silly, frivolous girls could not see or sense that I was immune to their remarks. I concentrated and studied, worked harder than ever, made certain that my marks were higher than those of anyone else.*

Lisa set herself a grueling pace, and the harder she worked, the harder she pushed. Summers were no different for her than other seasons—through Sun Chen's patronage, Lisa Han lived at Li Juan Academy year round, without vacation or holiday. *Where would I go? Back to the slum? I had no family there, no friends. I could be lonely at school as easily as anywhere else.* What few moments of relaxation she permitted herself, Lisa passed deep in romantic novels. More often than not she saw herself as the heroine of those books. *And Victor the hero.*

The years passed so quickly that Lisa was honestly surprised when the Headmistress informed her that her graduation ceremonies were only a few weeks off. Lisa was not surprised at all, however, to learn that she would serve as valedictorian for her class. The prospect of graduation dismayed her a bit. For the first time since her mother abandoned her, Lisa Han felt directionless. She was seventeen, tall, her lush figure and long legs reminding her daily that she was becoming as adult in body as she had been in spirit through most of her life. Her grades and honors would, she felt certain, win her entry and scholarship to any university she selected. But the Academy had become a home to her over the years she had been there. To be on her own again—the future both excited and frightened her.

A dozen years later she could still quote her valedictory address. *All those things I believed that afternoon, and said in such a strong voice. Discipline. Determination. Hard work and constant study. Commitment to yourself and to your world. Sentiments David Wellington would understand and endorse. Even those girls who had taunted me gave me their applause that afternoon. It was wonderful, the diploma that I clutched so tightly, the congratulations and embraces of my teachers, the reception and buffet following the graduation exercises. Commencement—but of what? I was eager to enter the world.* Not even the fact that alone of all the girls on graduation day she celebrated without parents or relatives could rob Lisa of her happiness.

And then she was drawn aside by the Headmistress. "Lisa, there is someone who would like very much to meet you."

They left the crowded reception and walked slowly to the Headmistress's spacious office. When they entered the office a tall, distinguished man rose from the leather chair facing the Headmistress's desk. He turned to face them and Lisa caught her breath. "Victor Sun Chen," she said in a hushed voice.

Sun Chen bowed to her and said, "Your servant, my dear Lisa." Nothing had ever sounded so wonderful. When he took her hands in his she thought she might faint. Lisa steadied herself and made herself stand proudly before Sun Chen. He was even more handsome than in the press photographs she had looked up. An inch over six feet tall, with a dark moustache clipped militarily short, the first hints of gray showing at his temples, Victor Sun Chen radiated strength and purpose. He was muscular, the tapered Pierre Cardin suit he wore emphasizing his powerful build. Lisa realized that she still wore her billowing blue graduation gown, and felt foolish, a child. She could not speak. When Sun Chen touched her elbow to usher Lisa to a seat, she felt swept along by a force almost tidal, unresisting. *I did not want to resist.*

"You have made me very proud," Sun Chen said once they were seated. He nodded to the smiling Headmistress. "I have of course been kept appraised of your grades. And I have kept every one of your delightful letters." His smile dazzled Lisa.

"You never wrote back," she said in a small voice.

Sun Chen shook his head. "I did not want to distract you, my dear. You had your studies to attend to, your work. It was enough that you took the trouble to write to me."

"Oh, it was no trouble!" Lisa blurted, then caught herself. "You made so many things possible for me. I owe you so very much."

Sun Chen raised a hand, silencing Lisa. "Let us not speak of debts now. This is *your* day." He glanced at the wide window behind the Headmistress. Late afternoon sunlight flooded the office. "Although I see that the day will be over soon." Sun Chen clapped his hands together and showed Lisa another stunning smile. "No matter. Soon this will be *your* evening."

"I . . . I don't understand."

"Surely you cannot think that I would allow all of your honors to pass unremarked?" He feigned a look of hurt. "Perhaps I *have* been too distant. Permit me to take you to dinner this evening. We will dine at a fine restaurant and have a toast to your academic success, to your future."

"But—"

"No objections, now. I really will not tolerate

them." His face grew sincere, concerned. "Let me indulge my pride. Have you ever been to a truly great restaurant?"

Lisa shook her head shyly. She felt so young, so foolish.

"Then that is what you deserve this evening. We shall feast together at Paris 1930."

Lisa had heard the restaurant's name before, knew that it was fabulously elegant and expensive. She thought of her uniforms, the only clothing she possessed. She would be so out of place. She could not embarrass so great a man as Victor Sun Chen by appearing dressed as a schoolgirl. Everyone would laugh. "I'm sorry," she forced herself to say, the words like ashes. "I have nothing to—"

"Lisa!" the Headmistress exclaimed. "Do not be ungrateful. Go to your room, now, and change your clothes."

"But—"

"Such argumentativeness!" The Headmistress shook her head. "You would think we have taught you nothing! Do as I say." Oddly, there was no anger in her words. Was she smiling?

Lisa nodded, then stood up.

"I will be waiting for you, Lisa," Sun Chen said.

The walk to her room seemed to go on forever. She could not stop imagining the comments of the other diners. They would find their amusement in the spectacle of a great industrialist taking a child to a fine French restaurant. Lisa could not allow Sun Chen to learn of her self-consciousness. It was contrary to everything she had taught herself. Lisa gathered her courage. She would wear the uniform proudly, and not permit herself to think of what others might say. Her mind made up, Lisa opened the door of her room.

And stepped into wonderland.

Brightly colored boxes were piled high on the surface of her dresser, with other boxes stacked on the floor beside her bed. Spread across the bed itself was a gorgeous silk evening gown, the color of shimmering emeralds. Lisa looked around frantically to make certain she stood in her own room. Her few belongings were in their familiar places. Lisa scarcely dared to blink, for fear that the treasures before her would disappear.

She heard a sound and turned toward the doorway.

A lovely, small dark-haired woman stood there, smiling. "Lisa, my name is Candace Caillou," she said, a French accent coloring her words. "I am an assistant to Victor Sun Chen." She smiled broadly, the contours of her face lovely. "Although this day he has asked me to serve as assistant to *you*. Here. Let us sort through your graduation gifts." Candace stepped into the room.

"My—" Lisa's voice failed, and all the years of restrained tears threatened to break free at once. She pressed her hands to her eyes.

"No, no," Candace said, coming close, putting a gentle arm around the girl's shoulders. "Be happy. This is your graduation day. Here. Come, cheer yourself up with all of these lovely things, won't you? You have an important evening ahead. Will you permit me to help make you ready?"

Lisa sniffled and managed a slight nod. "Please would you?" she said.

"Of course." Candace smiled again. "Now, let us get to work." Candace took a moment to survey her new charge. "Here. Go and shower, quickly, though! When you return I will have things ready for you." Lisa gathered her toiletries and retired to the bathroom down the hall.

When she returned to her room Candace studied her once more. "Such a pretty young woman," she said. "Here. Get into your underthings." Out of habit Lisa turned to the top drawer of her dresser, but Candace stopped her. "No, no, Lisa. Not those old things. Victor asked me to shop for you and I did. Top

51

to bottom, head to toe, *tu comprendes?* Of course you do, you who are so very smart." Candace swept a delicate hand in the direction of the bed. "Here. Put these on."

Lisa stepped forward hesitantly and touched the silken garments that lay upon the coverlet. The brassiere and panties were as light as gossamer. Lisa looked uncertainly at Candace. "Go ahead, Lisa," Candace urged in a warm voice. "Don't be afraid. It is time you learned to enjoy yourself."

Lisa took a deep breath and unknotted the belt of her simple, serviceable bathrobe. She slowly drew on the soft undergarments, shivering with pleasure at the way they molded themselves to her body. Candace was smiling. "Stockings, next," she said. "Then we shall do something about your hair."

For the next half hour Lisa relaxed and allowed Candace to minister to her. At last the beautiful Frenchwoman stepped back and sighed. Candace's dark eyes were wide with pleasure. "Now. You must look at yourself. Go ahead." She stepped to the closet and opened the door on whose interior was mounted a mirror.

Lisa faced the glass. For a moment she did not recognize the elegant Eurasian woman whose image was reflected there. *Can that be me?* The St. Laurent gown fit as though specially created for Lisa. Her cheeks reddened a bit when she realized how much of her full, firm breasts were revealed by the low-cut gown. The more she looked at herself, though, the less embarrassed she felt. *It is a gown for a woman,* Lisa realized. *For me.* Candace had drawn Lisa's long black hair up off her neck, and fastened it in place with a jeweled clip. The few cosmetics that Candace had employed—"Your complexion is perfect unadorned! Here. Just a touch or two for emphasis."—seemed wholly to have transformed Lisa's features. It was as though a stranger stood before her.

But I got to know her quickly enough.

"Oh, you are a beautiful woman, Lisa Han," Candace said. "Here. Just a few last things." Candace rummaged through the packages and held out a small, colorfully wrapped box. "May I?" Candace asked, toying with the ribbon. Lisa nodded, and watched closely as Candace unwrapped the gift. It was a velvet box with a hinged lid. "A special present from Victor Sun Chen," Candace explained. She opened the box, and smiled at Lisa's reaction to the jade earrings and choker it held. Candace fastened the jewelry in place, then stepped back. From another box Candace produced a tiny crystal bottle. "A touch of Chanel," she said, brushing the stopper against Lisa's ears and neck. "And now you are ready?"

Lisa looked nervously toward the door. "Will I—"

"You will do fine," Candace said. "Here." She removed the lid from another box. Inside lay a satin cape and matching bag. Candace draped the wrap over Lisa's bare shoulders, placed the bag in her hands. "Now, go."

Lisa took a step in the direction of the door, a bit unsteady in the Ferragamo shoes, which fit wonderfully but to whose high heels she was unaccustomed. Lisa stopped, pressed a hand against the doorframe, looked back at Candace.

"Go *ahead,* Lisa. Do not keep Victor waiting any longer, or yourself." Candace fluttered her hands. "Fly, now!"

Lisa walked slowly back to the Headmistress's office. Something happened as she walked. She felt a change come over herself. By the time she turned the final corner the shoes no longer felt alien to her. *I could dance,* she thought. Wonderland seemed suddenly very natural to her. Lisa looked at her hands to see if they were shaking. They were not. The gown hugged her hips, controlling her walk. She enjoyed it. *I was born to wear this. This is who I am.* She held her chin high, moistened her lips, and stepped into the office to present herself to Victor Sun Chen.

He was alone, the Headmistress having returned to the reception. Sun Chen stood when Lisa approached him. He stared openly at her, nodding a bit as his gaze traveled over her body. "My dear Lisa," he said, and offered his arm.

Before leaving the Academy Lisa and Sun Chen walked through the still-crowded reception. Lisa tugged gently at Sun Chen's elbow. He looked at her, his understanding obvious—he slowed their pace in order to give Lisa's classmates a good look at her. She felt a fierce surge of triumph at the surprise and jealousy on their faces. She told herself that it did not hurt a bit when she overheard one of them whisper, "Like her mother!" *No, I am not,* Lisa thought. She froze them with a long glare, then glided weightlessly beside Victor Sun Chen, bidding farewell to the Headmistress and teachers before stepping outside.

A vintage Rolls-Royce Silver Phaeton was parked at the lip of the walk leading from the front doors of the Academy. The uniformed chauffeur who stood next to the automobile held the door for Lisa, but it was Sun Chen who helped her into the spacious passenger compartment. Lisa ran her fingers over the rich leather upholstery. She was careful to sit perfectly straight, and folded her hands demurely in her lap when Sun Chen joined her. The chauffeur brought the automobile to life and it pulled smoothly away from the curb. Lisa treated herself to a single glance back at the Academy, and was more than gratified to see the other girls' faces pressed against the windowpanes. Lisa gave them her most dazzling smile, then turned her attention wholly to Victor Sun Chen. The chauffeur guided the Rolls easily between the tall stone columns that had for five years marked the boundary of Lisa Han's world.

How my world expanded that evening, she recalled as she walked beside David Wellington. The American's hands were pushed deep into his pockets, his shoulders hunched, his brow creased. *What is he thinking of?* Lisa wondered. She could not find voice to ask. Her own thoughts drew her back irresistibly.

Precisely at eight, after a leisurely sunset and early evening drive through the terraced hills surrounding Taipei, the Rolls had come to a gentle stop before the Ritz Hotel. During the ride Lisa and Sun Chen had passed as much time in silence as they had in conversation. What words they exchanged had been inconsequential. Lisa had answered a few questions about life at the Academy. Sun Chen had told her something of his pharmaceutical holdings, and expressed surprise when Lisa revealed how much she had learned of his company on her own. The silences had not been strained, but natural pauses. They had much to learn about each other, Lisa thought. Now Sun Chen took her arm once more and escorted Lisa into the Ritz.

Paris 1930 occupied a portion of the hotel's second floor. The restaurant's appointments were elegant, the service unobtrusive and superb. The maître d' showed them to a quiet table. Sun Chen spoke to a waiter, ordering a Chivas on the rocks.

"The same for me, please," said Lisa with what she hoped sounded like confidence.

Sun Chen's dark eyebrows darted up. "You wish a cocktail, my dear?"

"Of course," said Lisa calmly.

Sun Chen's smile was indulgent. "I think not. A Perrier with lime for the lady," he said to the waiter. "After all, you matriculated from Li Juan Academy today, not from university," he told Lisa.

"Whatever you say, Mr. Sun Chen." Lisa did not feel chastened at all. She had never had Perrier, either—it was all so new.

"Please. Call me Victor."

"Victor."

After that, Lisa left all ordering to Victor Sun Chen. His French was flawless, serving him well in an unexpectedly heated confrontation with the somme-lier. "I ordered champagne," he explained to Lisa after getting his way with the wine steward. "For both of us. I don't think it will hurt. However poorly that buffoon thinks it will complement our meal."

When she tasted the Krug 1958, Lisa could not believe that the wine steward had hesitated. There could be no more marvelous taste in the world. The bubbles tickled her nose, the wine her palate, just as in the novels she had read. She touched the crystal flute to Victor's, looking deep into his eyes. She sipped the champagne slowly, letting its magic warm her. For the first time she allowed herself to wonder how the evening would end. *Will he kiss me? Will we make love?* The circumstances of her upbringing had early made her wise in the affairs of men and women. She had no illusions. But her determination had frightened off any who had tried to take advantage of her in the slums. At the Academy she was insulated from men. Her knowledge remained second-hand. *I have never been kissed. Will I know how?* She ran a finger around the lip of the champagne flute. She stared at Victor. Her uncertainty vanished. If he kissed her, she felt sure, she would know what to do. *If we make love, he will teach me.*

They lingered over their meal, Victor explaining to her the subtleties and excellences of each course. When at last the dessert dishes were removed, Victor made a show of looking at his gold Rolex chronometer. "So late. A good thing you're not expected back at the Academy this evening. You would be in violation of your curfew."

"Not expected?" Lisa asked, and surprised herself by giggling.

"Your Headmistress and I agreed that you had earned a vacation, my dear. There is a suite here in the Ritz, booked in your name." He stood and held her chair so that Lisa could rise. "Come. I will take you there."

Lisa felt as though she were walking above the carpeted corridor. The champagne quickened her step, brightened her eyes. She dared to stand close to Victor in the elevator, leaned against him and rested her head on his shoulder. He idly stroked her cheek with his fingers, nothing intimate about his touch. Lisa replayed the evening in her mind, startled to realize that for all the romance she had imagined, Victor had been unfailingly polite, even a bit distant as they dined. *Have I misunderstood?* she wondered. *Perhaps I am simply a scholarship student after all. Surely so great a man as Victor must entertain himself with more mature women than me.* If there was to be no romance between them, she decided as they left the elevator, then Victor would not know of her disappointment. *He would think me foolish.* She stood patiently as he unlocked the door of her suite, then followed him into the rooms.

Taipei sparkled with lights far below. Lisa removed her cape and draped it over one of the chairs in the sitting room. Victor stepped to the bar and poured himself a cognac. He cradled the snifter in his palm and joined Lisa beside the picture window that overlooked Chungshan District. "And how have you enjoyed yourself this evening?" he asked.

Lisa turned away from the view and gazed up at him. Sun Chen extended the snifter, wafted it below Lisa's nostrils. The heady fumes made her dizzy. She watched as Victor sipped the cognac. "I have enjoyed myself so much, Victor," she said. "I never knew—" She could say no more. Nor could she stop the tears that filled her eyes unexpectedly. "You have made me very happy."

"You are crying," Victor said. He placed the snifter on a low table and brushed away Lisa's tears. More replaced them. "Why?"

"You have been so kind. So much has been done for me." She placed a hand on his arm, found herself clutching him. "Now, it is all over. It is—"

"All over?" He smiled tenderly at her. "Why, my dear, your life is only just beginning. Do not be sad."

Lisa reached up and pressed her fingers against Victor's cheek. "I am afraid. I am—" Her fingers moved to his neck. Lisa pressed firmly against him, tugging him toward her. "Please—"

For a moment Victor Sun Chen resisted her. *He thinks I am a little fool.* "Lisa," he said softly. "You want this?"

She was never more certain of anything. *He knew what I would say, what I would do. But that was a lesson I did not learn until later.* "Oh, yes," she had said. "Victor, I want you."

Sun Chen said no more, but drew her into his embrace. He lowered his mouth to hers, and Lisa sighed when their lips met. Her mouth opened like a flower to his kiss. Lisa's ears were filled with the rhythm of her heartbeat. She thought she could hear Victor's as well, pounding in time to her own. The kiss lasted almost forever, and when it broke, Lisa tilted her head back to enable Victor to touch his lips to her throat. The warmth she'd received from the champagne was nothing compared to the heat that flooded her now. The gown grew suddenly tight; she felt swollen, engorged. She could feel the fabric against her nipples, between her legs. Victor's fingers traced patterns on her back, making her shiver with pleasure. They kissed again, even more deeply, and Lisa felt as though she would faint. She pushed her hands beneath Victor's jacket, holding him tightly, feeling the muscles beneath his shirt. She found his throat with her lips, tasted salt. Victor's hands were in her hair, undoing the clip. Lisa's hair spilled down over her shoulders. She shook her head, and kissed Victor deeply. She did not think or hesitate when she felt his fingers find the zipper at the back of her gown, but stood tall, her shoulders held firm as he unfastened the dress and pushed it down. Lisa stepped out of the dress and kicked away her shoes as Victor removed his jacket and necktie.

She was not ashamed of standing before him nearly

nude, and reached out to unfasten the buttons of his shirt. Sun Chen took her shoulders and pulled Lisa to him. As they kissed he pushed aside her undergarments, ran strong fingers across Lisa's breasts. She tugged his shirt from his trousers, and then her hands moved as though of their own volition to his belt, undid the buckle, opened his trousers. She felt his hardness, the mass of him hot. Her fingers reached but Victor pushed her back, ran his hands down over her hips as he lowered himself, cupped her taut buttocks as he pressed his face against her thighs, found the center of her with his mouth. Lisa's vision failed. Blind, whimpering, she dug her fingers into Sun Chen's hair, urged him on until she felt herself burst into flames and swayed, moaning, to the thick carpet.

Her sight returned in time for her to see Sun Chen standing above her, stripping away his clothing. He dropped to his knees beside her, his hands caressing her breasts, fingers stroking her flat belly, tangling themselves in her soft nest of hair. "Victor," she said deep in her throat. He moved over her, kissed her once more. Lisa felt her legs open to the pressure of him, reached down to guide him into her. She studied his face, his eyes closed, every vein and cord of muscle on his neck standing out in tension, his mouth a thin drawn line. He pushed himself into her gently at first, but with more force. Lisa pushed back at him, felt something within her resist, then yield with a sensation so intense that she cried out, then felt him move within her, and moved herself beneath him, and around him, until Sun Chen shuddered and she lost herself completely.

Sometime that night we moved into the bedroom where I proved further how quickly I could learn, Lisa remembered. *And before the next day was out I had moved into his estate where I learned many more things. Among them, the nature of hell.*

She grew aware that she had stopped walking, that

59

David Wellington was watching her. "You're crying," she heard him say.

Lisa looked around. They were at the jetfoil pier. "How—"

"You're crying," David said again.

"No. I cannot be—" She touched her cheeks, found them wet. "I'm sorry—"

"What's made you so sad?" David produced a silk handkerchief, and Lisa dried her eyes. She did not answer him. "Lisa—"

She returned the handkerchief, composed herself. "David, I apologize. This is . . . I don't quite know what's come over me." Lisa made herself smile, and prayed that the effect was not ghastly. "Too much work, perhaps. Too many—"

David pressed a finger against her lips. "Shh, now. Whatever it is that has upset you . . . or frightened you. Don't be scared, Lisa." His touch moved to her cheek. *Like Victor,* she thought, but cut such thoughts off. *Not like Victor at all.* "Whatever it is," David was saying, "let me help—"

Lisa shook her head and stepped away from him. "Don't concern yourself, David," she said. "It really doesn't matter."

"It does to me," David said, letting her have her distance. "It matters very much to me."

"Then get over it," Lisa said angrily. "I'm really not worth it, you know," she said.

"Self-pity?" said David Wellington without pause. "You surprise me, Lisa."

"Self—" She caught her breath. "Why should you be surprised, David? We've worked together, but you don't know me. Don't delude yourself into thinking that you do."

"I know you, Lisa Han," he said firmly.

"No."

David moved close, following Lisa as she tried to back away from him. She pressed herself against the wall of a building, drawing back when David moved his face close to hers. His breath was hot and sweet against her skin. Lisa placed her palms against David's chest, but did not push. "I *know* you," David repeated. His mouth was close to hers. "Know you well enough to want to know more." He moved even closer. "To *want*—" He kissed her, then, and Lisa returned the kiss before realizing what she was doing. By then it was too late, and she opened her mouth to his. Their bodies pressed close.

When the kiss was ended an eternity later David stepped back. Lisa did not move, needing the support offered by the wall. *I should not have allowed that,* she thought. *It will not happen again.* "That did not happen, David," Lisa said in a voice more ragged than she would have liked.

"Oh, really?" Mirth was evident in his gray eyes. "You certainly could have fooled me."

"Stop it," she commanded. "This is not right."

"No? What's wrong with it?"

"David, *please*—"

He approached her again, but did not touch her. "Lisa, come back to Hong Kong with me tonight."

"I can't. You should know that."

"Why can't you? Give me a reason."

Lisa felt sensation return to her legs. She stepped away from the wall, out of the shadows and into a pool of light cast by a high streetlamp. She answered him calmly. "Because we have business between us, David. Vital, important business." She returned his stare. "Nothing more. I insist on that."

"But you won't tell me why?"

She shook her head. "No."

David surprised her by grinning. "Then there's hope." He glanced toward the jetfoil where the final passengers were boarding. "You're certain you won't come with me? I fly back to America in the morning. We could have a few hours together, anyway."

"Do not ask such things, David. I have told you they are impossible."

David reached out and playfully tweaked her nose. "Lisa, it's you who don't understand me."

"What do you mean?"

"After all the time we've spent together you should know that I have no use for *impossibility.* I just don't believe in it," David Wellington said. He clutched her shoulders, brought her to him, and kissed her once more, hard. "You'll see." He turned down the crowded pier, rushing with tourists and other businesspeople to catch the evening's last jetfoil back to Hong Kong. David boarded without looking back.

For a long time Lisa Han did not move. The deckhands removed the hawsers, and the sleek craft moved slowly away. Clear of the docking area, the jetfoil turned and began picking up speed. Lisa watched until its lights dwindled in the distance, her mind blank. She would not think of David Wellington in any terms other than business. There would be time enough.

After an hour she boarded a slow ferry, and passed much of the night riding in silence back to Hong Kong.

4

DAVID WELLINGTON PUT his Porsche 959 through its paces, devouring the miles of twisting mountain road that lay between Asheville and the Wellington estate. After midnight, he had the roads virtually to himself, and he made the most of it. The tachometer climbed, and engine roar filled the night. David's foot found the clutch and he pressed against its tension, downshifting through a series of sharp bends. David breathed deeply, pine-scented mountain air mingling with the aroma of the Porsche's leather interior. The road straightened and David accelerated once more. He felt exhilarated, as he always did when testing himself and his reflexes. Yet he knew that behind his excitement lurked a weariness that would catch up with him once he was home.

David had caught a scant half hour's nap during the Learjet hop from Atlanta to Asheville, his sleep fitful, and his waking moments filled with thoughts of Peng and omnigene. He'd barely slept on the plane from Hong Kong, using his time on that flight to scrawl his way through a notebook-and-a-half related to Peng's proposition. *Mostly related. More than once I caught myself doodling Lisa's name. Like a schoolboy.*

David grinned as he downshifted and felt the 959's tires bite into the pavement at the edge of a hairpin turn. David knew these roads as well as he knew his signature. He held his breath, accelerating even before the Porsche slingshotted out of the bend. The next mile and a quarter was almost perfectly straight. In daylight the road looked sheer over a hundred-foot drop. At night, road and drop were both swallowed by darkness and the shadow of the mountain that bulked huge on the left. Twin turbine whine filled the night. *It is the risk I enjoy,* David told himself, *much more than the speed.*

Tire squeal came close to drowning out the turbines as David guided the Porsche on a high gee trajectory through the next curve. For a second, centrifugal tug pulling hard, David thought he would lose it. He couldn't find the edge of his control; his reflexes were more dulled than he suspected. His knuckles whitened and a sudden cramp moved along the inside of his right thigh. The headlamps stabbed out into emptiness, the car threatening to follow, to fall.

Then the rear tires slewed, the beams swung back, found road. The curve receded behind him.

David shed speed and dropped the 959 into a lower gear. He kneaded his thigh until the muscle unclenched. He would take the rest of the drive at a steadier pace. Risk made little sense, he reflected, unless you were up to it, and tonight he wasn't. This time the Porsche would not prove the vehicle for his relaxation. He was still tense, a dull pain between his shoulderblades. There was a sexual edge to his tension as well. *I left more than just business unresolved.* He pressed his back against the contours of the leather seat. The soft glow of the dash illuminated the interior of the car. David thought of Lisa Han. Their kisses had been brief, but he had found in them the promise of great riches of response. *If she ever lets down her guard I am likely to be overwhelmed.* It was a likelihood he would welcome, and through the final ten miles of his drive he diverted himself with a pleasant fantasy, himself and Lisa marooned together, no omnigene, no responsibilities, no demands. *Only us.*

He found himself yawning by the time he turned onto the private, graveled drive that led through a thick stand of trees to Tallpines. The night air was filled with the scent of spring, evergreen and wildflower. David thought of the rainy season that soon would descend upon Lisa Han and her part of the globe. *She ought to be here, with me.* He did not doubt that she would immediately love Tallpines as much as he did. *As does everyone who sees it.* Approaching the final fir-shrouded turn, he slowed the 959 to a crawl. *I grew up here, and even for me it is always as though I am seeing it for the first time.* The Porsche emerged into the clearing which gave upon the great house. David braked to a stop, put the engine in neutral. He got out, stood and stretched for a moment, stared at his family's home.

The night was clear and moonless, the house a silhouette against a sky filled with stars. To the left flecks of starlight glinted off the long greenhouse in which James and Monica Wellington had pursued their botanical interests. Living and reception quarters were central, two stories sprawling wide beneath a high peaked roof. On the right stretched Tallpines' most recent major addition, a library and laboratory wing hewn, like the main house itself, of local stone and wood. James had commissioned the new wing as a retirement gift for himself, and it had been built by craftsmen descended from those who'd constructed the manor house itself. *Some of those men's names go back centuries in these mountains. As does my own.* There were larger, grander, more pretentious estates in the area. The largest of them all, an American castle, lay fifty miles away and dominated thousands of acres. *We have nine hundred acres,* David thought, resting a hand on the cool metal roof of the Porsche. *This is no Biltmore.* He grinned. *But, then, we're no Vanderbilts.*

The land had been acquired and Tallpines begun not long after the turn of the century. The estate was intended to serve as a summer retreat for Hugh Wellington and his family. *Old Hugh: great granddad.* Hugh Wellington had been born deep in the North

Carolina mountains, but left his home when barely past boyhood. He earned an education for himself at the state university, returned to Asheville and set up in business as a druggist. Wellington had built a comfortable living on the steady trade at his store. Not all of Hugh's long hours were devoted to filling prescriptions and tallying receipts. Hugh manufactured most of the remedies he dispensed, and two of his formulas—a tonic for weary blood, and a linament for aching muscles—found fame far beyond Asheville. By the time Hugh was thirty-five, he was a millionaire more than once, and the foundations of both Tallpines and Wellington Laboratories were laid. Fortune and reputation grew apace. *Then came granddad with Pandrex and Wellington Labs became first among equals in headache tablets and nonprescriptions. Dad carried us into prescriptions and specialized drugs, not to mention rarified research and genetic tailoring.* David stared at the house for a long time, the purring engine of the Porsche the night's only sound. As he stood there he was aware of how much he missed his father, how much he could have used James Wellington's wise counsel as he approached this difficult decision. But David knew he was on his own, and now it felt . . . unusual, *new.* In the five years since taking charge, David had close to doubled Wellington Laboratories' size, and expanded into the Asian market. He had had some rough moments and some triumphs of his own, but so far nothing like the accomplishments and contributions those from whom he was descended had made. Three generations before him found their own way. Now he had the tools and the contacts, he had the power, he had the strength. David stood taller.

And I'm going to take omnigene into the People's Republic of China. His mind was made up. *For better or worse.*

David climbed back into the Porsche and drove slowly up to the front of the great house, his tension gone. He wanted a long, scalding shower and a night's sleep in his own bed. He killed the engine and stepped out onto the raked gravel of the driveway. Hearing the crunch of footsteps, he turned to greet Tallpines' groundskeeper, Lem Evans. Lem carried a small flashlight, and its glow showed David the smile that wrinkled Lem's ruddy face. "David, welcome home!"

David shot a glance at the house's few lights. "Hello, Lem," he said, shaking hands. Lem's hands were calloused from decades of work, yet David had many times watched those hands delicately graft plant tissue together in the greenhouse. Lem's hybrids had won prizes. David had known him since childhood, and found it at times hard to believe that the avuncular figure he'd known as a boy now had grandchildren. "It's good to be back."

"That I'd imagine," said Lem, broadening his questionable brogue. "Of course, for myself I couldn't imagine ever leaving." He glanced around, lowered the flashlight. "We're missing your father."

"Sure," said David. How many times had he and James and Lem stood outside on a spring evening just as this? "But he's here."

"You can tell it best in the spring," Lem agreed. "When things start growing again. All the things he planted, we planted together. Those will be here forever." He sighed. "So will he."

"I'll look forward to walking the grounds with you this weekend. I assume we're adding to the plantings?"

"As always," Lem Evans chuckled. "A couple of lovelies from Peru. Flowering shrubs that we hope will acclimate."

"I'll wear my work clothes," David said.

Pleasure showed on Lem's face. "Ah, that'll be good." He clapped David on the shoulder.

David reached into the back of the Porsche and grabbed his shaving kit. Tomorrow morning was soon enough to bother with his luggage. "How is Monica?"

"Coming out of it, I think." James's death had hit her hard, and she had not left Tallpines in months. "She's been outdoors a lot, smiling more, sitting in the sun. But she's always got her nose buried in a book."

"Maybe she's getting back to work," David said. He hoped so. Monica's grief had not been dramatic or histrionic, but it had been persistent. *One of the reasons I let the mess with Hilary go on so long,* David thought with a mild pang of guilt. *It gave Monica such pleasure. No excuse, though.* "We'll get her out of the books on Sunday, Lem. Get her hands dirty, let her plant something."

The idea delighted Lem. "I'll count the hours 'til then, David. It'll do her a world of good." He squeezed David's shoulder. "Now, goodnight!"

"'Night, Lem," David said, and walked up the steps of the wide front porch, and into the house.

Inside, the silence matched that of the night. Karl Lewis, Tallpines's butler and chief of staff, was awake, but David had never known a time when Karl *wasn't* awake. Now he waved off Karl's offer of refreshment or assistance. "Got it all in hand, Karl," David said, and with a smile waved his Vuitton shaving kit.

Karl nodded and retreated toward the kitchen.

David climbed the carpeted stairs slowly. At the head of the stairs he turned left, toward his wing of the living quarters, down a corridor whose dark paneled walls were hung with framed photographs and mementos. *A blue ribbon for grade school swimming right next to my picture on the cover of Forbes,* David noted with some wryness. When it had become clear that David would be an only child, his parents had renovated half the second floor to make a spacious suite—virtually an apartment—for David. The rooms' decor had changed over the years, as childhood pursuits yielded to high school and college studies and those in turn to business responsibilities, but David continued to think of the suite at Tallpines as his home, far more so than his Atlanta townhouse, his San Francisco Victorian, or his Manhattan condominium. *I do not live here often anymore,* he thought, *but this is where I come alive.* He passed through the comfortable study that had once been his playroom, stepped into the master bedroom and stripped off his clothes.

He stood without moving for a while in the hot spray of his shower. His eyelids were heavy. He was pleased, in a way, that Monica had already retired. *No need for her to wait up for me. And I'm certainly not up to being welcomed back by anything other than my bed.* They could greet each other in the morning. They would have a lot to talk about. He could not predict how Monica Wellington would react to the news of Peng's proposal. Since James's death she had acceded wearily to every one of David's business decisions. But since his death she had also held control of thirty-four percent of the company's voting stock. *And the China offer is not something to be casually accepted or rejected.* He promised himself that in addition to talking business with Monica he would make an effort to involve her in outdoor work. The fresh air and fresh spring life would do her good. If she was at last beginning to emerge from her emotional cocoon, David wanted to see that the emergence gained some momentum before he left Tallpines.

David let the hot water play over him for another few minutes. He breathed steam deep into his lungs. When he stepped from the shower he toweled himself dry, then padded nude back into his bedroom.

Where he stopped, stunned. Hilary Bishop lay on his bed.

"Surprise," she said softly, showing David a smile, tossing her mane of blond hair. "Welcome home."

"Hilary—" David began, before realizing that he was still undressed. He moved quickly to the cedar wardrobe near the bed, and took his quilted Burberry robe from its hook.

"Shy?" Hilary teased. "In front of *me?*" She giggled, and wriggled her hips seductively. Her thigh-length Sanchez satin bedjacket began to fall open. Hilary wore nothing beneath the jacket except her perfect tan.

David belted his own robe tight. "I didn't expect to see you," he said.

"No?" Hilary replied in a tone of voice that made the word a dare. "Well, I promise you I will more than exceed your expectations." Her eyes were wide and challenging. It was a look David knew well. Hilary kept her wide eyes on David as she tucked her thumbs under the bedjacket's belt, and tugged against its loose restraint. The jacket fell completely open, revealing to David the lush body he had once found so delightful.

"Get out of my bed," he said flatly.

Hilary chose not to hear him, and flipped her hand as though to brush away his orders. She sank back against the pillows and moistened her lips with the tip of her tongue. "You're just tired," she said, her voice husky.

"I *am* tired, Hilary," David said.

"Come here."

"Too tired for this. Get out of the bed."

"David—"

"Now."

For a moment Hilary did not move, save to press her hands flat against the colorful quilt that covered the bed. "You're serious," she said at last.

David nodded. *I am indeed,* he realized. He could not deny that even as he stood still and obdurate, Hilary's body worked its magic on him. It would be easy to say nothing, to take her, but he would not. *This is ended.* He thought of Lisa Han. He stared at Hilary. *No need to be a total bastard about this: Hilary can't help being who she is.* "Come, now," he whispered.

Hilary's eyes flashed at David a second's worth of

knives, then began to glisten with tears. Her lower lip quivered. "Why?"

David sighed. "Hilary, don't. It's too late, we can talk this out tomorrow."

She shook her head and repeated her question, imploringly. "Why, David?"

"I think we both know, and just won't admit it. Didn't we find that out the last time we were together?"

"But . . . it was just a little *tiff,"* Hilary whimpered, her voice tiny and girlish. Her shoulders shuddered beneath the satin jacket.

"It was more than that," David said gently. He came close to the bed and touched his fingers to her cheek. Catlike, Hilary rubbed against David's palm. He brushed away tears with his thumb. "There's no way for this not to hurt. We had good fun for a while. Damned good times." He drew back his hand. "But that's all, and that's ended, now. Come."

Slowly Hilary closed the jacket and knotted its belt. It took obvious effort for her to raise her chin to a more even keel. Hilary swung her feet from the bed and stood up, looking David in the eye. She took a step away from him before speaking. "You're making a mistake."

David looked hard to find hurt in Hilary's expression, but there was nothing but hate. "I don't think so."

"No." Her tone was arctic. "Of course you don't. You wouldn't."

"Get some sleep, Hilary. We'll talk in the morning."

"Yes. You can bet we will." Hilary tried once more to kill him with her gaze, and when she failed walked quickly from the bedroom. She slammed the door shut.

For a moment David stood still. A dull ache had returned to the back of his neck and he reached up to massage it. He turned down the covers and hung up his robe. The sheets were cool and crisp when he slid between them, with only a hint of warmth betraying the spot where Hilary had lain. Some of that warmth, still, touched David. The relationship had lasted longer than any of his recent loves, and he knew that tomorrow's conversation would not be without pain. At last he closed his eyes, and fell asleep almost immediately.

In the morning he awoke with a start from a vivid dream of Lisa Han. They had been together, in some sort of danger, David recalled. Yet there was also a sexual edge to the dream. He lay still for a moment, breathing deeply, trying to recapture it, but the dream was gone, all details fleeting. David rubbed his eyes and sighed. He was climbing out of bed when there came a soft knock at the door.

"Mind if I come in?" Monica Wellington said, peeping around the edge of the door. "It's after eight! You two should—" She stopped, having seen that David was alone. She came into the bedroom. "Where's Hilary?"

David felt his stomach knot. *Whatever side of the bed I get up on will be wrong today,* he thought. "She didn't stay here."

"But—"

The timing, David reflected, was awful, but he had no choice other than to plunge right in. "I asked her not to, Monica."

"You what?"

David answered slowly. "I asked her to leave. She's in the guest room."

Monica was incredulous. "We went to a lot of trouble, David. She changed her schedule . . . we wanted to surprise you."

David covered himself with the sheet and stepped to the cedar wardrobe. Once he had donned his robe and tied its belt, he turned to face Monica. "I'm sorry," he said. "Hilary and I are . . . we have some things to work out."

Monica shook her head, dark bangs falling into her eyes. She brushed them away. "I think I'd better talk to Hilary," she said.

David nodded, and watched her go. *Not an auspicious start for the day,* he thought. He went into the bathroom and drew a steaming basin of water, and busied himself working shaving brush against soap mug. Splashing hot water on the stiff bristles, he took his time shaving, trying to calm himself, but the knot of pain at his neck dug in deeper. David dressed quickly, pulling on a favorite light L.L. Bean flannel shirt and gray Perry Ellis slacks. He slipped his feet into a pair of battered but beloved moccasins, fashioned by hand by mountain artisans. He stepped to the window in his study and looked down on Monica and Hilary seated at the wrought-iron table in the center of the slate terrace. David took a long breath of morning air, then walked downstairs to join them.

Hilary Bishop was dressed for a mountain spring morning, blond hair pulled back in a ponytail, Calvin Klein safari shorts and jacket reminding David again of the fullness of her body. Hilary saw him stop at the edge of the slate and stood up. "Good morning, David," she said, but made no move to approach him. Monica said nothing, nor did she look David's way. Taking his seat at the table, David poured a cup of Jamaican Blue Mountain coffee, and sipped it slowly.

David found himself picking at his plate, despite the fact that it was laden with his favorite fare: eggs and biscuits, grits and pungent country ham, fried apples. Finally he pushed his plate aside, and noticed that neither Hilary nor Monica had done much better. "Marjorie will be upset," David said, referring to Tallpines' cook.

The joke fell flat. *"I'm* upset," Monica Wellington

73

said. A sudden breeze toyed with her hair. "At your behavior, David."

"Monica—" he began, but Hilary would not let him speak.

"I'd like to talk for a minute," Hilary said. She took Monica's hand, and reached out to touch her cheek. "This is . . . not easy for any of us. But we're all adults, now, and we're all good friends, whatever David's and my status may be. I don't understand what's happened between us, and maybe David doesn't either. But we can't all sit here and sulk and fling accusations, Monica. David and I will have to work this out on our own." She brightened. "Besides, if we sit here in silence, we won't be able to talk business!"

David was surprised. He had never seen Hilary so solicitous. She seemed genuinely more concerned about Monica's emotional well-being than her own.

Taking a handkerchief from her pocket, Monica dabbed at her eyes, and looked directly at David. "Hilary's being too polite," she said coldly. "But she's right. There's business to attend to, and I'll leave you to it. I want to be alone for a while." Monica pushed her chair back from the table and returned to the house.

Hilary broke the moment of awkward silence, speaking with the same concern. "This is going to be hard on her. Since James's death I think she—" she broke off, then caught herself before composure failed. "She put a lot of stock in our . . . in *us*."

"Yes," said David.

Hilary looked closely at him, her brow wrinkled with concentration. "So did I."

David nodded. "It just went too far," he said. "I should have spoken up sooner."

Hilary pressed her lips tight together before speaking. "How long have—"

David shrugged. "Does it matter?"

After a moment Hilary shook her head, then sat

back. "I guess not. But there's . . . nothing there for me?"

She looked vulnerable, a posture in which David was not accustomed to seeing Hilary Bishop. "Good friendship," he said. "How about that?"

Hilary made her face brave. "If that's all there is."

"That's all," David said, and nodded.

Hilary looked away from him, gazing out over the immaculately maintained lawn that stretched from the edge of the terrace over hundreds of meters until it reached the perimeter of the thick forest that surrounded the estate. "It's so lovely here."

David's surprise deepened. This wasn't like Hilary, he thought, and disliked himself for his suspicions. But there was a storm of fury inside her—he knew that—and he could only wait for it to break loose. "You said you have business."

Hilary's shoulders rose before she turned to face him. "I do," she said. "A wonderful opportunity, in fact."

David raised a Wedgwood cup to his lips and sipped coffee. "What is it?"

"Ethan Drug is in serious trouble," she said. "The buyout their management leveraged is going down and it's going down hard." She spread her hands wide.

"And?" David asked. The news about Ethan was nothing new. The company had once operated a vast and profitable drugstore chain, but had expanded too fast. Management believed it saw an opportunity to reverse the company's downward trend, and had taken it over a year ago. They had made some progress, but still faced large financial challenges.

"And I know a way to turn that trouble into large profits," Hilary announced, her eyes gleaming.

David restrained himself from smiling: this was the Hilary he knew. "Go ahead."

Hilary's words came in a torrent. "There's no way Ethan can get itself out of its fix. But it's going to take them a very costly while to get to the point where they can abandon ship and come away with anything at all. That's where we come in."

"We?"

Hilary nodded vigorously. "Conditions of the buy-out restrain management from diversifying—they've got to operate those drugstores, and find a way to make them profitable. They can't."

"And we can?" David asked.

Hilary laughed at him. "Are you kidding? No one could. Ethan grew up in the old days, David, the dull old days of downtown drugstores with marble soda fountains. The marble's all chipped and cracked, and the only customers they've got at most of those stores are street people and old people too poor to move to the suburbs. Their day is gone."

"So how do we make them profitable?" David said.

"Close them. Board them up and tear them down."

"What?"

"As drugstores, Ethan's holdings aren't worth the property they stand on. But as *property*—the sky's the limit! Two hundred stores in a hundred sixty cities and towns. My studies show that of those, more than a hundred Ethan Drug Stores stand on property that's eminently developable, and terrifically profitable."

"Potentially," David said.

"Immediately," Hilary insisted. "Hell, the property's the only thing the company's got that's worth anything. And fortunately for us, they borrowed against it low, early on. It's the least of their debts, and the only one we'd have to worry about paying off."

"The only one," David said. The deal she had offered him was pure Hilary Bishop. *Monroe would be very proud of his little girl. And probably rather scared of her.*

"Sure." Hilary used her fingers to count off the stages of her scheme. *"One,* we take over Ethan. *Two,* we clean house—and I mean radically. There aren't ten stores in that chain that are worth anything. For appearance' sake, we pump some cash into those ten, begin shutting down some of the others. *Three,* we start doing a tax-time dance, taking every penny we can find. *Four,* we put together a package of desperation aimed at Ethan's creditors—"

"Which include Wellington Laboratories," David said softly. He was, he admitted, enjoying this performance.

"Sure, sure. They're into the Bishop Group for quite a bit as well. That's how I got started on this." She caught her breath and resumed her enumeration. *"Five,* after a decent interval—three months ought to do it—we start leaking the news that we've made a bad move, that Ethan's headed belly-up. We get the creditors on the bandwagon as early and cheaply as possible, again dancing our rears off for the IRS. *Six,* we fold up Ethan while holding on to the land, paying off in full any paper on the physical property, and paying off for a few cents on the dollar any outside creditors." An expression of triumph, almost feral, crossed her face. *It looks natural,* David thought.

"Seven, call in the bulldozers and the cranes and start putting up office buildings." She sat back smiling. "And that's how you turn what should be at most no more than an eighty- to ninety-million-dollar investment into a billion-dollar real estate group!"

David could say nothing, resisting the impulse to applaud. "You've told Monica about this?"

Hilary nodded. "It's why I was so concerned about her this morning. You should have seen her, David! Her eyes were more bright than I've seen them since the funeral. She even came up with a couple of twists and turns that will make the deal more profitable. She's got a good feel for this, it's going to do her a lot of good."

David refilled his coffee cup. He did not know what to say. He hoped Hilary was exaggerating Monica's enthusiasm for this scheme. *All I need is Monica getting this notion into her head while we're trying to work things out with the Chinese.*

Hilary was looking at him expectantly. "Well?"

He made himself smile widely for her. "Give me some time to think this through," he said. "Real estate development isn't exactly Wellington Labs' long suit, you know."

Hilary was not interested in objections. "We'll hire the talent for that," she said. "You should have heard Monica talking about it. We'll let *her* run it, get her more involved." Hilary hugged herself suddenly, a gesture that chilled David. "And all the money we'll make!"

"What about us, Hilary? You think we can do business together?"

"I know we can! Business on this scale—David, you're a fool to hesitate for even a second."

"Maybe I am," David said softly.

Comprehension dawned on her, and spread across her face. "You *are* hesitating."

"That kind of money always makes me hesitate."

"I've got a briefcase full of papers, studies," Hilary said. "Once you look at them—"

"I'd like to see them," David said. "Later."

Hilary narrowed her eyes. "You're soft, David," she said. "You always have been."

"Hilary—"

"You talk to me when you're ready to listen," Hilary said.

"Coming from you, Hilary, that makes sense," David observed. He rose from his seat. "You'll excuse me." Not yet eager to face Monica, David walked swiftly from the terrace and out across the lawn. He would sort it all out later.

Hilary's proposal was symbolic of the way she did business—and the way she had conducted herself during their affair. As he entered the forest, setting out along one of the pine-needled trails, he tried to recall if Hilary had ever really listened to him. The more he reviewed his memories, the more certain he became that he had never enjoyed her full attention. *Monroe's genes bred true,* David thought. The deal Hilary had offered represented much of what he disliked: the fastest, biggest deals were what mattered. *Not the best.*

He wondered what Hilary would say about Peng's proposal. The potential of a base in China and the perfection and introduction of omnigene were immense, far greater than Hilary's dubious billion dollars. *But it will be the work of decades,* David thought. *China will not come easily. Why should it?* He could not see himself wearing the hat of a high-level real estate developer, counting skyscrapers with Hilary Bishop. That was too easy. *I'd rather shake the world,* he thought, then realized that Hilary would be incapable of thinking in such terms. For all her obvious ambition and delight in talking of billions, Hilary, like her father, was hopelessly small time. The Bishops, father and daughter, were always ready to strike a deal and collect their earnings, but they also liked to leave the conference table with their earnings in hand as soon as possible. They had no desire to stick with a project over the long run. Monroe, and now Hilary, thought of business commitment in terms of months, maybe years, never in terms of a lifetime.

David stopped beneath the bower of an oak tree that had been huge when his father was a child. Lost in thought, he did not hear Hilary approach, but was not startled when she spoke. "David. What has happened to us?"

"We've ended," he said simply.

Hilary reached out to touch him, but David stepped back. "No acting, now," he said. "You and me. No roles."

Hilary slowly lowered her hand. "Someone else?"

David thought of Lisa Han, but said, "No."

"Didn't it mean anything to you? Just another affair?"

David remained silent, and held his face impassive.

"Won't you even take the trouble to say a final goodbye, then? We've been together a long time, or have you forgotten? You stood beside me while my daddy was buried. I thought you *cared.*"

"I did," said David. "I do."

"And you treat me like this," Hilary said with a small, disbelieving smile. "Who do you think you are?"

"You have to ask that, and you don't know why we're finished? Hilary, we don't even know each other."

She stared at him, her chin quivering, then broke past and ran down the path into the woods. After a moment he followed slowly, catching up with her at the edge of a quiet glade.

"You carved our initials here," Hilary reminded David. She did not turn toward him. "Which tree was it?"

"Hilary, don't," David said.

"Don't what? Don't think about what's ending between us? Don't think about how happy I've been?"

"We haven't been together for a good while, Hilary. Not really."

"I love you."

Had she ever spoken those words before? David could not remember.

As Hilary stepped deeper into the glade, sunlight filtering through leaves struck her hair. "Here it is," she called back to David.

Reluctantly David stepped toward Hilary. He had carved their initials here after a turbulent hour of lovemaking on the carpet of leaves. Hilary had looked like a woodland goddess, pagan, smeared with dirt, legs splayed. When he finished the carving, their lovemaking had resumed with even more ferocity. David felt himself grow warm at the memory, tried to chase it away.

Hilary pressed her fingertips to the crude heart that

circled the letters. Her back was to David, and he saw her shoulders shaking beneath the jacket. *Don't cry, Hilary,* he wanted to tell her. *It won't work.* He said nothing, waited.

A moment later Hilary turned around. She surveyed David languidly, then stepped back, pressing herself against the trunk of the tree. She reached up and untied her ponytail. Her hair spilled free to cover David's initials in the carved heart, while her own remained in clear sight. *Nice,* David thought, and kept his eye on the carving. A hard kernel of fury was growing in his stomach.

With a toss of her head, Hilary said, "Remember when you made that carving?"

"Don't do this, Hilary," he said.

She was having none of his warning. "I remember it." Her voice was warm and hoarse. "I remember it often." Her shoulders rose and fell as her right hand moved to the top of her safari jacket. "Some days I can't stop thinking about it, remembering it the way it was here, wanting it that way again." Her fingers worked at the buttons.

Hilary's look was hard and challenging, but David told himself how easy it would be to ignore that challenge. All he must do was turn and leave. Hilary popped another button free and the jacket was open to her midriff, barely containing the swell of her breasts. David's heartbeat was sluggish, sensual; his groin felt tight. His anger grew within him.

"Don't you want me like that again?" Hilary said. She ran long fingernails up the deep cleft between her breasts.

David's throat was dry and tight. He was as sensually aware as he had ever been in his life; cool air against suddenly sweatdamp skin, the whine of a mosquito, light in Hilary's hair, the throb between his legs. It all ran together in a red haze. *Go!* he told himself. But he did not.

"That time did it for me like nothing before or

since," Hilary murmured. She liberated the last of the buttons. Her eyebrows arched. Her fingers nimbly worked the brass buckle at the waist of her shorts, then the zipper. Golden curls caught a glint of sunlight. "Can't you do that for me again?" she asked, tilting her head back to expose the pulse of her throat.

I have an answer for her, David thought, and nearly moved forward.

"I think you can," said Hilary. She pushed her shorts down, revealing her golden pubic tuft. Hilary stroked herself, and shuddered. "You've *got* to, David, I've got to have it again." She stroked herself more furiously, her curls beginning to glisten with excitement. "Nobody ever made me come the way you do, David," Hilary said, her voice hoarse and breathy.

David's own breathing was ragged, his penis thick in his trousers, an insistent weight. Yet he might have been rooted to the spot. He could not take Hilary, but he could not leave.

Hilary rotated her hips, rubbing herself against the trunk of the tree. "I need your big cock in me, David," she moaned. "I need it in me so bad. I want to feel it all up in me." She licked her lips and her eyes grew bright with a new idea. "I want to *taste* it. You always loved that. I want it in my mouth, want you to come all over me."

David was ready at that moment to move forward and take Hilary as hard as he could. But she was impatient, and broke her lewd pose to demand, "Well?"

"No," said David. He had seen through her now—she had no chance at all. A cool breeze rustled through the glade.

Hilary put both hands between her thighs. "I'm so wet," she cried. "David, please!"

But the breeze had cooled David in more ways than one. "Come back to the house when you're finished, Hilary," he said, and felt uncommonly good doing so.

"We need to talk about your development project. A minute or two should do it."

Hilary's features became ugly, the planes of her face rearranging themselves as anger stormed through her. "You son of a bitch!" she spat as she jerked up her shorts. "Who do you think—"

This time David answered her. "I am David Wellington. And I don't believe you have ever known what that means."

Hilary was off the tree and at him, her hands making claws. For a second David thought she might actually swipe at him with her nails. But Hilary caught herself and sought to draw blood with words instead. *"David Wellington,"* she said. Her tone was as ugly as her expression. *"Scion*—oh, yes—of a stupid redneck headache pill! Well, my friend, that is so much less important than *you* think—"

"Stop it."

"Don't you *dare* tell me to stop it!" she screamed. "You Wellingtons have always thought you were so smart, so fine, so *genteel.* All your talk of business *ethics."* From Hilary's lips the word sounded foul, an obscenity. "You're such goddamned fools. Monica knows it—she saw your father coming and got exactly what she wanted: a rich, foolish, old husband with one foot already in the grave."

"Shut up, Hilary."

She ignored him, her invective climbing. "Poor Monica. Good God, the prospect of having to live with you Wellingtons even for a jackpot payoff is enough to make me vomit. Well, Monica's played the grieving widow part brilliantly for the last year, and maybe it has all paid off for *her.* But just thinking about having to go to bed with that old—"

David slapped Hilary, hard.

The force of the blow froze her for several seconds. She turned away, stumbling as she struggled to fasten her clothes. Hilary had not gone ten feet when she whirled on David once more. "The funniest thing is,

David, that *our* sex was never that good. Never even close." She clapped her hands together. "And that day here. I'm sure *you* remember who took charge. Remember all the things *I* taught you."

"Goodbye, Hilary." His voice was leaden.

"Oh, I'm not through with you yet. You'll know when I'm done—when you're wrung out and hung up to dry."

David watched until she was swallowed by the forest.

5

WORKING LATE INTO a Hong Kong evening, Candace Caillou surveyed the progress she had made with the piles of material that covered her rosewood desk. Most days, the immaculate gray ultrasuede that covered the walls of her office soothed Candace. She had selected the office's art carefully, with striking prints by the Japanese master Hokusai making both contrast and complement to the Picasso lithographs that Candace loved. Neither Picasso nor Hokusai could comfort her tonight. She pushed her Brayton International executive chair back from the desk. Candace stepped to the window. Her office's perch on the 32nd floor provided a fine view of the tip of Kowloon Peninsula and, beyond, the glittering lights of boats plying Victoria Harbor. Candace pressed her fingertips against the cool glass and stared out into the night.

Eventually her attention was distracted by her own reflection in the window. *I am forty this year,* she thought, although the image cast back at her could have been that of a woman a decade younger. *I have kept my figure and my features.* She reached up to pat back into place a curl of still lustrous black hair. *And I have even begun to buy back some of my integrity.* Candace sighed. *That of course is Lisa's doing as much as my own.* Finally she turned from the window and walked to the handsome étagère which held a Baccarat crystal decanter of the Armagnac she favored. Candace poured a healthy dollop into a snifter and wafted it beneath her nose, the heady fumes invigorating. Candace carried the snifter back to her desk and placed it carefully in the corner of a blotter trimmed with hand-worked leather.

Spread out before Candace were memoranda and reports, studies and comments, all highly confidential, outlining the steps by which a business relationship between Wellington Laboratories and the People's Republic of China would be realized. Another sheaf of papers offered in-depth and equally confidential scenarios projecting the consequences. The most exciting of the scenarios—as heady as the Armagnac!—showed Wellington's rise to dominance of the world pharmaceutical industry, and the adoption of omnigene as the wonder drug of the century. The darkest—and not by any means the least likely—painted a picture of disaster for all concerned. A bright red folder was filled with the same sort of studies, these focused upon the part to be played by Lisa Han Ventures. *LHV will earn its fees, and its points in the deal. But we will also earn a great deal of enmity throughout our region.*

Candace idly tapped a gold Cross pen against the edge of her desk. *And of course there is Victor.*

Over the years since she left him, Candace Caillou had trained herself to think of Victor Sun Chen as infrequently as possible, but when he did intrude upon her thoughts she felt a wave of revulsion. *Such a fool!* she was accustomed to telling herself on those occasions. Her thoughts tonight were different. The revulsion was still there, but it was joined by a certain grim joy. *It is good that I—that we—hate him so deeply. That way we will never lower our guard.*

Unconsciously drumming the pen against the desk in a steady staccato, Candace admitted to herself that a constant guard might not be enough this time. *We have always been wary of Victor.* The papers before her revealed, among all the other things, the degree of difficulty in which Sun Chen lay at the moment. It would be easy, perhaps a matter of months, to topple him from the perch he'd occupied for so long. No analyst showed Sun Chen remaining a power in pharmaceuticals a decade hence. *He has finally extended himself too far. It is a direction on which I helped set him, years ago.* Candace held the pen still. *And for all the years since he has had the security to . . . toy with us. Now, cornered, he will likely grow desperate.*

Whatever enjoyment or gratification she had taken from her position as Sun Chen's executive assistant was long gone. The many wounds remained fresh, would never heal. That, Candace sometimes felt, was also a good thing. If she knew all too well how deeply Victor Sun Chen could inflict pain, she also knew that she possessed the resources to endure it. He could be a charming man, even as he engaged in torment. She had seen him take pleasure from ruining a competitor. He had told her, once, that she, too, would be ruined by his whim. "But it will take time," Victor had said. "You must wait."

He sends reminders of that promise, she thought, suddenly chilled. From the opening of LHV's first, small office, each step taken by the company had been accompanied by the arrival of a bouquet from Victor. *We received them when we opened our suite here, and in Tokyo. If things proceed as expected, we shall open an office in Beijing within the month. What shall Victor do then?*

Sun Chen's bouquets, those lovely gauntlets, served notice of confrontation. *And Victor has won more than a few of those,* Candace remembered. Two of them had been important deals, transactions she had assembled herself. In one instance the unexpected death of a principal had led to the deal's collapse. *Of course there was no proof, any more than Wellington has found proof linking Victor to the deaths of its employees.* The fact that there had been no flowers yet led Candace to hope that Victor had no idea of David Wellington's China ambitions. But those ambitions, and Sun Chen's troubles, were greater than ever before. *He may be playing with us already.*

Candace sipped some Armagnac and turned back to her work. Sun Chen's place in her thoughts, however, was immediately taken by David Wellington. She had met him several times during the Kwang take-over, and spoken with him frequently by telephone. *Lisa Han talks of him with a life to her words that I have not heard in years.* That frightened Candace, for it resonated with the greatest and most devastating loss Lisa Han had ever faced. *It must not happen again,* she thought.

By the time Candace finished her Armagnac, her mind was completely focused upon her work. Figures and forecasts danced for her as she manipulated them, putting together an arrangement that would best serve Marianne Ingwer, who would be handling the negotiations in Beijing. The more she shaped the data, the more bold the whole prospect became. This was what Candace lived for, her *profession,* those moments when her expertise became electric, when her every aspect was focused fully upon financial structures and corporate strategies. Even Victor Sun Chen became for Candace simply another, albeit dangerous, player in a grand game.

Hilary Bishop was back at the main house at Tallpines in five minutes, and out of it in ten. Monica was sitting in sunlight on the terrace when she saw Hilary emerge from the woods. She raced across the lawn and was at the terrace before Monica was well out of her seat. Monica had never seen Hilary so angry. Her clothes were disheveled, her face red. "Hilary, what—" Monica began, but Hilary slammed every door she came to, then flew up the stairs.

By the time Monica reached the guest room, Hilary was throwing clothes into luggage. "Let it go, Monica," Hilary said angrily when Monica touched her shoulder.

"But you can't just—"

"Can't I?" Hilary zipped shut her Vuitton suit bag, and jerked up her other luggage. "I'm gone," she said, elbowing past Monica. She cut Karl Lewis off with a curt obscenity when the butler offered assistance with her luggage. "Just get me to the airport. *Quick!*" Karl hurried to fetch the Mercedes.

Monica followed Hilary to the front porch. Hilary tossed her luggage down to the gravel drive, then paced back and forth as she waited for the car. Monica tried once more: "Hilary—"

"Dammit, Monica, I do not want to hear it. That bastard and I are through." The long blue sedan pulled around the corner of the house and came to a smooth stop at the porch. Karl popped open the trunk and reached for Hilary's luggage. Hilary bounded from the porch and outmaneuvered Karl to jerk open the passenger door herself. Before she got in she looked up at Monica. "You think hard about Ethan, and don't take too long. I won't wait for you and you won't have that bastard on your side if you come in. You call me—*soon.*" Hilary got into the Mercedes and slammed the door. Monica could not see her through the tinted glass.

Karl looked up at Monica, his face tight with concern. *I've never seen him other than impassive,* Monica thought. She waved him on. *James and I used to joke about stoic Karl. James*—the thought vanished as Karl brought the Mercedes to life and eased away. For a moment Monica was tempted to run after the car. It had all been such a whirlwind—she was only just realizing that Hilary was actually leaving. Monica took a step down the porch stairs, but caught herself. She had seen Hilary like this before—there would be no calming her down for a while.

A ray of light bounced back from the rear window as the Mercedes passed out of sight among the trees at the edge of the drive. Monica turned and passed through the house to the terrace, to wait for David.

David lingered in the woods for more than an hour, the forests around Tallpines calming him as always. His moccasins leant him stealth as he moved rapidly along trails he'd known since childhood. David caught a glimpse of a fox darting over the top of a hill, and a doe and her fawn taking water at a brook. He lay on his belly beside a familiar pool and watched bright trout dart like bullets through water that was crystal clear. He lingered by the brook long enough for the sun to find a route through the thick trees, turning the surface of the water reflective. The face that stared back at David seemed in many ways new to him. Hilary had given him a few lines around the eyes, some more gray hair at his temples, but now he had taken his freedom from her. He had a world to reshape, and was prepared to concentrate fully upon that. *And Lisa,* he thought with a smile. He rose from his position and made his way slowly back toward Tallpines.

The buzz of the telephone startled Candace Caillou. She glanced at her watch, amazed to find it after eleven. To the right of her blotter, neatly stacked and initialed, stood evidence of her absorption. She had gotten through most of what faced her. Tomorrow, when she met with Lisa and Marianne, they would be able to initiate work on the nuts and bolts of entry into China. A smile spread across her face. The phone buzzed again. After four rings, the service would pick it up. On a whim, Candace answered.

Lisa Han began to scold her immediately. "Candace! I know you too well. I didn't even *try* your flat."

It was good to hear her voice. "How was Tokyo?" she said, hoping to cut off Lisa's lecture. This was no new argument between them. *And Lisa pushes herself far harder than I do myself.*

"Candace—it's after eleven!"

"I had work to do."

"We all have work to do," Lisa said.

"Where are you, Lisa?"

"Kai Tak International. And, yes, Tokyo went well." Candace heard Lisa's soft chuckle.

"Of course it went well," Candace said. She swiveled her seat to face the window. "And you will be pleased with the package I've put together regarding Pinetree." She used the code word assigned to David Wellington.

"No flowers yet?" Lisa asked in a somber voice.

"No."

"Good." After a moment Lisa said, "Are you tired?"

"Not particularly," Candace said with a patient sigh. "But I promise I won't stay much longer."

"No, no. I wasn't lecturing. I'm still too up to sleep, and I'm famished. Hungry?"

Candace realized that she was. "Where?"

There was a second's silence during which Candace pictured the thoughtful expression, eyes shut, lips pursed, about which she'd often teased Lisa.

"Plume," said Lisa Han at last. "We've earned it."

"So expensive!" Candace blurted, her bookkeeper's instincts unstoppable.

"Tokyo was *very* successful," Lisa replied. "My treat."

Candace gave in. "When?"

"I'm clear of customs. Forty-five minutes? You'll call and secure a table?"

"Done," said Candace. "I'll see you in forty-five minutes."

Candace called the restaurant and reserved a private table. She took a moment to straighten her desk, locking away the confidential files. A glance at her watch told her that she had plenty of time before joining Lisa. By the time she reached ground level and emerged from the elevator, Candace had decided to walk to the restaurant. She set out down Middle Road, turned right on Nathan, and made her way to Salisbury. High clouds hid the stars. *Rainy season soon,* she thought.

The nighttime streets did not frighten her. Candace could take care of herself. She had a certain fatalistic outlook as well, derived in part from her years of working with Sun Chen, and in far larger part from the years just after she left him. *He has had people close to me and Lisa killed. And if he wishes he could kill us with very little effort.*

She was so young. Candace never forgot the dreamlike expression on Lisa's face when Candace fetched her from the Ritz Hotel in Taipei. It was the morning after Lisa's graduation. *Such romance in her eyes. I did not tell her that others had felt that way about Victor, that in my time I had shared his bed. Nor did I give her any hint that she was no more special than any of the other girls he'd honored with scholarships over the years. I helped bundle Lisa's things, and listened to her silly chatter about how wonderful Victor was, and took her by car to Victor's estate.*

"It's magnificent! A palace!" Lisa had cried as the Rolls-Royce entered the terraced grounds surrounding Sun Chen's mansion. She turned to Candace and clutched her hands, every word laced with disbelief. "I am to live here?"

Candace nodded. *"Oui.* Victor would be very pleased if you would stay here." *I did not add: until he tires of you.*

Lisa sank back against the leather seat. Her eyes sparkled with tears. "Oh, Candace, dreams *can* come true. I never allowed myself to believe that before."

It was month before she realized that some dreams are nightmares. And by that time I was as fond of her as a sister.

Lisa Han settled easily into the routine of Sun Chen's household in the hills outside Taipei. When Victor was in residence there—no more than three nights a week—Lisa shared his bed. Candace watched with disgust as, upon learning that Victor was coming home, Lisa began dressing for her evening with him. *She would make herself into a whore—and think only silly thoughts of love.* The girl who while Victor was away could most often be found curled into a chaise with a serious book, now became a seductive woman. She wore gowns or lounging suits cut to display as much of her skin as possible, while still leaving Victor some secrets to uncover. On such nights, when she walked in the garden, Candace was sickened by Lisa's cries of pleasure.

The real Lisa came out when Victor was away. Lisa's intelligence was sharp and subtle, an amalgam of hard study at the Academy, vast reading on her own, and the brutal experiences of her early years. Candace held her silence, but found it excruciating that a girl so wise in so many ways could hold such illusions about Victor Sun Chen. *No one had ever been kind to her before. How could she have known?*

That summer, Candace made it a point to go out of her way to extend little courtesies and attentions to Lisa. They talked often in the gardens, and Lisa spent an hour or two each day in the office from which Candace managed Sun Chen's personal affairs. When Victor was elsewhere, it was a wonderful summer.

But summers end. It took only six weeks for Lisa Han to begin feeling like a pampered, but caged, animal. She moved through the garden as though stalking, and jumped at the slightest distraction. Her night cries grew louder and more frantic as Victor moved beyond the edge of experimentation toward those acts which gave him the greatest pleasure. Some mornings Candace found Lisa crying in the garden, her face puffy, her movements stiff and painful. She was learning, but she would not admit the truth of her lessons. Lisa shrugged off Candace's suggestions that she escape. Such talk was foolishness. She loved Victor.

Lisa's mind was restless, even when Victor was away. University was much in her thoughts. *She would light up when I told her about the Sorbonne, about the excitement of classes alongside those who share your age and interests. She made the mistake of carrying her enthusiasm for education into the bedroom with Victor.* Candace tasted bile.

Lisa Han's dreams died, for the first time, on an evening in late summer when Sun Chen appeared unexpectedly at his estate. Candace and Lisa were in their favorite corner of the garden, looking over brochures from various American universities. In recent days Lisa was dreaming of studying finance in America so that she could return to help Sun Chen increase his fortune. *She was still clinging to her fantasy—but I could see in her eyes that she knew the truth.*

"Here," said Candace, leafing through a brochure from Dartmouth. She found a photograph of boys and girls together. "All the young men you can meet!"

Lisa shook her head vehemently. "How can you say such things, Candace? I belong to Victor for now and always." She reached out and touched the brochure. "I shall miss him while I am at school."

At last—*too late!*—she searched for the nerve to speak bluntly to the child. "Lisa, you are fooling only yourself," she began.

Lisa paid no attention. From the long drive that led to the house came the sound of an approaching vehicle. Lisa jumped from her chaise and scurried to the low wall that surrounded the garden. "It's Victor!" she called. Candace could not tell what emotion Lisa's voice held. "He's come to surprise me," Lisa said, almost haltingly. "That's what it is—he has come for a surprise." She nodded twice, then hurried through the house to greet Victor at the front door. Candace followed her.

By the time she reached the front of the house,

Victor's car had rolled to a stop. Candace watched immobilized as Lisa skipped to the Rolls-Royce, then fell back. Sun Chen emerged from the car accompanied by a young woman. *No older than Lisa. Not nearly so lovely, but for Victor: fresh, new.* The smile he showed Lisa was fearsome, all teeth, lips drawn back. Lisa stood without moving as the new girl brushed past her and entered the house.

"Victor—"

"You *will* pardon me," he told her. "I *do* have a guest to entertain."

"But, Victor . . ." Lisa's voice was tiny.

"I'm certain one so smart as you can understand. It was your smartness, indeed—" He reached out and stroked the underside of Lisa's chin. "Most girls your age, Lisa, remain fresh and . . . undisturbed far longer than have you. You were too smart for your own good. You wanted horizons, and did not comprehend the importance of my walls."

Lisa's shoulders slumped.

Sun Chen was not finished. "I think perhaps Kiri will enjoy your room, my dear. Candace will help you select a few—a *very* few—of your things, and prepare your severance." He beamed. "You see? I am not an ungenerous man, after all. You will have enough, if you are careful, to see yourself established."

"What will—" Lisa could not complete the sentence.

"You underestimate yourself," said Sun Chen. He grinned. "Why, in your own way, you are as talented as any woman I have known. And there is always a market for such talents." He reached to touch her once more, but Lisa stepped away. "Very well," Sun Chen said. "Goodbye, Lisa." He hurried up the steps to the house, pausing only to nod at Candace. "Deal with this." He vanished indoors.

Candace Caillou drew a ragged breath, then walked slowly to Lisa's side. She put her arm around the girl's shoulder and tried to pull her close, but Lisa would not be moved. "I am a fool."

"Oh, no, no," Candace said, as soothingly as she could. "You're still a child. This hurts, but—"

Lisa broke away from her. "I'm no child," she said. "We both know what I am, what I have become."

Candace shook her head. "We know what *he* tried to make of you, dear Lisa. But you were too smart. He said so himself. Look at yourself. Your whole future lies ahead."

Lisa only laughed at her and ran into the house.

Candace found Lisa in her room, stretched across her bed, weeping. Candace sat beside the girl, stroked her back. "Lisa. Here. Don't. He is not worthy of your tears."

From another part of the house came the sound of high-pitched feminine laughter. It was followed by a cry that was different, throaty, sensual and frightening at the same time. Lisa ran from the bed to her bathroom where she was sick.

When she emerged her eyes were red, but her shoulders were firm, her head held high. "Does he think I will kill myself?" she asked Candace.

She forced herself to answer with brutal honesty. "One did. He did not notice. Lisa, he has forgotten you already."

Candace saw that the words stung Lisa like a slap. But the girl did not flinch. "He is mistaken, then," Lisa said. "Did you see that girl?"

"Yes."

"Does he really think that she is like me?"

"Yes."

"Candace, he is wrong. I could see it in her eyes. And in my own." Lisa measured her words. "Victor is finished with me. But I must assure you, who are my friend, that I am not yet done with him."

There was no emotion in these words, yet Candace did not doubt the conviction that underlay them.

Victor has made an error, she thought, *and an enemy.* She knew what must be done, and clapped her hands together. "Here. Let me help you." Candace went to the closet and produced suitcases, arranged them on the bed and opened them. "Gather your things, Lisa. Make yourself ready."

"Victor said a *few* things, only." Her smile was bitter and determined.

Candace gave a short laugh. "He will not notice this, either." She looked toward the closet, the dresser. "Take serviceable clothing, practical things. Leave the whore's costumes for this new one. *Here!* I will be back shortly." Candace had several things that had to be done quickly, and hurried to her tasks.

When she returned she found the suitcases fully packed, closed, and in a neat row by the door. Dressed in a crisp poplin suit over a blue silk blouse, Lisa looked very young. Pain and hurt had been replaced in her eyes by a cold, hard light. "I will miss you, Candace," Lisa said. "You have been a friend."

I who dressed her that night for Victor to pluck, Candace thought. She nearly wept. "I will miss you more than I can say, little Lisa."

"No. Not 'little' Lisa any longer. Not ever again."

Candace nodded solemnly. "Have you any plans?"

Lisa's chuckle was ghastly, and she cut it short. "How could I?"

"Where, then?"

Lisa shrugged. "Down to Taipei. I have a little money, I'll find something." She turned away from Candace. "Not what Victor thinks."

"No, Lisa, of course not. Here. Look at me."

Lisa faced Candace. "Yes?"

"There is a taxi in front. It will take you to the airport. At the Pan American counter you will find waiting for you a ticket to San Francisco." She held up her hands to halt Lisa's protests. "No. Do this. And take this with you." She pressed an envelope into

Lisa's hands. "There is five thousand dollars, American. It will help you get established, help make it easier for you to begin your studies."

"Studies?"

"Yes, Lisa. Berkeley, I think. It is a good school. I have contacts there and nearby. Call me on the office line when you reach San Francisco. I shall have things well under way by then." She touched Lisa's cheek. "Now, go!"

Lisa took up her suitcases and stepped tentatively toward the door. She had not gone far when she dropped her luggage and rushed to embrace Candace. "How can I—"

Candace stroked Lisa's hair, calming her. "Be strong, Lisa." She hugged her tight and then released her, touching a handkerchief to her eyes. "Go!"

As the cab pulled away, Candace was pleased to see that Lisa sat straight, not once looking back.

The memories, so vivid and unexpected, had filled Candace's thoughts as she walked from the office. Now the egg-shaped dome of the Space Museum loomed on her right. Directly ahead stood the Regent Hotel, in which Plume was located. Around Candace, even at the late hour, bustled travelers and well-dressed diners, the elite of Hong Kong's elite. *How far we have come since that afternoon.* Candace wondered how much farther they would have to go.

David faced Monica across the iron table on the terrace. The sun was high. Since returning from the forest, David had listened patiently to Monica's catalog of his evils. He did not know what a good thing he had had with Hilary. He did not take Hilary seriously as a businesswoman. He did not take Monica herself seriously as a businesswoman. He would never be able to fill his father's shoes.

That last stung David. When Monica had pursed her lips to curse him, David recognized the expression: it reminded him of Hilary. In the glade, in the moment of anger, he had dismissed Monica's accusations. *I even struck Hilary for Monica's honor,* he thought. Now, he wondered. *Hilary had succeeded, at least, in planting doubt.*

"Hilary is heartbroken," Monica was saying.

"Hilary will get over it," David replied. "So will I."

"That's all? That's all you two meant to each other?"

David looked closely at Monica. Was there a calculating determination in her eyes that he had not noticed before? He thought of the way she had looked at James when he was alive, of the love that had shone in those eyes. Could they hide someone as scheming as Hilary? In many tastes and manners, he saw now, they could be twins.

"That's all you have to say?" Monica insisted. "That you'll both get over it?"

"We're different people," David said. He pushed back his chair and rose from the table. "It wasn't right between us. And, yes, we'll both get over it. That's all."

"Hilary was right," Monica said, her voice shrill. "You are a son of a bitch."

"Be careful," David shot back. "You're talking about our family."

He left her fuming on the porch and went inside to shower.

Candace made her way through the lobby of the Regent, pausing briefly to gaze at the unparalleled forty-foot-high view of Victoria Harbor. She didn't linger—Plume offered a fine vista of its own. Candace made her way slowly down the long, carpeted staircase that led to the restaurant. A tall dark-haired man in a white silk dinner jacket smiled at Candace with unmistakable invitation in his blue eyes. Another night, she might have been tempted. Tonight, though, she returned only a smile that thanked him for his attention. He stepped aside to let Candace pass into Plume.

Soft music from an accomplished Filipino trio greeted her. The restaurant's owners were proud of their ten-thousand-bottle wine cellar—the vintage collection was on display. Candace gave her name to the tuxedoed maître d'. He nodded. "Miss Han awaits your arrival."

Lisa stood as Candace approached. She wore a colorful Jenny Kee peplum jacket over a slitted but businesslike skirt. A simple cravat was knotted at the throat of her silk blouse, and above the cravat blossomed Lisa's smile.

"Hello, Candace." The women brushed their cheeks together, then took their seats.

"Welcome home, Lisa."

"Thanks. It's good to be back." A waiter fetched a Glenlivet on the rocks for Candace and a Bombay gin Martini for Lisa. As they waited for their drinks, Lisa briefly outlined the results of her stay in Tokyo. When she finished, she took a sip of her Martini. "Now, let's talk of Wellington," she said.

Candace organized her thoughts, drew a breath, and began. "Marianne met with Peng this morning. They're already mapping out a strategy that will see them through the bureaucracy." Marianne Ingwer was LHV's resident China hand, having guided more than one of Lisa's clients through the intricacies of doing business with the People's Republic.

"Is Peng hopeful?"

"More than ever, according to Marianne. He's quite eager to commence actual work." Candace took a sip of Glenlivet.

"That must await David's final go-ahead."

"The sooner he gives the word, the sooner we can get started."

Lisa nodded. "Still—put yourself in his position. A stumble now could be devastating."

"Everything will run smoothly," said Candace, and raised her glass. "To Wellington Laboratories."

Lisa touched her own glass to Candace's. "To Wellington. To the beginning of a new world."

Candace sighed. "Lisa, your thoughts are always on the future."

"Where else?" Lisa cocked her head slightly, as though puzzled. "The past, after all, is dead."

Hilary Bishop was still livid when she reached the Baltimore airport late that afternoon. She fumed while she waited for her luggage to emerge on the baggage conveyor, and raced the engine of her silver BMW as she endured a delay at the exit from long-term parking. She invited a speeding ticket as she raced toward her apartment, ready to give the police a piece of her mind, but for once no cooperative cops could be found. On an angry whim she screeched to a halt at a small student bar near Johns Hopkins, not too far from her apartment. She took a stool and ordered a double vodka on the rocks. She had every intention of getting very drunk.

Hilary was an ounce into her second glass when she noticed the broad-shouldered, tall young man grinning stupidly at her. He couldn't have been much past twenty, doubtless some corn-and-potato-bred midwestern student. The more Hilary started at him, the more he grinned. She beckoned him at last with a crook of her finger, and indicated the stool next to hers. Hilary hooted with laughter when he told her his name was Zeke. After two more drinks apiece, Hilary picked up the tab and led him to her car.

Monica took dinner in her room. After picking desultorily at her meal, she turned her attention to the sheaf of papers Hilary had left and lost herself in them, and in their promise. While she found some minor flaws in the plan, Monica shared Hilary's perception that a takeover and development plan, properly executed, could turn a small investment in Ethan into a large fortune. *Of my own,* she thought. At nine she gathered the papers together and walked downstairs.

She found David alone in the spacious library. A small fire crackled in the large hearth. David's back was to Monica, and for a moment she did not call attention to herself. She looked beyond David, to the long shelves laden with books. Each volume bore a neat white catalog tape on its spine. *James's room,* Monica thought. Above the fireplace hung a portrait of James. There had been days over the past year when Monica could not bear to enter this room.

Now she took strength from his image. James had encouraged her always to set and follow her own course. "David," she said.

James's son turned to face Monica. "Speaking to me?"

Monica came more fully into the library, but was careful to maintain a distance from David. "We have to talk."

"Agreed."

She stared at him for a long while before speaking. "I'll say no more about you and Hilary, David. You're right: that lies between the two of you."

He nodded, almost imperceptibly.

"I'm disappointed in your response to her plans for Ethan, however." Even as she spoke, Monica felt estranged from herself, as though she were addressing David and listening to herself at the same time. She sounded cold and without emotion. "She told you I was interested?"

His nod was more obvious this time. "She did."

Monica took a breath. She looked up at the portrait of James, at the features she had known so well. This was not easy. "I remain very interested, David. I think we should join her."

David Wellington frowned. "It's a mistake, Monica. It's not our kind of opportunity."

"Because Hilary brought it to us," Monica said.

"Because of the kind of business it is." David took a step toward Monica, a hand held out. She retreated, and he stopped where he stood. "All right."

"There's a lot of money to be made there."

"I don't disagree," David said evenly. "But there's also a lot of potential for disaster. And even if it all swings exactly as planned, you're tying up a great deal of capital and entering a field that's . . . not for us."

"Us?" Monica said.

David did not answer her, but went on speaking. "And there's a problem with timing. We're going to have our hands full very shortly."

"Oh?"

"I met with Xiang Peng while I was in the Orient," David said.

Monica was surprised to find herself smiling. "How is he?" She and James had passed many pleasant hours in Peng's company. Monica especially liked all the old stories Peng told so well, stories of James's youth, of what he'd been like as a young man.

"He's well," David said. "He sends his affection."

Monica's smile dwindled. "What has this—"

David took a breath and spoke clearly, slowly. "Wellington Laboratories has been extended an opportunity to participate with the People's Republic of China in a major pharmaceutical manufacture and distribution joint-venture."

"You're serious?"

"Absolutely." David's eyes were bright. "We'll be manufacturing our full line. As well as new products."

"Which are?"

"We'll be taking omnigene to China."

Monica felt breathless. "Good God," she whispered. "How did they find out?"

David glanced toward the portrait above the hearth. The sides of his mouth rose in a grin. "How else?"

"James?" Monica felt dizzy.

David handed her a cream-colored envelope. She looked at it, saw her husband's handwriting, carried it to the velvet-covered Kittinger sofa that faced the fire. She sat down unsteadily, and opened the envelope. *He used to write me little love notes,* she thought. *Always in a funny peacock-colored ink.* Monica had every one of James Wellington's notes to her, still. She looked at them often. *This letter is to David,* she realized as she stared at the stationery. Her hand shook as she read James's words. When she was done, she looked up at David. "He expected to be alive to see . . ."

"He deserved to be," David said.

Monica glanced at the letter again. "But with James gone, what does Peng expect from us?"

"Dad's death doesn't change the offer, Monica. You and I can do this. It's too important to pass by."

Her breath came only with difficulty. "We? David, I don't know."

A smile lighted his face and he took two long steps toward her. "Sure you can, Monica. Don't underestimate yourself so. It's been rough, but it's time for you to engage yourself, get *involved.*" David stood over her. "And there's nothing more important or involving for us than the Chinese offer. It's the opportunity of the century."

Monica moved out of David's shadow. *Typical of him to misunderstand me,* she thought. Her voice was firm. "I simply meant that I'm not sure how wise the venture is."

David looked surprised. "You can't be serious."

"Can't I?" Monica stepped away and moved close to the fireplace, resting a hand upon the massive slab of black walnut that formed the mantel. The hand-hewn wood bore the gouges of traditional tools, and Monica ran her fingers lovingly over the wood.

"David, this could be a disaster," she said at last.

"Don't be ridiculous."

"I'm not," said Monica coldly. "Oh, this is a wonderful opportunity for the right company—"

"Wellington Labs."

"Perhaps—if your father were still running the show," Monica said, more cruelly than she'd intended. She watched David flinch, and disliked the pleasure the sight gave her. But she would not relent: "Without James, I see too many problems. We're better off joining Hilary."

David did not hide his sudden anger. "We're done with Hilary."

"Are we?" Monica said. "James left me a large part of the company, David. Or have you forgotten?"

"Not enough to force me into the Ethan takeover."

"Enough to pay my way on my own," Monica said sharply.

"You don't know what you're saying."

"No?" Monica smiled. "David, I check every day. Bright and early each and every morning I check on just how much my shares are worth." She tilted her head and wrinkled her brow. "And they're worth quite a bit."

"They'll be worth more after China."

"Or less. After all, the rest of your adventures in Asia haven't been terrifically profitable, have they?"

David ignored her. "Omnigene's time has come. You and I both know that. Hell, you were as excited as Dad when the breakthrough came."

"It made him happy for me to be excited about omnigene," Monica made herself say. She wanted to hurt David, to wipe the smugness from him. There was a timbre and an edge to her voice that she had not heard in years—a cruel, hard, harsh edge. "And I *liked* keeping him happy."

"Then Hilary was right?"

"About what?"

David did not answer her immediately. When he spoke, his voice was heavy. "Hilary told me how you

105

set your sights for a wealthy husband, and reeled Dad in."

Monica would not let David stare her down. "I kept James very happy, David. We had six years together. You saw him. What do you think?"

"I think he was so lovesick he didn't know what he was doing."

"Hardly a flattering portrait of James," said Monica. "Or of me."

"I think Hilary painted you just right, Monica," David said bitterly. "I think Hilary showed me just who and what you are."

Monica held her chin high. "Isn't it funny, David, that you'll dismiss Hilary in an instant when she's talking business—but you hang on her every word when it suits your purposes."

"You're making a mistake, Monica."

"So concerned about my welfare?"

"We were . . . family."

"Were we? I don't remember your seeking my advice once! You always went running for your father."

David stared hard at Monica. "I'm taking omnigene to China."

Monica nodded. "I'll even wish you luck." She made her voice sweet. "Just let me know before you move too far. I'm going to need resources to go after Ethan. I'd hate to sell too soon—but I'd hate it worse if you ruined Wellington before I got free." She started for the door.

"You're going to join Hilary?"

Monica stopped and faced David once more. "Don't be too quick to make assumptions about me, David. And don't ever underestimate me." She watched him for a moment to make certain her message had gotten through. But David saw and heard only what he wanted to. Monica left the library, slamming the mahogany door hard behind her.

* * *

For a while David paced back and forth in the library, seeking to release some of his tension. *I could not have handled this more poorly had I tried,* he thought. At last he wandered to the long Kittinger sofa and sat down facing the fireplace. The flames had burned low, but a bed of glowing embers remained.

David did not look at the portrait of James Wellington, but could feel its presence nonetheless. He found himself thinking of his father's last years, of the sudden and unalloyed joy James had derived from marriage to Monica. David could hear him: "Just to be in her presence cheers me."

David heard other words, as well. From his deathbed, his speech slurred by stroke, James had charged David with a responsibility: "Care for Monica. Watch out for her."

Gradually David raised his eyes. The portrait captured all of James Wellington's strength of purpose, the glow of confidence that shined in his eyes. David wished suddenly that he could make some sort of promise. Taking omnigene to China without Monica's backing might split the company, and with all the irons David currently had in the fire he doubted if he could afford Monica's shares. And he couldn't retreat from China—there was too much chance of omnigene becoming lost for years in a bureaucratic black hole.

David sighed heavily. He would not solve his problems tonight. He stood and stretched, then bent to close the glass doors of the fireplace. Tomorrow was Sunday, and he and Lem would be spending the morning in the garden. He looked forward to working deskbound muscles, to wielding a shovel and feeling dirt on his fingers. He remembered his earlier resolution. *Get Monica outdoors.* If they could just talk, he would do what he could to steer her onto a more sensible course. "She sets her own course," he remembered his father telling him, early in James's courtship. "It's one of the things I love most about her."

* * *

Sleepless, at last Monica threw back the embroidered silk coverlet and climbed from the huge pencil-post bed. In the sitting room that adjoined her bedroom a tall Baker bookshelf held a variety of both business and entertainment reading material, but when Monica scanned the shelves nothing caught her attention. She was too fully aware of what she had said to David—

To sell my interest in Wellington. To leave all this behind.

But another thought nagged at her: *China!*

Away from David, she could admit the appeal of so bold a plan. Her heart beat more rapidly as she considered the effect such a move would have upon her industry. *But to endorse it would mean once more to yoke myself to a Wellington, to follow his lead.*

Monica settled herself onto a Duncan Phyfe recamier. *With Hilary I would at least be closer to following my own lead. If the deal is as good as Hilary says.*

She thought of the things David had said to her, of the way he had said them. Her indecision faded under the sudden force of her anger. She could play the game every bit as well as David. Her mind made up, Monica reached for the telephone.

Zeke may have looked stupid, but he stood well over six feet tall and, stripped, proved rock-hard with muscles and arousal. They were hardly inside her apartment when Hilary began removing her clothes, casting them in the general direction of a severe Ecart sofa upholstered in white. When they were both nude, Hilary led Zeke roughly and shoved him back onto the edge of her wide waterbed. She dropped to her knees before him. There was no teasing prelude, no coyness, no hint of romance. Hilary clutched Zeke's erect organ with both hands, took it within her lips, her mouth, her throat, tearing at him until he exploded and for a moment thereafter.

During the following hours she dared him repeatedly to exhaust her, but he could not. It was barely midnight when Zeke protested that he was worn out. Laughing at him, Hilary moved past Zeke on the bed, its satin sheeted surface rippling sensuously beneath her. A small Tiffany lamp in a far corner cast the room's sole, soft light. Languorously, Hilary stretched to reveal herself, opening her legs, pushing Zeke's face down until he gave her what she wanted. She was riding the crest of a climax when the telephone on the Louis XIV table beside the bed gave a soft chime.

"Don't you *dare* stop!" Hilary hissed as she reached to answer the phone. "Yes?"

"It's Monica." A soft sigh came across the miles. "I've been thinking, talking with David."

"Why don't you tell me about it," Hilary nearly crooned, sinking back against the pillows, her hips rising and falling against Zeke's bowed head. "Why don't you do all the talking?" she said, and as she listened to Monica, Hilary heard hints that helped her toward the beginning of the biggest thrill of all.

After she hung up, Monica pulled her Calvin Klein bedjacket tight around her. She had taken a step, she realized, perhaps the largest step since her marriage to James. She bit with perfect teeth at her lower lip. Hilary would welcome her into partnership; knowing Hilary, the inevitability of the partnership was already being taken for granted in Baltimore. Monica could straighten that out later—Hilary would also need to learn not to make presumptions about Monica's course of action. If they were to do business together, it would be as equals.

If we do business . . . Monica knew that it would be even easier to take the next step, one that could upset every arrangement David Wellington had made.

Well, why not? What did she owe him?

Monica was in no hurry to answer those questions. She rose from the recamier and walked to a wall hung with dozens of neatly framed photographs, mostly of her with James. *My gallery,* she thought. Monica pressed a hand to her lips as she studied the pictures. James and Monica Wellington at the White House. In London and Tokyo, even Moscow. Another picture showed her and James with Xiang Peng during a visit to Beijing. Had James and Peng talked even then? *James mentioned nothing to me,* she thought with some pain. But she also recalled the eagerness with which Peng had spoken of the reforms sweeping through the Chinese government. Those reforms would make it easier to do business in China. Easier to foster learning, generate scientific advances. All of which would ultimately benefit the people not only of China but of the world.

I could be a part of that.

But she was not certain—not after her conversation with Hilary. Monica turned her attention to another, older picture, a favorite from her days at college. Monica and Hilary stood side by side before the riding stables at Hollins College in the hills outside Roanoke, wearing matching riding habits. It was springtime, and the air was clean, the sun bright. Monica remembered many such mornings with Hilary. *We both look so fresh and innocent,* Monica thought.

She had met James Wellington a month after the picture was taken. *And decided within minutes that he was the one. I even told Hilary as much.* Monica and James were married barely a year later, and it was some months after that before Monica realized, to her amazement and Hilary's amusement, that she had fallen deeply in love with her wealthy, older husband.

Tonight, as every night since James's death, Monica missed him desperately. David and Hilary could divide the world between them if she could just feel James's arms around her once more. But that was past—James was dead and it was time for Monica to get on with her life. She pressed her fingernails into her fists, determined not to remain lost in her grief.

Coming alive again, that was what this was all about. She would find her way, her own way, use her resources to create a life for herself.

But Monica leaned closer to the photograph, looking hard at the two red-cheeked young women with the same eyes, the same makeup, clothes, and posture, the same smile.

6

DAVID SWUNG THE heavy mattock, heaving it up high and then bringing it down hard from the peak of its arc. The blade bit deep into the earth. David drew a sharp breath and levered the mattock out of the ground, opening the gouge wider. He tightened his grip and swung again. Where he worked would be a flowerbed by summer's end.

For the first time in days David could feel some of the accumulated tension in his body begin to dissipate. He pushed himself to greater exertion. Stripped to the waist, covered with a sheen of perspiration, David swung the mattock into the face of the earth again and again, losing himself in the mindlessness of the activity, surrendering to the rhythms of his work.

Monica did not make her presence known until, with a last great groan, David buried the head of the mattock deep in the ground and stepped back, his chest heaving.

"Sublimating?" Monica Wellington said slyly from behind him.

David turned to face her, surprised to see her wearing a wide smile. He returned to her a grin of his own, immediately determined to hold their conversation on an even keel from the start. As he looked at her—luminous this morning in bright Kamali culottes and colorful blouse, her dark hair gleaming in the early light—his grin became genuine. "Flagellating," he said. "Punishment for my sins."

Monica's eyebrows rose. "And what sins are those?"

112

David shrugged. "Talking before I think, maybe." He stripped off his suede work gloves and tossed them to the ground. From his back pocket he took a wide bandana and mopped sweat from his face.

"Been thinking?" Monica said.

"Nonstop."

"Me, too."

David claimed his workshirt from the low branch on which he'd hung it. "Ready to give it another try?" he asked as he buttoned the shirt across his broad chest.

"I think we'd better."

David and Monica walked together around the garden. "I was too rough yesterday," he said. "But China wouldn't be easy under the best of circumstances." He put a strong hand on her shoulder. "I could use you with me on this, Monica. There's a lot to be done."

"I called Hilary last night," Monica said without hesitation. "Before you say anything else, you need to know that."

David nodded, his jaw clenched. "You're joining her?"

"Not that quickly, David," Monica said with a dash of impatience. "But, yes, I am going up to Baltimore to take a long look at her dossier on Ethan. Hilary and I had talked a great deal about the takeover before you bulled home on your high horse."

David caught himself before too quickly responding. He bent low to examine a bed of iris, descendants of a rhysome he and his father had planted three decades ago.

"You'll give me warning before you sell your shares?" he said at last, turning to face her.

"Dammit, David, I haven't decided to sell! I have a stake in Wellington just like you. I want what's best for the company—"

"Monica, I *need* you with me in China. I'm serious." He gestured toward a low marble bench overhung by the bower of a tall oak. Sitting together, David started to walk her through the complications that lay ahead. He had barely begun when Karl came from the house with a remote telephone unit.

It was Ling Tze-Han, director of Wellington's Taiwanese operations. His voice was thick with urgency. "David—we've been hit hard at Kaohsiung."

David thought of the ultramodern facility, barely two years old, that he'd constructed on the outskirts of the picturesque Taiwanese port. The plant was a model of the latest pharmaceutical technology, turning out Pandrex and other Wellington products at a rate far higher than that of any other manufacturing plants. David's grip tightened around the plastic body of the remote phone. "How bad?"

"Very. There was a shipment of chemicals coming in by transport truck. Security found nothing irregular. Once inside, though, once the truck pulled into the loading bay . . . the explosion itself killed at least eleven. There were incendiaries. The plant's still burning. You can see the flames for miles."

Sun Chen, David thought, and recalled Lisa's warnings. "I want to know who did this—and I want the evidence hard. You understand?"

"Already on it."

"Start rebuilding as soon as the fires are out. Nobody gets laid off. Spend what you have to—this time the bastards don't win." He broke the connection, and told Monica.

"And in the midst of all this you're going ahead?"

"As soon as possible."

Monica left the bench and stood beside David. "Be careful," she said and reached up to touch his face. "I mean that."

David believed her. "I'll be leaving this afternoon."

"Taiwan?"

He took a moment to think. "Not yet. When I go back it'll be to announce the Chinese venture. I've got some work to do before that."

114

"Just a bit," Monica said, laughing.

"Where can I reach you in Baltimore?"

"I'll be staying at Hilary's apartment."

David could not resist: " 'Step into my parlor . . .' "

"I'm all grown up, David. You never know—you might end up joining in the Ethan takeover yourself."

In Baltimore, Hilary Bishop stared with some annoyance at the young man who lay naked and snoring upon the tangled sheets of her bed. *Zeke,* she thought. *God!* But he'd had his uses, and Hilary had explored every one of them during their long and strenuous night. She stood nude before the tall mirror that faced her wide bed. Hilary grinned wickedly at her own reflection, examining her figure, appreciative of the fullness of her firm breasts, the taut curve of her hips. *Zeke had appreciated it, too,* Hilary thought, looking back at the sleeping student, *several times over.* She had, in fact, lost count at some point during the night, and for a while had allowed herself the hope that Zeke would prove inexhaustible. But the ability to respond even to Hilary Bishop's lush charms had at last failed him, and with a satisfied but slightly sheepish smile Zeke had shrugged, closed his eyes, and immediately begun to snore. Leaving Hilary still wide awake, adrenalin-filled, her thoughts racing.

She had many things to think about, many plans to make, but her thoughts returned continually to David Wellington. The more she thought about David and his treatment of her, the angrier she became. She had seethed during the flight to Baltimore, but that was nothing compared to the way she felt now, and she did not delude herself that Zeke had been anything more or less than an instrument through which to vent at least some of her rage.

Monica Wellington's phone call had provided Hilary with the beginnings of a far more potent instrument.

She would not use it too quickly. Hilary wanted the

edge of her fury to ease a bit, lest she make a mistake. *Daddy always said that being too angry can be your undoing,* Hilary recalled. She made a pirouette before the mirror, stretching, tensing her muscles, working out the kinks. *"Got to have a goal, little girl,"* Daddy used to say, *" 'specially when you're mad. Got to know where it is you're going, what it is you're going to do when you get there. Then, little girl, you can use your anger to move yourself right along the way."*

Hilary had listened closely. Monroe Bishop's sound guidance had over the years helped his daughter transform her hot temper into a tempered tool. Now, as she stretched and exercised to the accompaniment of her own reflection, Hilary could feel some of her tension relaxing as well. Her rage was being transformed into a hard, cold kernel of pure determination.

"Got yourself a goal, little girl?" she heard her father ask.

Sure do—bring down David Wellington and his company.

"Got yourself a plan?"

Not yet, Daddy—but it's there, it's coming.

"Got yourself someplace to go?"

Oh, yes.

Hilary was breathing hard, her breasts rising and falling, a sheen of perspiration glistening on her tanned skin. *Someplace to go.* She thought of what Monica had told her of David's own plans. *Someplace to go,* she thought again, and looked at the illuminated numbers on the clock beside her bed. It was still Sunday morning, and she wouldn't be able to get any of her people going for another hour or two. She could wait. Hilary counted to herself the things she would need. *More from Monica.* That was the head of the list, but it was also the one item that would have to wait a few days. She recalled their college bull sessions. More than a few planned study nights evolved into wide-ranging discussions that ended only with the first light of dawn. Other girls in the dorm chattered away over fashions or boys. *But Monica and I kept our eyes even then on bigger targets.* Now new targets were centered in the sights. *I'll have her with me by Thursday.*

She wanted a better picture of David Wellington's situation in the Orient, as well as a solid idea of the competition he faced. She could pump Monica on that subject as well. *I'll need to know any of his eastern allies as well.* Hilary made a mental list of the personnel she would put to work on this. She wanted her best, and she wanted their full attention. She added another item: *Who gains the most if Wellington goes down in the Orient?* Hilary might need allies, too. She slowed the pace of her exertions, stopped, rose to her tiptoes, then settled lightly down.

Hilary looked back at the bed. Zeke had kicked away the covers, revealing once more his perfectly proportioned body, the muscles of an athlete, a foolish sleeping smile. Lower, Hilary could see the first twitchings of renewal, that sweet stirring that was exactly what Hilary wanted now that her plans were in place.

Hilary's heartbeat slowed to a steady, thudding rhythm. Her own arousal burgeoned with warmth that flowed down through her thighs and made her toes tingle. Heat expanded beneath her belly, nipples growing stiff, cheeks reddening. She climbed in beside Zeke's sleeping form. Even as Hilary pressed her cheek against Zeke's growing hardness, then climbed higher to touch her lips to his throat, her thoughts were filled with her plans for Wellington. Distantly, as though an echo, she heard her father: *Revenge got no place in business,* he was saying. *Look out for your own dealings first, little girl.*

But Zeke was coming up out of his sleep, pulling Hilary insistently to him. Her father's words faded, and in minutes she surrendered herself to sensation alone.

The road from Tallpines to Asheville climbed in a series of long stretches and sharp turns up and out of the valley in which the estate lay. David pulled the Porsche off the road at the high end of one of the switchbacks, the last spot from which Tallpines was visible before mountains and trees obscured the view. David got out of the Porsche and walked over to the lip of the hill to gaze down at the estate where he had grown up.

Sunset and the high perspective made Tallpines and its setting seem exceptionally tranquil. The long graveled drive appeared as a pale ribbon winding through the trees to reach the emerald expanse of the manicured lawn. In the center of the lawn stood the great house itself, the long glass arm of the greenhouse extended to one side, terrace and wings also reaching out like something organic. Until James died and Monica sealed the house into mourning, Tallpines had always struck David as a living thing. Now it was coming alive again.

David grinned ruefully. *Whatever else, home was lively this weekend.* That was good, *whatever else.* Some of the shadows that had lurked through the mansion since James's death had now been exorcised.

But there were other shadows pressing in on David now, other deaths to mourn. He thought angrily of Kaohsiung, of the fires still burning there. *More good people sacrificed on the Wellington altar,* he thought bitterly. Monica as well had seemed shaken. David hoped that she carried her disquiet with her to Baltimore. If she were on edge, she would be more likely to see through Hilary. And if she didn't see through Hilary, there would be no way for him to buy out her stock and support the growing losses that plagued him in areas of the Pacific Rim.

* * *

The last traces of twilight lingered as Monica made her way up the gently sloping hill to the spot where James Wellington was buried. She stopped at a huge poplar whose shade sheltered the small cemetery, running her fingertips over the tree's bark before stepping closer to her husband's headstone. She studied the inscription which James himself had written: *The search for truth, the sharing of discovery, the responsibility to help.* Monica thought of David, of Hilary, of who she could help.

Myself, she thought. *It was James who taught me how to come truly alive—and for so long in return I lived to give him happiness. Since his death I have lived in so many ways for his memory. Now I am on my own.* She felt a desolation that she had come to know well—but now the desolation was joined by something new, a gathering energy whose final form she barely suspected.

Monica stood for a long time beside the grave, as though waiting for some sign that she was setting the right course for herself. No sign came, and Monica found herself crying a little. It was not the first time she had stood on the spot and wept, but today she dried her eyes before she returned to the house. And once inside, she settled herself at her desk and began in earnest to map her own future.

As soon as the Learjet was airborne David set to work arranging the elements he would need to maintain momentum in the Pacific and at the same time prepare some insulation for himself should Monica force his hand. He could not allow her stock to find its way to the open market, as outside shareholders were not likely to see the beauty of Peng's proposal or the long-term potential of David's Pacific strategy. Nor was it too soon to begin preparing his defenses in Washington for the inevitable battle once Wellington Labs' entry into China was announced. The media would be after him as well for comment on the

Kaohsiung explosion and its ramifications for Wellington Laboratories. *A rock,* he told himself, *and a hard place—with me in between.* David did not complete his notes until the Lear was circling on its final approach to Atlanta.

He buckled his seatbelt, but did not put away his notebook. *Losses,* he thought, only half-seeing the numbers that would have provoked most businessmen toward safer strategies. He pondered the preparation, the hard work and study, the unrelenting effort that had gone into the generation of those . . . *losses.* David slammed the notebook shut as the Lear's tires touched down. He breathed deeply, seeking to make his mind a blank.

David hurried from the jet to the sleek, low Vector that was parked at a corner of Wellington Labs' hangar. He thumbed the Vector's lock and pivoted the door up, lowering himself into the Recaro seat that was molded to the contours of his body. He brought the car to life and on a sudden whim switched off the cellular phone housed beneath the instrument-laden dashboard. Any calls would be routed to his house, where the valet could take them. David ratcheted the lever beneath his left hand, putting the Vector in gear. The traffic on I-85 was moderate, keeping David from really opening the Vector up, but he flew past the 100mph mark on one stretch, and abandoned the highway earlier than was his custom, driving the back way into Buckhead. As always David enjoyed piloting the Vector through the streets lined with some of Atlanta's most stately architecture. The Vector looked like a spacecraft among the plantations.

Gerald Schulz, David's valet for nine years, greeted him at the door of his Buckhead townhouse, his face set in grim lines. "Ling Tze-Han is waiting on the line for you, sir," Gerald said, taking David's briefcase and helping him off with his light Lauren jacket.

Calling back for "Southern Comfort, neat," he

stepped to the wide Washington desk that was the centerpiece of the book-lined study. Drawing a breath he lifted the phone. "Go ahead, Ling."

Ling's voice was heavy. "Whoever did it knew what they were up to, David. It'll be tomorrow before the fires are out, latest report." He sighed, his weariness clear over the telephone. "Two firemen are dead. The plant's going to be a total loss."

Gerald entered the study and handed David the glass. David took a long swallow and let the liquor burn him. He breathed deeply. "Do what you can for the families of those lost. My instructions regarding rebuilding remain the same. Start tomorrow."

"Will you be coming over?"

"Not immediately."

"David, we could use you here for morale. If you don't come, I fear that a message of acquiescence will be sent—"

"Surrender? Don't be absurd."

Ling was insistent. "We need a message."

"There's one coming," David said. "Watch the papers tomorrow. Any indication who was behind the bombing?"

"Of course not." Ling laughed bitterly. "There never is."

"But we both know who it was."

"Yes."

"Well, my friend, there's a message coming for him as well. I'll call tomorrow." David hung up.

Gerald stood nearby, expectantly. "The press, sir. They've been calling throughout the evening. Do you have a statement?"

David took another swallow of Comfort. "I have a lot of statements. We'll talk to the papers tonight, and I'll be available for television first thing in the morning." He glanced at the crystal-domed brass ship's clock at the edge of his desk. "Give me an hour, then put the reporters through. *Times, Post,* and *Journals* —Wall Street and Atlanta—first."

"China Post?" Gerald asked. It was Taiwan's largest and most influential daily.

"Of course. Now, get to it. I'll be ready in an hour."

Gerald nodded and left the study, closing the door behind him.

David sat alone in the silence, nursing his drink. After a moment he pressed his thumb against the CSI ProTech seal that guarded the contents of the lower right-hand drawer of his desk. The seal read his thumbprint and the drawer glided open. David withdrew a folder labeled *Omnigene* and added his father's letter to it.

Staring at the file, David thought of all the work and secrecy that had gone into the development of omnigene. A special laboratory facility had been constructed, staffed with a handful of dedicated and brilliant scientists committed to the project. That handful of men and women, David reflected, possessed more concentrated brainpower than any like group in the world. They had given James Wellington their absolute loyalty, and in return he had given them the tools they needed to forge an advance that would change the face of medicine forever. After James's death, David had been gratified to find their loyalty transferred to him. He would see them soon, and test their loyalty with Peng's proposal. David uncapped a Montblanc pen and made a note at the head of a fresh legal pad. He would fly to the laboratory tomorrow. He had little doubt what their answer would be. They would do what he wanted.

But was that enough? There was a far easier and less risky alternative.

We've done a good job with omnigene, and we've kept it to ourselves this long. Why not go ahead and announce it here, put the slow bureaucracy into motion, make the unnecessary changes the government will insist upon, congratulate our people on the Nobel awards that will be theirs, watch the value of the company soar as a result of the publicity.

And wait years for testing in triplicate and quadruplicate and worse to be completed, perhaps twice that long for the public to benefit.

Not the least of the benefits of so safe a course would be to defuse Monica's departure. *I might even be able to hang on to some of the Pacific operations.*

David stared at the report and the handwritten letter from James Wellington that flanked it. He thought of brilliant Elizabeth Jonklaas and jovial, confident Wang Derui. He thought of the pride which had always shone so clearly on the faces of the technicians at Kaohsiung. *Losses.* How could he write them off? *They lie dead while I am suspended in indecision.* How could he send such a message to Sun Chen? He slammed his palms down onto the surface of his desk, hard enough to make his palms tingle.

No!

He looked again at the ship's clock. Twenty minutes remained before he must answer the questions of the press. That was time enough. His mind was made up. David picked up his telephone and dialed Hong Kong.

When Lisa Han came on the line he said, "Put it in motion." The words sounded good to him, they sounded *right*. "Lisa, let's *go!*"

HILARY MET MONICA at the Baltimore airport, fetching her in the silver BMW that she drove with considerable élan that left Monica slightly breathless by the time they arrived at a deco Charles Street building. The smiling, gray-haired concierge attended to their luggage while Monica and Hilary rode to the penthouse together.

No matter how many times she visited, Monica was always surprised by Hilary's apartment. Its fixtures all chrome and burnished steel, bright walls broken by Bauhaus windows, upholstered pieces covered either in dark leather or unblemished white weaves, Hilary's home was as striking as Hilary herself. In the wide, Carrara marble–floored entranceway Monica stopped to admire a new piece: a beautifully configured neon sculpture that glowed green and blue in the shape of an abstract swan.

"Electric Leda," Hilary said with a giggle. "Isn't it just wonderful?"

Monica thought of the carefully collected art and *objets* at Tallpines, most of them stately pieces from the nineteenth century. "Cutting edge, Hilary. Where you always are."

"Isn't it the truth! Come on."

Monica draped her coat over one of the three Le Corbusier Grand Confort armchairs that faced Hilary's wrought-iron fireplace. She stretched, breathing deeply. A long corridor, tiled floor to ceiling in a black and white chessboard pattern like something out of Alice in Wonderland, led to the kitchen. Through that corridor now appeared a slender, delicately featured young man dressed in modish livery and bearing a silver tray with crystal flutes and champagne bucket.

"Meet Stefan," Hilary said to Monica. "He's just incredible in the kitchen. I asked him to put together a little something for us this morning."

Stefan placed the champagne service on the polished surface of an ebony Andree Putman table, offering Monica a slight bow before turning to the champagne. Monica accepted a crystal flute filled with Moet & Chandon Brut Imperial. Before she could sip the champagne, Hilary stepped close with her own flute and offered a toast.

"To us," she said with a brilliant, unstoppable smile. "Hilary and Monica together again—just like old times!"

Monica focused her attention on the delicious wine for a moment, not wanting too quickly to say anything to Hilary. Stefan emerged from the kitchen with another tray, this one bearing an iced silver bowl mounded with dark Beluga caviar rimmed with lemon wedges, the bowl itself surrounded by triangles of pale toast. Monica busied herself with the Beluga.

Hilary was talking excitedly, pacing about the richly carpeted living room with her champagne. "We're going to knock this industry for a loop, you and me," she said. "David's never going to know what hit him."

Monica spoke softly. "David can hit back," she said.

"Can he now?" Hilary's voice was thick with contempt. "Against both of us? Come on!"

"Don't underestimate him, Hilary."

Hilary would hear none of it. "David's got his hands full right now, wouldn't you say? Or is he used to having his factories blow up every day?" The morning papers had been filled with the story of the explosion at Wellington's Kaohsiung facility. David himself had been interviewed on *Today, CBS Morning News,* and CNN.

Monica finished her champagne, its bouquet making her heady—she could not resist a pun. "His hands may be full, but he's got plenty of tricks up his sleeve."

"You always were clever," Hilary said, stepping close and stroking Monica's cheek softly. "More than David. Whoever's out to get him—"

"Victor Sun Chen," Monica blurted, as much to see Hilary's response as anything.

Hilary nodded. Did her eyes grow brighter at Sun Chen's name? "I thought as much. David mentioned him once or twice when we . . . before he got to be too good for me."

"Are you being fair?"

"Was he?" Hilary snapped. "And fair or not, this Pacific Rim scheme of his is going to backfire—" She swung open the black lacquered doors of a huge deco armoire to reveal a small computer. Hilary's fingers flew over the keyboard, calling up information. "Your stock's already lost two points this morning, Monica."

Monica held out her champagne flute for Stefan to refill. "We can afford it," she said.

Hilary chortled. "You've been cooped up in those mountains too long! Nobody can afford to take a loss. Especially not when you're going to be selling soon."

"Selling?"

"Well, we're not going to be picking up Ethan out of pocket change."

Monica began to laugh softly. "Cutting edge, Hilary."

"Nowhere else," said Hilary Bishop. "Let's get down to work."

The minute David Wellington was finished with his media responsibilities, he left for the airport. He was ready to move fast, and in several directions. His week's agenda would take him across much of the country. Perhaps the most crucial of his stops would be his Chicago meeting with Odell Wellington,

James's cousin and, outside of David and Hilary, the only person who controlled more than five percent of Wellington's stock. David would meet with Odell midweek—first there would be an unannounced layover at a Wellington facility that few were aware of.

Shortly after two, the Lear touched tarmac at Wellington Envirotech in the desert near Taos, New Mexico. The guards who stood sentry at the landing strip and the high fence that surrounded the installation, as well as the landing strip personnel, believed the signs that were posted throughout the small complex—WELLINGTON ENVIROTECH: MAKING A CLEANER TOMORROW.

David Wellington, and the five scientists who formed the core staff of the facility, knew more. They were waiting for him in the conference room. David quickly took his place at the head of the long polished mahogany table, the Brayton chair yielding comfortably beneath him. He looked from face to face, measuring the concern he saw in the expressions of the gathered scientists. These were the people who along with his father had made the breakthroughs leading to omnigene. David drew a breath and began.

"You have heard by now of the disaster at Kaohsiung. Ling Tze-Han briefed me again as I was en route here. The death toll is already twice what the latest media reports claim. The facility is a total loss."

Ellen Siebert spoke up, her blue eyes clouded with pain. "David, what does this have to do with us?"

"A great deal, perhaps," he said, then gave them the rest of it. "I'm ready to take omnigene to market."

The scientists' faces registered their surprise. David thought of how much he owed them all. Ellen Siebert, whose skill at manipulating genes and chromosomes made possible the healing combinations posed theoretically by Ernest Schliemann and Ranajh Chandrasingh. The group was completed by two biophysicists, Leonard Rogers and Rhonda MacLaren, who worked in concert with the others to develop specific arrangements of omnigene—which would target and eradicate specific diseases. For these five the New Mexico facility had been virtually a monastery for the past four years. Yet it was a monastery equipped with the world's most advanced medical, laboratory, and computer technology, all of it dedicated to omnigene.

Ernest Schliemann got over his surprise first. "You are going to throw us to the dogs of the FDA?" he asked in his pronounced German accent, provoking soft laughter throughout the room.

David spread his hands wide. "Could I do that to you?"

"What, then?"

"I am going to lend you to the doctors of the People's Republic of China," he said. "You'll be working in an installation even newer than this. And we're going to get them to pay for it."

The idea of sending the scientists to China immediately had occurred to David on the flight to Atlanta yesterday. He had broached it to Lisa Han over the telephone last night, and she had instantly seen the advantages. The scientists could join her representatives in Beijing, answering any technical questions the PRC might pose. Further, the omnigene team could study firsthand the Chinese's ability actually to provide the facilities and support that Peng had offered.

Rhonda MacLaren fixed David with the cold blue-eyed stare he had anticipated. "Who pays for all of this isn't our concern," she said. "Who publishes the findings? Who gets the credit, the—"

"Nobel?" interrupted David. "I don't blame you. The credit for every bit of this remains with you five. You've earned it ten times over. And once the advance is announced—"

Her eyes flashed anger. David knew what her next question would be: *When? How long?* He could hear her frustration, see the annoyance on her sharp features. "David, it's all very well for you to look for ways around FDA and NIH. But you know as well as I do that we could have made an announcement when your father was still alive—we could have been well on our way to domestic approval in the time you've spent looking for something more 'expedient.'" She pressed her lips tightly together. "Now we're going to wait while you do business with China?"

David kept his own tone firm, even. "No one appreciates your patience more than I do, Rhonda. But I also appreciate the fact that omnigene must be brought to the market *our* way. China may provide us with more control than we could obtain elsewhere. It's worth the wait."

"Is it?" she demanded. "To you, maybe."

"To all of us," David said. He looked at the scientists gathered before him, knowing that each of them agreed at least in part with Rhonda's objections. Their project was too exciting and they had put too much of themselves into it not to be eager for the acclaim that would accompany the announcement of omnigene. And in the recesses of each of their minds, David knew, was the fear that tomorrow, or the next day—while *they* waited—some other scientist, unconstrained by David Wellington, would announce his or her own breakthrough.

"Six months," David said. "A month to crack the deal. Two months to get you in place in the PRC." He gave them his best grin. "And another season for propriety."

"And then?" Rhonda asked.

"Then we have the biggest scientific press conference in history," said David.

Ellen Siebert spoke up. "And if the business with China can't be resolved within a month?"

David did not hesitate. "Then we strike a deal with the most agreeable of our existing market nations. And we throw the biggest scientific press conference in history. Immediately."

"I'll give you that month," Ernest Schliemann said. He produced a huge-bowled meerschaum from a pocket. "And if it's China I'll go the other five."

Ellen Siebert, Leonard Rogers, and Ranajh Chandrasingh offered their assent.

For a moment Rhonda MacLaren said nothing. Then she spoke carefully. "Four weeks, David. From today. And then you set a date for the announcement or I swear I'll publish on my own."

"Four weeks from today, Rhonda, if I don't have a solid commitment—I'll foot the publishing bill myself."

David stood before the group for only another moment, then turned and left the room.

Victor Sun Chen folded the *China Post* sharply and dropped it onto the squat stone table beside his wicker chair. A bird sang sweetly from the bamboo thicket that filled one corner of the walled garden. Sun Chen clapped his hands hard to silence the music.

The flames at Wellington's factory in Kaohsiung had barely been extinguished before David Wellington was all over the media, announcing his determination not only to rebuild in Kaohsiung and on an even grander scale, but also to bring to law the person behind the bombing and the other acts of terrorism that had plagued Wellington Labs in recent months. *Person:* singular. The ashes at Kaohsiung were being sifted for evidence. Wellington was assigning its every resource to finding the arsonist.

Bold talk, Victor Sun Chen thought, *but empty.* David Wellington could shift ashes until the universe itself was a cinder and he would find nothing. Did he think that Victor Sun Chen employed any other than the very finest talents? The Kaohsiung firebombing had been the work of Neil Kintang, the very best of Sun Chen's people in the deadly professions. Kintang would leave no evidence, any more than when he dealt with Elizabeth Jonklaas or that buffoon Wang Derui. Sun Chen had intended to use Kintang when he initiated the next move in his campaign to drive David Wellington from the Pacific Rim. But Kintang insisted upon laying low for several days, and suddenly Sun Chen was unwilling to wait. The next move, Sun Chen hoped, would be the final move, an elegant and terminal checkmate. It must come soon.

Sun Chen had many friends and contacts throughout the world, and from them he had lately begun to receive disturbing hints that David Wellington was after something much larger than simply a marketing foothold in the Pacific Rim. Lisa Han was involved as well, causing Sun Chen to wonder, not for the first time, if the pleasure he'd derived from toying with her destiny over the years since she left his house was worth the difficulties she had on rare occasions caused him. More often, Sun Chen blocked Lisa's ambitions, placed obstacles in her path, even struck hard at those with whom she was close. But he had let her live, nor had he struck at Candace Caillou, whose complicity had made possible Lisa's flight in the first place. He was saving them, until the time was right, until their deaths could be properly and fully savored.

Now Lisa Han worked with David Wellington on a project involving the mainland. What could it be?

Sun Chen laughed harshly. Did it matter? He looked at the gold Rolex on his right wrist. It would be late afternoon in America. He hoped it was a lovely day for David Wellington. The American did not have many days left.

David had learned in his youth that his father's cousin Odell was a man who could give good, honest advice, and that was something that David was more than ready to welcome at the moment. The omnigene team was on its way to Beijing by now, routed on separate flights through scattered airports to call no attention to themselves. It was all beginning, David thought, and Odell had a right to know.

David arrived in Chicago shortly after ten on a bright Wednesday morning, a long chauffeured Lincoln carrying him immediately to the Drake Hotel. He and Odell had reservations for eleven in the Cape Cod Room. David was a little early and ordered a Stolichnaya Bloody Mary while he waited.

Odell, punctual as always, was escorted to David's table at eleven exactly. A beautifully pompadoured shock of carrot-red hair belying his seventy years, immaculate in Brooks Brothers broadcloth and yellow bowtie, Odell beamed at his young relative. "Davy, it's damned good to see you," he said, extending a hand that swallowed David's. Odell turned to the maître d'—"Jack Daniels, rocks, double," he said with a nod and a wink.

"Been readin' about the Taiwan thing," Odell said. "Seen you on TV the other day. Been watchin' what's happening to my shares." Wellington Labs had dropped a full four points before rallying. "What's going on over there anyway?"

David spread his hands wide, and waited until Odell's drink was delivered before he spoke. "Some of our competitors play this game a little differently from what we're used to," he said, and outlined his difficulties with Sun Chen.

Odell took a swallow of bourbon, closing his eyes as he savored its bite. "Maybe you need to change the way you're playing—or get out of that particular game."

"I'm not getting out," David said.

"Then you better have something planned."

David grinned at him. They placed their orders, and once the waiter had retreated David spoke firmly. "How much did Dad say to you about omnigene?"

The older man's bushy eyebrows rose slightly. "Not a lot. Told me that there weren't twenty-five people in the world who knew about it. We looked at some of the science—it's a programmable phage, essentially. The doctor tells it what to go and get and it goes and gets it." His green eyes twinkled. "James said that he thought it wouldn't be too long before it was even better—a worker gene that can go in and repair nerve damage, rebuild old arteries, whatever you want it to."

David nodded. "It's nearly here. Another six months and we'll be ready for the announcement. And the team is more than ready to announce." He gave a quick account of his meeting in New Mexico.

The waiter returned with broad steaming bowls of Bookbinder's redfish soup. Odell took his time with a spoonful or two of the dark chowder laced with a healthy dollop of sherry. "Ought to help the stock when you do announce," he said finally.

"Maybe not," said David.

Odell put down his spoon. "What do you mean?"

"One of those twenty-five people Dad told about omnigene was Xiang Peng. He's offered to let Wellington bring omnigene and the rest of our line into China. And put it to work right now." In a soft voice David explained the details of Peng's offer.

Odell did not reply until his empty soup bowl had been removed and replaced with a platter of perfect cherrystone clams. He squeezed lemon over them. "Government's going to raise hell about this," he said, and popped a clam into his mouth.

"Screw 'em," David said and grinned wolfishly. "I've seen too many good pharmaceutical products disappear for years to keep the bureaucrats happy. I want omnigene out in the world, doing good."

"And makin' money."

"You're damned right," David said.

Odell Wellington nodded somberly. "You better do some prep work, boy."

"I'm flying to Washington this afternoon."

"I reckon with you, me, and Monica behind this what few other shareholders there are can't do much. By the way," he said in a tone that let David know the question was not at all incidental, "how *does* Monica feel about this?"

David took a deep breath before answering. "That's the kicker to all this, Odell. Monica may be putting her block on the market." He sketched the Ethan takeover. "If I can't swing the shares I'd like to be able to count on you to keep them in the family."

Odell Wellington sat back in his chair and studied David. "You always were honest, David."

David did not understand, but said nothing.

Odell explained himself. "Monica called me last night. Had a good long talk with her. Her version of the story's same as yours. Even asked me the same thing—wanted to know if I'd guarantee her stock. To keep it in the family."

David's stomach was tight. "Then she's going to sell?"

Odell shook his big head. "Don't go jumping off like that, son. She's not even close to having her mind made up. But the important thing is she's thinking about what's best for the company, too."

"What do you think?"

"I think you better get on down to Washington and see what you can put together. I told Monica I'd buy her out if that was what she wanted." He fixed David with a hard stare. "But even if I do, that's going to leave you in control of more than 50 percent, which means I got all my money tied up in a company that may be in a pile of trouble. You show me you know what you're doing."

"I know what I'm doing," David said firmly.

Odell cocked his head and studied David for a long time. "One more thing. I think you ought to pay close attention to what Monica has to say. You know, my cousin James wasn't any fool; he made a smart move when he married Monica, and he always took her dead serious. That's good advice."

After a moment David nodded, and Odell rewarded him with a wide smile. "Anything else?"

Odell pursed his lips. "Might start thinking about how this Sun Chen's playing. Might want to start learning some new rules."

8

SENATOR NANCY NOLAN Wade was an old and trusted friend of the Wellington family and had visited often at Tallpines, for the company of her dear friend James Wellington as well as for the healthy contributions the Wellington family made to her campaign chests. Her coffers were low, she explained to David over lobster *en chemise* at Le Provencal. Nancy was tall and full-figured, elegant tonight in an Anne Klein white linen dress that emphasized rather than hid her stature.

"I've had some tough fights before, David, but this is shaping up as the biggest yet." Early indications were that her opposition would be Thomas Sinclair, bright, articulate, well-funded, and backed by a coalition of fundamentalist right-wingers. "I've fought for some pretty unpopular causes over the years," Nancy said. "And Sinclair's going to bring every one of them home to haunt me."

David cut through the delicate crepe that was wrapped around thick chunks of fresh lobster. "But no skeletons from the closet," he said after he swallowed.

Nancy shook her head. "Hell, no. They don't need them. Stand up for science education and you're an enemy of the people's right to be ignorant. Put in a word for women's rights and you're out to tear down the social structure of the family."

"What about genetic engineering?" David said.

Nancy's jade eyes flashed with humor and annoyance. "You've got to be kidding! Tamper with the

136

'natural order of things'? Create life in the laboratory —it's as evil as original thought!"

"Then what do you suppose they would say about an American genetic engineering company moving some of its elements to the PRC?" David asked in a low, even voice.

Nancy Nolan Wade did not miss a beat, although she did lower her own strong voice. "I would say that the company ought to be more worried about the FDA, the FTC, and probably the FBI. What in the name of God are you up to?"

"Something worthwhile," David said. He lifted his wine glass and sipped the exquisite Montrachet. "Something that may require all the help I can get on the Hill."

"Sounds that way. Care to tell me more?"

"Off the record?"

"Raise your right hand and swear you're not about to commit treason?"

"How about if I raise money for your campaign instead?"

"Even better," Nancy said. She fingered the single strand of perfect pearls that circled her neck. "I'm all ears."

They were on cognac and coffee by the time David was done. Nancy wafted the snifter of Remy beneath her nose. "I can think of about half a dozen agencies and at least two departments that are going to be all over your case for this, David."

"What kind of help can you give?"

Nancy sighed. "I thought you'd get to that." She was silent for a moment, considering. "You're not going to transfer them the technology itself?"

"No. Their people will be running our machines— and they're going to help pay for the facilities."

"That's a plus. But there's the whole political thing—a lot of people are going to accuse you of selling your country out."

David's grin was feral. "Fuck them! Tell them I'm

putting the screws on the Russians by way of China. How can the Soviets handle the publicity when the old gray Politburo flocks to Beijing for a shot every time they've got a cold?"

Nancy smiled. "Not bad at all. And of course none of this need come up until the breakthrough is announced—"

"Six months after entry. Pandrex and the rest will be well on their way to being established in China by then."

"All to your advantage."

"Of course." David finished his cognac. "Now, tell me honestly. If I kept it here at home, went through all the regular channels of testing and approval—how long?"

"In today's climate? For an advance as large as the one you've hinted at? Six years, minimum."

David nodded. "Then I'm doing the right thing."

Nancy's laughter was rich and warm. "Well, my dear, so am I, but that doesn't mean I won't get beaten next year."

"You won't," David said firmly. "And neither will I."

David had left his Jaguar in a parking deck not far from Le Provencal, and after seeing Nancy Nolan Wade into her limousine, he strolled slowly down 20th Street. The evening had grown late as he and Nancy turned from business to family matters. It turned out that Monica had called Nancy from Baltimore—they were going to lunch together late the following week.

"Give her my best."

The senator was surprised. "You're not going to see her while you're here?"

David shook his head. When he explained a little of the tension that lay between him and Monica, Nancy frowned. "I didn't promise you that getting Washington's approval for the PRC venture would be easy," she reminded David. "But it's going to be harder if Wellington Labs is falling apart internally. Your Ps and Qs need to be in perfect order, David. Perfect order. Now, sure I can't give you a lift?"

David wanted to walk. He rounded a dark corner in the direction of the parking garage where the Jaguar waited. Few people were on the street. Lost in thought, David barely had time to turn and see a tall man loom out of the shadows toward him.

David dropped into a defensive crouch, raising his left shoulder to take the force of the blow from the cosh his assailant swung fiercely. David's shoulder exploded with pain, his left arm going numb even as he drove his stiff-fingered right hand deep into his attacker's solar plexus. Adrenalin surged and David took a wild satisfaction at the *chuff* of air escaping explosively from the man's lungs. The cosh struck David's cheek, but the blow had lost much of its force. David pivoted, seizing the mugger's right arm by the wrist, jerking it down hard. Bone cracked and a high-pitched squeal echoed through the night.

Rough hands seized David from behind. He saw just in time the wicked glitter of a long knife, and writhed against the grip enough for the blade to bite into his shoulder rather than his neck. Even as the knife cut him, David was using the inertia behind the blade to swing the new assailant up and over his shoulder and bring him down hard on the sidewalk. David stomped a heel down hard onto the knife-wielder's right kneecap, hearing it shatter before all noise was drowned by screams of agony. David spun to face his first attacker.

The mugger with the cosh was backing away from him, his right arm hanging useless at his side. David advanced slowly, senses alert, his numb arm beginning to throb back to usefulness. He was on the verge of pressing his attack when he became aware that his target's attention was focused on the road behind him. David dove for a doorway just as a car pulled parallel and four shots from a silenced pistol pounded into the wall where David's head had been just seconds before. David rolled, kicking at the man whose arm he'd broken. There was a shout from down the street as the attendant at the parking garage at last emerged and ran toward them.

Lights were coming on as the man with the cosh raced past David, helped the other assailant to his feet. The car was screeching away even as David's attacker pulled the door closed. It was gone around the corner by the time the garage attendant reached David's side.

"Jesus Christ! What happened?" the attendant said.

David was out of breath. He leaned back against the building for support, becoming aware that his right shoulder was bleeding. He drew air deep into his lungs, seeking to control the pain that coursed through him. His heart was beating wildly. He pushed himself away from the building, eager to be off the street before anyone else became involved.

"Did you get a look at them?" the attendant demanded.

"Not really," David said, and managed a grin. "I was busy."

"Catch the license on the car?"

David shook his head.

"Well, come on down to the office. We'll get an ambulance, call the cops anyway."

David walked slowly beside the young garage attendant, his thoughts racing. "There's fifty in it if you keep this to yourself," he said as they reached the garage.

The attendant looked quizzically at David. "You got to have a hospital, man," he said, staring at the dark stain spreading across the shoulder of David's light jacket.

"A hundred," David said. He looked hard at the

young man. "But not a word to anyone." David hurried into the attendant's small office cubicle where he wouldn't be seen. "Got a bathroom here?" The attendant jerked a thumb at the far wall. David stepped into bathroom, removed his jacket and opened his shirt.

The wound looked worse than it was. David pulled a handful of paper towels from the dispenser and held them under cold water before pressing them to the wound. He might be able to get by without stitches— for a while at least. And suddenly he had someplace he wanted to go, fast. There was a small first aid kit on a shelf above the sink, and David rummaged through its contents. He improvised a bandage, taping it tightly in place before buttoning his shirt.

David drew a deep breath against the throbbing in his shoulder, then stepped back into the cubicle where the attendant waited expectantly. David reached into the breast pocket of his jacket and got his wallet. He handed the attendant two new hundred-dollar bills.

"Absolute silence," David said to the young man.

The attendant stared distrustfully at the bills, then slowly reached out to take them. "I just don't want no hot water, understand?"

David smiled at him. "Don't worry."

"How come you don't want no cops?"

David made his voice mysterious: "There are people who don't need to know I'm in town. Now, how about getting my Jag?" The attendant, obviously convinced he'd played a part in a deadly piece of government business, nodded soberly and rushed off to fetch David's car.

The concierge at Hilary's building drew himself up to his full height when David Wellington sought entry. David had done what he could to clean himself up, but his jacket was torn and bloodstained and the ugly weal across his cheek did little to reassure the concierge that David was the sort of visitor his trusting tenants would appreciate. David waited patiently while the doorman called Hilary's apartment. The concierge frowned over the telephone, but nodded to David and let him pass.

David leaned against the burnished wall of the elevator as he rode up. His head throbbed and the knuckles of his right hand ached. His shoulder had stopped bleeding, but twice during the drive to Baltimore he'd thought he would pass out. But he wanted to see Monica—and more importantly, he wanted Monica and Hilary to see him. He mustered his energy and stood upright as the car glided to a smooth stop.

Monica was waiting at the elevator doors, and she gasped when she saw David's condition. "My God! What—"

David waved her questions aside. Monica walked beside him into the penthouse, where David collapsed into one of the Corbu Grand Confort chairs. "I need a drink," he said raggedly. "The stiffer the better."

Monica nodded and stepped to the bar. She poured two healthy bourbons and brought one to David, who sipped the liquor greedily, welcoming its warmth. Monica seated herself facing him.

"Where's Hilary?"

"Out. A date."

David closed his eyes for a moment, but grew dizzy and opened them again. He looked around the apartment where he had once spent so much time. "Just a simple little cottage," he laughed.

Monica would have none of his bravado. "Dammit, David, what happened to you?" she demanded fiercely.

David reached up to gingerly touch the bruise on his cheek. "A little something from Sun Chen, I think," he said, wincing. "Help me get fixed up?"

"Of course. We'll use my bathroom."

David stripped off his coat and shirt and sat on the

lip of the onyx bath, "You need stitches," Monica said after she examined the knife wound.

David shook his head. "I'll have it looked at tomorrow. I don't want to risk a hospital tonight." Frowning, Monica delicately washed his wounds clean and covered them with deftly fashioned butterfly bandages. Her fingers were cool and soothing against David's skin. "It's good to see you," he said as she completed her ministrations.

Monica placed the cotton gauze and surgical tape back in the medicine cabinet. She examined the shelves. "Hilary won't have a Pandrex in the house anymore," she laughed. "Want an aspirin?"

David shook his head—it only ached a little now. "Another drink, though. And some talk."

"Go ahead," Monica said once they had returned to the living room and she had replenished their drinks.

"I want you to be on your guard, Monica," David said. "I don't think Sun Chen will try to hit at me through you, but stay alert, keep your eyes open."

"You're sure he was behind this?"

"They tried to make it look like a street mugging, but I'm sure. How many muggers are backed up by a chauffeur with a silenced gun?"

Monica closed her eyes for a moment. "Kaohsiung. Now this. David, I don't know."

David sipped his liquor, ready to change the subject. His appearance here had made his point better than hours of conversation and argument could have. "I had lunch with Odell today. He told me you two had talked."

"That's right," Monica said, her manner suddenly and unmistakably defensive. "What are you going to tell me? That Odell won't back my play now? There are plenty of others who will."

"Not at all. In fact, Odell's quite interested in both projects, China and Ethan. Although he's quite rightly concerned that the company not get crippled in the process." He wanted to keep her talking about Ethan. Let her think about this attack tomorrow, after he was long gone.

"We can't have it both ways, David."

"Can't we? I've been looking over Ethan's portfolio, too. And there's something there that—"

He was interrupted by the sound of the penthouse door opening and closing, heels clicking against Carrara marble, Hilary's high-pitched giggle. "We'll just *see* what you have to offer!" she was laughing as she entered the living room at the side of a broad-shouldered, dark-haired man in a Cardin suit. When Hilary spotted David she stopped short, her eyes flashing anger.

"What the fuck are you doing here?" she spat.

"Sometimes I just get a little homesick for the old place," David said as he rose from the Corbu chair. "Nice to see you again, too."

Hilary ignored her companion, and flashed her anger at Monica. "Why the hell did you let this bastard in?"

"Hilary, he was—"

By now Hilary had noticed the bloodstain on David's jacket. "What happened?" she asked mockingly. "Hurt yourself and come running to Monica?"

David finished his drink and stood. "I'd better be going."

"Yes," Hilary said. "You're right."

David winked at Monica. "Walk me down to the car?"

Monica started to object but David shot her a sharp look and she caught herself. "Of course."

David stared at Hilary, as though trying to spot the woman with whom he'd once been in love. She was nowhere to be seen. "Nice to see you," he said to Hilary, then faced her companion. "Good luck," David said to the man, and added an extra touch of cheer. "You're going to need it."

Monica stood with David outside the building for a

while. The evening was cool, with a few high clouds gliding past the moon.

"I'm flying to New York the first of the week," Monica said. "To meet with the people at Ethan."

David said nothing for a moment. Then: "Good luck."

She smiled at him. "Whatever happens?"

"Whatever," David said. He offered her a grin, and outlined Rhonda MacLaren's concerns about the timetable for taking omnigene to China. "So make your move in the next couple of weeks, or things might *really* start going to hell."

"I don't think I'll need two weeks."

David said nothing.

"And Hilary?" Monica asked.

"Oh, Hilary may have her uses yet," David said. He looked at his watch. It was past two. "I'd better be going."

"You will see a doctor?" Monica asked as David moved to his Jaguar.

"Right away," David promised.

"But you wanted me to see this first. Didn't you?"

David had hoped his motives weren't so transparent. "You always were smart," he said, and reached out to squeeze Monica's hand. "And I wanted to see Hilary."

"And Hilary to see you." She squeezed back. "You'd better get smarter yourself," she said.

"What do you mean?"

"I think I see it in your eyes. Sun Chen. You're going to have to play this his way."

David shook his head as he climbed into the Jaguar. "No. Sun Chen's going to lose. I'm playing to win."

9

OVER THE WEEK since the explosion at Kaohsiung and David's call initiating actual work with the People's Republic, Lisa Han had come to look forward to her daily conversations with him. Not just because each conversation moved their business an exciting step or two further ahead, but also for the pleasure of his long-distance company. Early on they had agreed to alternate the timing of their calls, so that during one conversation David spoke from Atlanta morning while Lisa responded during Hong Kong night. The next day, their roles were reversed. Lisa Han could not decide at which hour she liked David Wellington best.

When it was morning in America, David was exuberant, overflowing with energy and excitement, ideas flying scattershot, all of them ultimately related to omnigene and its introduction into China. Sometimes David's energy level was almost too high for Lisa, who would gently remind him that for her it was already night. "Then we need to get together and work more . . . synchronously," David would reply, slight traces of southern accent rounding the edges of his words.

At night David was more restrained and reflective, even philosophical. Sometimes he talked of his father, or the ongoing uncertainty he faced from Monica Wellington. Sometimes he talked for hours. *And I hang on every word,* Lisa Han realized.

She curled the fingers of her right hand inward until the long nails bit into her palm, making white marks.

She stared at the many-buttoned communications console that rested on the left corner of her wide teak desk. *The telephone is so safe,* she admitted to herself, *and isn't that why I permit our conversations to go on so long? I can trust myself with him so long as there is a world between us.*

A light on the console flashed and the unit emitted a soft *beep.* Lisa's dark thoughts were swept away. David's was the only call to be permitted through the switchboard to Lisa this morning. She drew a breath and lifted the phone. "Good morning," she said.

"Good *evening,* Lisa Han," said David Wellington. His chuckle was rich. "It's Friday night, here. We really must do something about our time zones."

"You're already rearranging whole industries, David. Would you rework the face of the globe as well?"

"Nothing so ambitious. I was thinking of something more in the line of a visit. Say, you to America? A few days earlier than planned?"

Lisa silently chided herself for such silliness as a flutter danced through her stomach. "You tempt me," she offered, "but my desk is piled high with work, no small portion of which pertains to your interests. And I'll be in San Francisco by the end of next week."

"That's fair enough," David laughed. "No small portion of my interests pertain to you."

Lisa sighed. "There's work to be done."

David was silent for a moment. Then: "I won't give up, you know."

"Neither will I."

"If we're lucky, one of us will win in the near future."

"We're going to need our luck, David. And our courage."

David's voice was strong. "We're going to need everything we've got, Lisa. But we've got everything we need."

"As an aphorist, I think you are hardly Confucian."

"Maybe not. But as an aphorist I'm an amateur. As a businessman—nobody's beaten me yet."

"Perhaps that is why Sun Chen is so interested. He enjoys being first."

David was silent for a moment. When Lisa had learned of the attack she had been willing to abandon it all—no gain was large enough to offset David's death. His response to her concern had been curt. "I'll not make my life more valuable than those Sun Chen's already taken—I'll not give him the satisfaction." He had promised to keep himself under cover and, indeed, there had been no further moves against him.

But there will be, Lisa knew.

"I have a first planned for Sun Chen," David was saying. "And it won't be long in coming, either."

Lisa said nothing.

"What do we hear from China?" David said.

Their telephone link was protected by the latest in CSI scrambler technology, but Lisa still felt nervous discussing omnigene over the phone. It was one of the reasons she was flying to San Francisco to meet with David in person. "The bureaucracy continues to resist certain of our demands. They want a more participatory role in the technology."

"I guess *so!*" David snapped.

"According to Marianne, the arrival of your people is helping to relax the situation." Wellington's scientific team had been gathered in Beijing since yesterday. Xiang Peng had hosted an extravagant dinner to welcome them, a dinner attended by many of the People's Republic's leading scientists. Against Lisa's wishes, the dinner had received some small attention from the press. That had been David's idea: another way of letting Sun Chen know that the stakes were increasing.

"I spoke with Ellen Siebert this afternoon," David said. "The Chinese scientists seem to understand the benefits of the deal as proposed. They're thinking in the long term. Five years from now, when their people are tallying up their own Nobels, I may regret this."

"As I mentioned, David, it is not the scientific community from which we face objections. But the bureaucracy, while changing, is entrenched. Some of their attitudes are quite hard to overcome. It is perhaps time to consider areas in which we might compromise. Flexibility, David, may be called for."

There was a long silence from David's end of the conversation. At last: "Dammit, Lisa, I *am* flexible. The fact that I considered this offer in the first place shows that. You know as well as I do that there are a dozen other countries that would cut me a deal for omnigene. The Chinese know it, too."

"None of those countries offer you an opportunity like this, David. None of them can even come close."

"And there's not another pharmaceutical company in the world that can give the Chinese what I can."

"All I'm saying, David, is that you're up against a great willingness to be patient. They may choose to wait you out."

"Let them." David's words came quickly, his tone clipped and brusque. "I'm already up against a long wait *here*. That's what this is all about."

Lisa stared for a moment at the wide window, against which heavy raindrops pelted. "Marianne has relayed to me the latest Chinese requests. May I outline them for you, at least?"

"Go ahead," David said sharply.

"Primary among the points of contention is their request that they be allowed to carry some of the other products outward." Marianne had told Lisa that the Chinese were particularly interested in over-the-counter drugs, and were pressuring for a concession that would let Chinese-manufactured Pandrex flow throughout the Pacific Rim and even on into the Basin.

"Absolutely not," barked David. "I will not sell my people down the river. Peng knows that."

"Of course. He *does* understand your position. And so do I, and Marianne. But there are people who hold more power than Peng, although they possess far less vision. Some distrust the whole capitalist transition that's sweeping China. Others object to your insistence upon control of omnigene technology. They feel that such an arrangement leaves you with the upper hand."

"You're damned right it does," David said.

"And if they choose not to deal?"

"Then we don't deal. Simple enough for them?"

Lisa smiled. "That, of course, is precisely the posture Marianne and I are presenting in Beijing."

That earned a quick chuckle. "Like minds."

Lisa felt obliged to prod David with some of the deal's other complications. "And what do you hear from Baltimore?" she asked.

David did not rise to her provocation. In an even voice he said, "Monica's still reviewing the situation. She expects to fly to New York with Hilary next week to meet with Ethan's management. She promises we'll know something by the time you reach California."

"Will she be casting her lot with Hilary Bishop?"

"Can't say yet. But Monica knows Ethan inside out, and the way Hilary's got this planned, the deal may actually make money."

"Your stock's gained back most of what you lost after Kaohsiung," Lisa said. "Can you afford it if she wishes to sell?"

"Hard to say." He grew impatient. "Whatever it is, I'll handle it."

"Of course."

"You don't sound convinced."

"I—"

"It's because of the damned phone," David said unexpectedly, his voice rough. "If you were here—if I could look you in the eyes, take you by the shoulders and *show* you . . ."

"I can see clearly from here, David," Lisa said,

looking through the window, now blurred with rain-drops, at boats plying across stately Victoria Harbor. "I don't want your determination to get in the way of options worth discussing. You may face circum-stances in which compromise is necessary."

"With omnigene? I can't think of any."

"David, I simply think we should be aware that a compromise in China might offset any losses Monica forces you into. Compromise on the product outflow. You've already lost your largest plant; replace it with one on the mainland and let the PRC pick up con-struction costs. Your operations throughout the Rim will thus be streamlined, with the savings that im-plies. Why not?" she asked, anticipating his answer.

"Because that's not the deal I want," David said, as though on cue.

Lisa found herself smiling. "The Occidental busi-ness mind never ceases to amaze and disturb me."

"I wouldn't want to disturb you, Lisa," David said. His voice had grown deeper. "Are my conditions causing you much trouble?"

"It's what your commission buys, David," said Lisa warmly. "And it's going to be a large commission."

"Worth every penny."

"Marianne and I are with you, but before this is through we'll probably have to give the Chinese something, if only something symbolic. Be thinking of what that should be."

"I'm already making notes. I'll have everything ready by the time you reach San Francisco. And from there, with luck, to Beijing. Together."

Lisa would not acknowledge the nuance in David's words.

He became more obvious. "You're certain you won't accept the guest room at my home in San Francisco? All the amenities—and the door locks soundly, should you be worried."

Lisa allowed herself a small laugh. "I'm sure you have a key."

"Well—"

"No," she said more firmly. "My reservations are already made at the Huntington. It's better this way. More . . . professional."

"All work and no play, Lisa," David warned.

"Gets David Wellington's requirements met," Lisa finished for him. "And since we have the compromise question settled, I suppose I had best get in touch with Marianne."

"So soon?"

"There's work to be done. We'll talk tomorrow."

David offered no further objections, and she felt a pang of disappointment when he said, "Goodbye, Lisa."

She replaced the phone on the console. The Austrian businesswoman would be pleased, Lisa knew. The first time Lisa and Marianne had reviewed David's conditions and opposition to compromise, Marianne had smiled like a wolf and said, "Of course. What else would such a man want?"

But that was during the planning stages, and now the long negotiation was under way. Lisa had kept from Marianne the details of David's domestic complications. She wanted her associate to be working from strength. Should disaster loom, Marianne could think quickly on her feet. Lisa asked her secretary to place a call to Beijing.

Tall, extravagantly long-legged, with shining blond hair that fell in open curls about her lovely face before cascading down over her wide shoulders, Marianne Ingwer attracted a great deal of attention as she made her way through the streets of midmorning Beijing. Her carefully tailored dark Geoffrey Beene suit caught the eye of several of the men she passed. Marianne smiled. While here and there in the crowds that swirled around her were women whose clothing was colorful and even stylish, the fashion revolution was moving through China more slowly than the economic reforms. Nor was the PRC yet so accustomed to foreign businesswomen that its citizens could easily ignore one who would have garnered stares in the most refined sections of Hong Kong or London. *I am someone special,* said Marianne's relaxed and confident posture and stride.

Lisa Han knew it, and had turned over to Marianne virtually complete control of their side of the negotiations. Far from being bothered by the parameters David Wellington set for those negotiations, Marianne endorsed them. If the Chinese were going to become capitalists, let them learn from masters. Marianne relished the opportunity.

She had been with Lisa Han for just over four years, and sometimes Marianne felt that there was an almost telepathic connection between them. Too many of her previous employers had been only too happy to saddle Marianne with reams of restrictions before sending her to do busywork, insisting that she check even the most fundamental of moves with them. Fortunately one of her errands brought her into contact with Lisa. *And thanks to Lisa it was much sooner than I'd hoped.*

Marianne approached the newly constructed building that housed the offices of the China International Trust and Investment Corporation. At 29 stories, the CITIC headquarters towered over all else in the city, a fitting symbol of the latest revolution to sweep China. By now, Marianne felt at home in its maze of corridors and small offices. CITIC was in many ways the most influential, and certainly the most innovative, of the bureaus transforming the government's growing fascination with capitalism into action. Yet even here, Marianne had quickly discovered, capitalists were not completely trusted.

Marianne smiled when she spotted Xiang Peng in the lobby. Peng offered Marianne a slight bow. "So," Marianne said as they stepped toward the elevators. "Next stop, the office of Dhao Zhu." It was to be her first meeting with the man who, Peng had told her, could greatly smooth the path toward completion of a deal with Wellington Laboratories.

Peng nodded. "I will introduce you. Then I must return to David's team: we're meeting with representatives of the Biophysical Institute this morning."

"On my own," Marianne said as the elevator doors closed.

"Indeed," said Peng. "And you will need grace to emerge from this meeting unscathed."

"Oh, I'm very graceful."

"Which is why I am optimistic, Marianne. But, remember, Dhao Zhu is a hardliner in regard to what Western firms must offer to do business in China."

"Do you think we face a battle?"

Peng considered that for a moment. "I would say that we face a—*hurdle*. It could be that Dhao Zhu will see immediately the brilliance of our proposition." Peng beamed at her before showing a frown. "Or it could be that he keeps us waiting in his office before dismissing us without fair consideration. I have heard of this happening."

"Not to me," Marianne said firmly.

Peng held up a cautionary finger. "Be careful," he whispered.

"I will," Marianne said, "but I, too, have the reputation for being a hardliner. Shall we see what happens when like minds meet?"

The elevator doors opened and Marianne and Peng stepped out.

Although she longed at least once a day for the serenity and seclusion of Tallpines, Monica Wellington had managed to grow accustomed to the Bauhaus comforts of Hilary's penthouse. "This'll be just like old times!" Hilary exclaimed shortly after Monica had moved in. Monica discovered quickly just how accurate that prediction was. Stefan and the cleaning woman who arrived early each morning had their work cut out for them. Hilary still tossed her clothes hopefully in the direction of chairs or dressers, the garments more often than not landing on the floor. *Just like college, except there was no cleaning woman then.* Memories came back: *I did all the work.* Monica couldn't help wondering at first if Hilary's habits were less sloppy when it came to business.

The worries vanished almost immediately. Hilary's preparation was thorough and well organized. The documents Monica had reviewed at Tallpines were merely prelude to the stacks of material Hilary had arranged in the penthouse's library for Monica to review. Monica staked out the library as her own domain, and moved into it early each morning, staying for long hours of work each day. She plowed through the material nonstop, making lists of suggestions and ideas, refining Hilary's plan for the takeover and liquidation of Ethan Drug.

Even the best of her suggestions received only the most peremptory comments and responses. Since the night of David's unexpected visit to the penthouse, Hilary's mind had been elsewhere and it did not take Monica long to discover where. Hilary was fascinated by Victor Sun Chen. Whenever David's name came up in conversation, Hilary responded by calling him "that redneck son of a bitch!" and then pressing Monica for information about Sun Chen and the pressure he could put on David. Monica dodged the questions as best she could, but it was clear that Hilary had other, accurate sources of information.

Their discussions came to a head over Saturday lunch. Stefan had prepared golden brown Baltimore crab cakes and delicately seasoned *pommes frittes,* served in the dining alcove off the kitchen. The meal served, Stefan faded unobtrusively into the background.

Hilary chewed a bite of crab cake, then fixed Monica with a stare. "What's David up to in the PRC?" she asked.

Monica struggled to contain her surprise. "David's in Atlanta," she said.

Hilary rolled her eyes. "Don't do this, Monica, I'm in no mood to play." Her eyes were puffy from a long night's exertions—Hilary had brought home a new man last night, their lovemaking prolonged and uninhibited. The noise had interrupted Monica's sleep twice.

"I don't know what you're talking about."

Hilary shook her head angrily. "That won't work, either. I know you and that son of a bitch are still talking. And I know that he and a Eurasian bitch named Lisa Han are up to something. This has a direct bearing on what we're planning, Monica. So open up."

Monica waited a long moment before answering. David had warned her that this moment would come, but the advice he'd given did not make Monica's play any easier. "The Chinese are interested in certain Wellington Labs products," she said at last, speaking slowly.

"Import or manufacture?"

Monica took a breath. "Manufacture."

Hilary whistled, a long, low note. "No wonder this Sun Chen is worried. David can produce pharmaceuticals in the PRC for less than on the outside. He can flood the market."

Monica said nothing.

Hilary grew reflective. Monica fancied that she could almost hear Hilary's thought processes whirring through ramifications and complications. "This has a bearing on our Ethan plans, too," Hilary said finally.

"It could."

"Could, hell! Word of this gets out on top of the Kaohsiung explosion, and it's going to look pretty bad for David Wellington. Almost like he had it planned."

"Don't be absurd," Monica said.

Hilary ignored her. "And if *that* happens, it could play hell with your stock. You'd better make up your mind to sell, and get it over with before the bottom falls out."

Monica studied Hilary a long time before speaking. "Lisa Han is meeting David in San Francisco next Friday," she said deliberately. "I'll have made my move by then."

Hilary nodded her agreement. "Friday," she said idly before falling silent. She ate some of her crab cake, and took a sip of Pouilly-Fuissé before speaking again. "By Friday, you'll have had a good look at Ethan Drug in person, and we should be ready to go ahead with a little expansion of our own."

"We'll have had a look," Monica corrected.

"No, I've been meaning to tell you. Something's come up and I'm going to be leaving town late this afternoon. I'll be gone for a couple of days."

A chill skittered up Monica's spine. "Where?"

"No, no," Hilary said. "You kept your secrets from me, remember? Besides, Ethan isn't the only iron I've got in the fire and you *are* still a member of the competition after all. I can't tell you everything. You go see McDaid at Ethan, get things moving. I'll be back before the end of the week. You can give me a report when I'm home." Hilary stood up. "Just like old times."

Monica sat alone at the lacquered table, thinking of what she had done.

Nestled in her first-class seat, taking advantage of every amenity Northwest Orient had to offer, Hilary Bishop hurtled toward Taipei. The meeting that awaited her excited Hilary in a way more electrifying than anything she could recall. Everything she had accomplished and learned since leaving David at Tallpines was about to come together.

10

VICTOR SUN CHEN walked slowly, calmly, through his gardens. The wait, he had often thought, equalled the excitement of the climax. Sun Chen had waited for many things in his sixty years, and in that time he had savored many resolutions. This afternoon gave the promise of a key to the resolution of a relationship that had begun many years ago. Sun Chen had enjoyed each of his duels with Lisa Han, and felt a certain wistful regret in the knowledge that this latest duel would be the last. He recognized in Lisa so much of himself.

When Sun Chen heard the Rolls-Royce pull up the drive, he drew a slow breath, taking a moment to straighten the lines of his crisp Cerruti suit. A moment later his secretary ushered Hilary Bishop into the gardens.

Hilary was taller than Sun Chen had expected, and as cool as an iced drink in her green silk Bill Blass jacket and skirt. A Tiffany chain glittered at her throat, and the blouse she wore was generous in what it revealed of her full, firm breasts. Hilary's handshake was strong, and she held her head high as she took a seat facing Sun Chen across a small stone table. Sun Chen directed his secretary to fetch refreshments.

"I met your father once," the Taiwanese said after a tray bearing tea and small sandwiches had been placed between them.

"Yes?" said Hilary, deftly taking over the duty of pouring tea for both of them.

"A fascinating man. A brilliant businessman, I think."

"He was all that," said Hilary. Was there an element of defiance in the look she gave Sun Chen?

"And yourself?" Sun Chen asked, lifting a Wedgwood cup to his lips. "Do you share his talents?"

"Some say I do."

Sun Chen sat back in his wicker chair and studied Hilary. "Then let us get to it. I am curious to know what this mysterious transaction you offer will cost, coming as it does from so brilliant and beautiful a businesswoman as Monroe Bishop's daughter."

Hilary's eyes narrowed for a moment. "Shall we say that this is in the line of a professional courtesy?"

"I do not follow." Sun Chen's cup made a delicate clink as he replaced it on its saucer.

Hilary laced her fingers together. "I have no intention of charging for what I bring you."

Sun Chen showed disbelief. "Altruism? You must forgive me, I am unaccustomed to such gestures. What would your father say?"

Hilary shook her head, blond curls rustling over her shoulders. She fingered the chain in a gesture that was almost coy. "Hardly altruism—that's more David Wellington's line, and Wellington is what I bring you."

Sun Chen displayed no reaction. "This was implied when we spoke by telephone," he said. "Now you have flown all this way. Speak freely."

Hilary nodded, took a breath, and began to tell Sun Chen of the deal David Wellington and Lisa Han were striking with the mainland Chinese. Sun Chen could sense the enjoyment Hilary derived from delivering the information as a flush rose to color her cheeks. She stabbed at Sun Chen with her fingers as she made her points, her breathing rapid, her pupils dilated. "You see, Victor, should this news be made public it would cast the Kaohsiung explosion in a whole new light. To show that David destroyed his own factory in order to pave the way for a deal with the communists—"

"You think he is responsible for Kaohsiung?" Sun Chen asked.

Hilary snorted her laughter. "Don't be absurd." Her gaze was calculating, holding more than a trace of a dare. "Whoever dealt with Kaohsiung is far more talented than David." She was audacious enough to wink at Sun Chen.

Sun Chen spread his palms wide in a display of innocence. "And why have you come to me with this information?"

Hilary would not play. "I'm not stupid, Victor. We both know that you've tangled with David several times. You couldn't frighten him away by killing his people and sabotaging his plants. And whoever you hired to hit him in Washington obviously lacked the skills to do the job right."

Sun Chen sat still and did not speak. The idiots who had botched the attack on Wellington still angered him. Sun Chen held his anger inside. The next time, he would send Kintang with all of his special skills. And Kintang would not fail.

"You're either going to have to kill David or ruin him," Hilary said. "He does not scare."

"Everyone scares, my dear," said Sun Chen, his voice as cold as steel. He made no attempt to deny Hilary's allegations. "I gather your information is accurate?"

"You can depend on it," Hilary said, her tone cocky. "You could bet David's life on it. But you're going to have to move quickly—Lisa Han is joining him in San Francisco on Wednesday. They'll be moving fast after that."

"And you offer no conditions for what you've given me? Surely you must get something out of this."

Hilary smiled broadly. "By Tuesday morning I'll have put pressure of my own on Wellington Laboratories. When this is all done, who knows? It might be Bishop Laboratories—and I assure you, we would be out of your region quickly."

"Yes," said Sun Chen. "I can imagine what your assurances would be worth." He stared hard at her for a long moment. "Is there anything else?"

Hilary tossed her head, her curls cascading. She raised her chin and revealed the pulse of her throat, leaning forward a bit to purse open the lapels of her blouse. Sun Chen could see the fires grow brighter in her eyes. Her color deepened. "I don't fly home until late tomorrow," she said. Hilary's pink tongue darted out to moisten her full lips.

Sun Chen looked at her, imagining how it would feel to impale himself within her. He did not doubt that Hilary would respond with an energy and a hunger to match his own. Finally Sun Chen stood up. Hilary rose gracefully from her seat, and took a step toward him, stopping when the Taiwanese gave a curt shake of his head. "You will pardon me for speaking bluntly," Sun Chen said to Hilary. "But I learned long ago the folly that occurs when one such as I fucks my own kind."

Hilary laughed softly. "Oh, Victor, surely you know the advantages of allowing yourself at least *some* folly once in a while."

She dropped to her knees before him.

At some point Hilary and Sun Chen moved to his bedroom suite, but they did not sleep.

He had surprised her in the garden with the ferocity of his response. Kneeling before him, Hilary had slowly unfastened Sun Chen's belt and opened his trousers. Before she could reach inside his pants to clutch his penis, Hilary found her arms grasped tightly. Sun Chen pulled her up to him, holding her with a stern grip. Sun Chen's dark eyes were hot, his voice thick and hot.

"Strip," he said, and released Hilary. "Slowly. For

me." He lowered himself slowly into his seat, his eyes never leaving her.

Hilary had a moment's hesitation. There might be others watching. But the moment passed. Donning a seductive, sullen pout, Hilary removed her Blass jacket and dropped it casually to the pebbled surface of the terrace. *Let them watch,* she thought as her fingers worked the buttons of the pale peach Givenchy blouse. An audience would just make her performance more exciting. She swayed back and forth slowly before Sun Chen, her blouse falling open. After a moment, her eyes locked with Sun Chen's, Hilary shrugged off the blouse. Hilary was not wearing a bra. She ran her hands up her abdomen to her breasts, and felt her nipples grow stiff against her palms. Hilary's breathing grew more deep.

"The rest," Sun Chen ordered.

Stepping out of her pumps, Hilary undid the clasp at the waist of her skirt and pushed it down so it fell to her ankles. Hilary stepped out of the pool of material and faced Sun Chen clad only in minuscule silk panties, taupe stockings and garter belt. She gracefully lifted her right foot and placed its sole on the edge of Sun Chen's chair, between his legs. For a second she held the foot motionless. Then she inched it forward until her toes pressed against the hardness at Sun Chen's groin. With tantalizing slowness she released the clasp and rolled the stocking down the length of her tanned leg, caressing her flesh as she did. Hilary tossed the stocking aside and even more slowly removed her other stocking. She wiggled her bare toes against Sun Chen's crotch.

Sun Chen placed his hands on Hilary's taut buttocks, pulled her to him, burying his face against her silken panties. His breath was hot against Hilary and she felt an electric shiver dance up her spine. Sun Chen's fingers found their way inside the waistband of Hilary's panties and he urged them down slowly, his tongue licking at her flesh, his teeth nipping at her. A soft, low moan escaped Hilary's lips.

"Now," Sun Chen said when Hilary was completely nude. He leaned back in his chair as Hilary once more lowered herself to her knees. She reached up to touch his face, then slowly unknotted his tie, opened the buttons of his Ermengildo Zegna shirt. Sun Chen's body belied his age—he was muscular, his hairless chest firm and smooth. Hilary raised her mouth to his nipples and bit them into stiffness. She worked her way down his torso.

Hilary cried out with delight when she pushed aside Sun Chen's trousers at last to reveal his stiff penis. It was beautiful, thick and hard, and she pressed her cheek against its throbbing warmth. A single perfect drop of semen glistened at its crown. Hilary's pink tongue darted out to capture the droplet, and Sun Chen's cock gave a lurch in response. Hilary closed the fingers of her right hand tight around Sun Chen's hardness; her left hand found the weight of his testicles. She squeezed with both hands, eliciting a guttural grunt from Sun Chen. Hilary lowered her mouth to Sun Chen's penis, capturing the glans between her teeth, gently biting down. His hips began to rise and fall, his hands found her shoulders and kneaded her flesh.

Hilary tasted Sun Chen as he grew stiffer, felt the weight of his balls increase. With the index finger of her left hand she probed back farther, found the tight ring of his anus and pressed against it until it gave way and granted her entry. Sun Chen shuddered and Hilary worked harder with her other hand. Sun Chen arched his back, pushed suddenly with his hands to force Hilary's mouth away as he came, his ejaculation scalding her flesh as it spattered against her cheeks and breasts.

In a single, fluid motion, Sun Chen rose from his chair and drew Hilary to him. He mashed his lips roughly against hers, his tongue a fierce invader, his hands everywhere at once. Hilary felt her own heat begin to mount, her pulse rising, her breathing growing ragged, her cheeks flushed. She followed in a daze as Victor Sun Chen led her from the garden, through a doorway and into the recesses of his bedroom suite. His erection had diminished hardly at all and when he pushed her down onto the bed, Hilary opened her legs for him to penetrate her. But Sun Chen had something else in mind.

Quickly stripping away his remaining clothing, he bent and roughly drew Hilary's knees over his shoulders, locked his fingers into the firm flesh of her thighs, stood slowly until he was upright. Hilary was suspended upside down, blood racing to her head. She cried out as Sun Chen's mouth found the cleft between her thighs. He insinuated his tongue into her moist center, lapping, probing until he found her clitoris. Sensation exploded through Hilary as Sun Chen licked and bit at her. Her heels beat rhythmically against his shoulders. A first tentative orgasm swept over her, followed immediately by another, larger one. Then she was coming nonstop, again and again until the largest blast of all lifted her up and out of consciousness.

She was not gone long. Hilary came deliciously back to her senses as Sun Chen shrugged her knees from his shoulders, and lowered her to the bed. Still standing, he moved deeper between her thighs and placed the tip of his penis against her wet opening. Hilary moaned as Sun Chen entered her in a single harsh stroke. Once imbedded, he did not pause, but pulled back to plunge once more into her, lifting her up with the force of his assault. It had never been like this for Hilary—she found in herself a level of response that frightened her. Crying as she came, Hilary tightened herself around Sun Chen, set her own rhythm to match his, and lost herself once more as he exploded inside her.

"Folly," Sun Chen said as he lowered his weight onto Hilary. "You will drain me dry."

Hilary clenched her inner muscles once more around his still stiff penis. "Evenly matched, I'd say," she whispered against his ear. "Not folly."

Victor Sun Chen laughed and rolled off her. He left the bed and padded nude to a Chippendale highboy that stood against the near wall. Hilary watched as Sun Chen poured Scotch from a Baccarat decanter into crystal glasses. He brought the drinks back to the wide bed but did not immediately offer Hilary one. When Hilary reached for a glass, Sun Chen held it just out of her reach. Then he moved the glass and touched it to Hilary's breasts, splashing a bit of amber liquor onto her skin. Sun Chen bowed over Hilary and sucked the drops of Scotch from her hard nipples. Hilary sighed, moved closer to Sun Chen, reached once more for his penis.

Sun Chen chuckled again and moved away from Hilary. "You are greedy," he teased. He handed her a drink, sipped at his own. "Glenfiddich," Sun Chen said. "I serve only the best."

"I'll say," Hilary chuckled. The liquor blossomed against her palate. For the first time she looked around Sun Chen's cavernous bedroom. Wonderfully enameled vases held delicate quince branches, their blossoms a delicate contrast with the room's dark walls. The walls themselves were hung with framed erotica, Indian and Asian drawings and prints depicting every imaginable sexual act—and some that had never before occurred to Hilary.

"I can see what your greatest pleasure is," Hilary said to Sun Chen. She sat up in bed, feeling his warmth ooze from inside her and onto her thighs. She reached into the pile of clothing Sun Chen had discarded, and found his Cerruti jacket. Deftly, Hilary removed the silk handkerchief from the jacket's breast pocket, and without any self-consciousness, used it to mop Sun Chen's fluids from herself.

"These?" Sun Chen said, indicating the erotica with a wave of his hand. He took another swallow of Glenfiddich, then shook his head. "A preferred pleasure perhaps—but not my greatest pleasure."

Hilary put the towel aside. She stared at Sun Chen's hard penis, wanting to feel it again inside her. "Well, what *is* your greatest pleasure?" she said huskily.

Sun Chen was silent for a long moment. "Perhaps money," he said at last. Laughing, he added, "Although I do not think the decor would benefit from framed bills, francs, pesos."

"You said, 'perhaps,'" Hilary prompted.

He nodded. "As with you, I'm certain. The money is . . . symbolic."

"One hell of a symbol," chortled Hilary.

"Indeed, indeed. But it is the power it represents that is my greatest, as you say, pleasure."

Hilary's desires grew insistent. "But the sex—"

"Sex *is* power," said Sun Chen with sudden force. He finished his drink in a single swallow and stalked to the highboy to pour himself another.

"It's pleasure as well," Hilary said.

Sun Chen's smile was ambiguous. "You're a sensualist, my dear," he said. He sat on the mattress beside her. Unexpectedly he pushed his right hand between Hilary's thighs, caught her clitoris between fingertips, pinched hard until Hilary cried out half in pain and half in pleasure. "And there are sensations ahead that you will not soon forget." He released his grip upon her. "But, first, I think we should have a little entertainment."

Sun Chen stretched to reach the massive black walnut headboard. He pressed against it and a panel swung open, revealing an array of shining switches and controls. He flicked a switch and with a whirr the curtains against the far wall drew back, revealing a tall Mitsubishi projection television system.

"Videos?" Hilary asked skeptically.

Sun Chen snorted. "Perhaps I should have said that

we would mix business with pleasure. Tell me, have you ever met Lisa Han?"

Hilary shook her head.

"Then you have a treat in store for you." Beside the projection set stood a massive Korean armoire. Sun Chen went to it and swung open the black lacquered doors to reveal shelves lined with carefully labeled videotapes. He selected one from the top shelf and pushed it into the VCR that stood on the armoire's bottom shelf.

As he returned to bed, Sun Chen spoke with as much excitement as Hilary had yet heard from him. "Lisa was one of my girls, you see. One of my . . . reclamation projects!" The words made him laugh deeply. Sun Chen took a remote controller from the bedstand and brought the tape player to life.

The huge screen showed the interior of Sun Chen's bedroom. Hilary compared the image on the television with the reality that surrounded her. Some of the paintings were different. The Chippendale was a new piece, not shown on the screen.

"This was some time back," Sun Chen said. "And the quality is better than we had any right to expect— so many of those days were captured on film. The video revolution had not yet arrived. Now my whole collection has been transferred to tape." His breath eased out in a hiss. "Here! Look!"

Onscreen a delicate Eurasian girl entered the bedroom in a shimmering brocaded robe, loosely belted at her slender waist. Her black hair was worn down, falling nearly to her waist, framing a perfect face whose dark eyes were beautiful even on tape. She could not have been more than seventeen.

"Lisa—" Hilary began.

"Lisa Han," said Victor Sun Chen between clenched teeth.

Behind Lisa a door opened and Victor Sun Chen entered the bedroom. He was younger, his body having not yet acquired the solid, muscular thickness that Hilary now knew so well. But the cruel good looks were there: he was as darkly handsome then as now. Sun Chen wore a lounging robe, in a darker shade of green but otherwise identical to Lisa's. He approached her and grabbed her shoulders, turning her to face him. Lisa took a step backward, unbelting her robe as she did so. Her back to the camera, Lisa stepped out of the robe. Her lithe young figure was revealed to Hilary as she pirouetted for Sun Chen, a graceful ballet that Sun Chen interrupted with a sharp slap against Lisa's flank. Lisa stumbled and Sun Chen caught her, bending her at the waist. He pushed her down until her face pressed against the bed, and held her there with one hand while he stripped away his own robe.

Sun Chen's erection was fierce onscreen and, Hilary noticed, equally angry now. Her hand strayed to his hardness. Her eyes returned to the screen. Hilary was not prepared for the brutality with which Sun Chen took Lisa from behind. She cried out herself in unison with Lisa's image, and involuntarily tightened her grip. Sun Chen flexed himself against her.

The tape showed Sun Chen furiously taking Lisa, pounding himself into her and against her until he exploded and she collapsed whimpering onto the bed. Sun Chen was merciless, striking Lisa's buttocks with his hand. For a moment the girl did not move. Then she gathered her strength, pushed herself up from the bed and turned to face Sun Chen. She licked her lips, and lowered herself to take him into her mouth.

"You see?" Sun Chen said. "She was such a good student."

Hilary watched the action on the screen. "And this is the Lisa Han with whom David is involved? Who is causing you such difficulty? How—"

Sun Chen's eyes were also focused upon the television images. "Of all my girls, Lisa was the smartest, the most ambitious. It has been my great pleasure over the years to watch her continue to grow." He sighed softly. "Of course, there have been times when I have had to . . . *intervene* in her life—"

"Playing God?" Hilary asked.

"Hardly!" Sun Chen's laughter was harsh and ugly. "But playing, yes. I have the time and the money, the resources to indulge myself. I keep track of my girls. I know which among them become courtesans, and which become common whores. I send flowers for the graves of those who have died."

"And Lisa Han?"

Sun Chen took Hilary's shoulders and pulled her to him. His hard penis pressed against her. "I will send flowers for her grave, too," he said. And then Hilary was lost in sensation.

Shortly after midnight Victor Sun Chen slipped from the bed where Hilary Bishop snored softly. He drew on a long robe, and took the decanter of Glenfiddich and a glass with him to the study that adjoined the bedroom. Sun Chen poured a drink, then placed the decanter on the teak desk at which he often worked. He did not sit down now, but prowled around the study, thinking.

Arranged neatly in a row on a shelf facing the desk were a dozen tiny jade Buddhas, each more than a thousand years old. Sun Chen had acquired the pieces at great cost years ago. He remembered now the delight Lisa Han had taken in them. Most of his girls, upon seeing the jade, or any of the other items in Sun Chen's collection, had asked about their cost. Lisa, though, had identified them immediately as works representative of the jademasters of the Chou Dynasty.

He wondered if he might not have waited too long to deal with Lisa. It was not the first time the question had occurred to him. Sun Chen had provided Lisa with obstacles, and delivered to her difficulties that would have stopped strong men. But Lisa's ambition was fully the equal of his own, and would be interrupted only by death. More superstitious than he ever publicly admitted, Sun Chen was not fully certain that even death could halt Lisa's spirit. He would know soon enough.

The finality of the thought disturbed him. Lisa was a link to his past. Even now he could recall, without the aid of videotape, the details of their lovemaking, the reservoirs of passion that she released for him, until her ambition got in the way. Sun Chen was sometimes curious about the course their lives would have taken had he not evicted Lisa so quickly. But then her ambition and intelligence had seemed unnecessary, irrelevant to the use he had for her. Only as the years passed did he come to realize that he should have been less hasty in dismissing her.

At least I have not been hasty in ending her life, he thought. Scotch burned his throat. He was without sentiment, yet suddenly wished very much to see Lisa Han. It occurred to Sun Chen, not for the first time, that Lisa had arrived in his home already possessing ambition, already honing her intellect. He had given her a taste of the real world, its pleasures and pains, and that taste she had taken with her when she left. She had come a great distance during the intervening years. *I would like to look into her eyes as she dies,* Sun Chen thought.

Sun Chen finished his Scotch and stepped to his desk to pour another. His mind was made up. He punched the intercom that connected him with Angelica Nevins, the English secretary who was the latest in a long line of assistants that had included Candace Caillou. No matter what hour of the day or night he paged her, Angelica always sounded crisp and efficient. "Sir?" she answered.

Sun Chen drew a breath, feeling a familiar feral stirring deep in his stomach. It was beginning. "Have Neil Kintang join me here for luncheon tomorrow."

"Very good, sir. Anything else?"

"Just Kintang," Sun Chen said, and broke the connection.

There was a rustling at the doorway to the study. Sun Chen looked up to see Hilary Bishop framed there, magnificently nude, her hair still bed-rumpled, lips puffy from his kisses, her firm breasts and flat belly bearing tiny red bite marks. After viewing the tape of Sun Chen with Lisa, Hilary had enthusiastically agreed to Sun Chen's suggestion: Hilary's wrists and ankles were discolored where the bonds had chafed her. She stepped closer to Sun Chen's desk, then stopped, her long legs splayed wide. Her hands strayed to her pubic triangle. She began to stroke herself slowly.

"Couldn't sleep?" she asked Victor Sun Chen.

"Just a bit of work to do," he said. He stood up. Hard again, his penis pressed against the robe he wore.

"Is your work done?" Hilary's fingers worked more rapidly. Her eyes were bright and dilated.

"I'm just begun," Sun Chen said.

Hilary smiled. "Wouldn't want you to leave your desk," she said slyly. She maneuvered herself to the edge of the enormous desk and sat down on it. "So why don't you just fuck me here?"

11

DAVID WELLINGTON WINCED as he reached for the tall glass of Perrier. After leaving Hilary's penthouse last Wednesday night, he had visited a friend on the medical staff at Johns Hopkins and had him clean and stitch the wound. No records of David's visit with the physician were made. The wound still ached, and the black eye from the cosh blow was only just beginning to fade. It was late Sunday night and he was seated in the lounge of his Learjet, cruising high on a course for San Francisco. David maintained an expansive home on Russian Hill, and he planned to pass the next few days secluded there.

He took a sip of the sparkling water. Arrayed before him were the latest figures from the Pacific Rim and Basin. They subtly confirmed his ambitions, showing growth in Wellington Labs's share of the Japanese analgesic market, a substantial increase in the number of Australian hospitals relying upon Wellington chemotherapy packets, a lower than anticipated flow of red ink from the chaotic Philippines. If he could hold on, the whole region would become profitable before another five years had passed.

Ahead of schedule, David thought. Was he reading too much into the figures? The latest issue of *Fortune,* just published, claimed that he was. A short article, "Wellington on the Road to Xanadu?," related in the magazine's typically arch prose the Kaohsiung disaster, and went on to paint a bleak portrait of the future of Wellington Laboratories in the Pacific. And they hadn't used a flattering photograph of David to accompany their text.

A little more intriguing were the article's hints that Wellington's future might include mainland China. Although omnigene was a secret, David had not hidden his people's presence in the PRC, and *Fortune*'s researchers and writers made no effort to restrain their speculations. David glanced again at the piece's concluding paragraphs:

> Wellington Laboratories may have been able to weather mounting losses in the Pacific, but the loss of the Kaohsiung facility changes the climate dramatically. David Wellington has already loudly announced his intention to rebuild in Kaohsiung, yet within days there were Wellington personnel on the mainland. Admittedly it is a scientific rather than a business delegation in Beijing at the moment, but James Wellington himself more than once used scientific exchange and innovation to pave the way for business.
>
> James Wellington built a large and hugely profitable pharmaceutical company with such enlightened policies, but even he never undertook an expansion so grand as his son's. There is no denying the appeal offered by the People's Republic to a dedicated expansionist like David Wellington. But China—and the entire region he seeks to penetrate—may require more resources and resourcefulness than he has yet shown.
>
> The nations of the East offer many profits, but also more than a few prophets. Oriental sages have counseled patience for centuries, but David Wellington, for one, does not seem to have listened.

David sighed and closed the magazine. This was not the first time the business press had underestimated him. A grin crossed his features as he imagined the journalistic reaction to the Chinese reality in the works.

The misguided article served other purposes. David

was using the press as another tool with which to pique Victor Sun Chen. He wanted the Taiwanese off his guard, so eager to have done with David that he would make mistakes. *And when Sun Chen stumbles,* David thought, *I will have him.*

Then darker thoughts loomed, and he saw with perfect clarity the obituaries written for his death and Lisa Han's, the articles detailing the collapse of Wellington Laboratories. David leaned back in his seat. He pressed a hand to his throbbing shoulder, closed his eyes, and was borne on toward San Francisco where he would lie low and await the arrival of Lisa Han.

Neil Kintang could have earned one hell of a freelance living anywhere in the world, but he had voluntarily indentured himself to Victor Sun Chen eleven years ago and never once regretted it. Sun Chen saw to it that Kintang lived very well indeed, always traveled luxury class, and received a generous bonus upon the successful completion of each assignment. Neil Kintang never failed.

Sun Chen was also careful to give Kintang plenty of warning before a job. A meticulous man who planned his work with the utmost attention to detail and execution, Kintang liked that. It was the details even more than the execution that made his work so enjoyable, his career so fulfilling. Kintang took pleasure from assembling the elements of each job, acquiring the right tools, putting together the proper timetables. As he developed those timetables, Kintang often allowed a measure for toying with his targets. Some employers might have found that unprofessional, which was another reason Kintang appreciated his special relationship with Victor Sun Chen. Among the many things they had in common was a delicious patience, a willingness to stretch out their pleasures.

Now, as he guided his white Saab 900 Turbo along

the snaking route that led through the hills to Sun Chen's estate, Kintang felt a tingle of anticipation. It was sooner after his work in Kaohsiung than Kintang would have preferred, but he gathered that Sun Chen had a reason for his haste. Certainly he had a reason for insistence upon Kintang; the fools in Washington had ruined an easy hit. Kintang was never clumsy. When the call from Angelica Nevins arrived in the small hours of the morning, Kintang had had a premonition that Sun Chen's next assignment would be David Wellington. And Kintang's instincts were usually correct.

He steered the Saab through the gateway in the high stone wall that surrounded Sun Chen's house and grounds and parked beneath the porte-cochere. He smiled at Angelica, waiting on the patio.

The smile she gave him in return was all business. "Mr. Sun Chen is awaiting you in the garden," she told Kintang emotionlessly.

Kintang took a moment to run a languorous gaze over Angelica. She was every inch the English working girl, her trim form quite nicely packaged in a cheerful Karl Lagerfeld print. "Lead on," he said.

She raised her strong chin a bit and showed Kintang a look that was nearly defiant. *Does she disapprove? he wondered. Does she even know what my relationship with Sun Chen is? Not that it mattered. I could thaw her,* Kintang thought, *so that she would never freeze again.* But he said nothing as he followed her through the hallway that led to Sun Chen's gardens.

Kintang hated flowers. As always here, though, he masked his distaste, donning a broad smile as Sun Chen rose to shake his hand.

"Neil," Sun Chen said heartily as they clasped hands. "It is always such a pleasure to see you."

"It's always a pleasure to be called."

Sun Chen wagged a friendly finger at Kintang. "Even more of one, this time, I think you will find," he said as they took their seats.

"Luncheon will be served shortly," Angelica said. "Would you care for a drink, Mr. Kintang?"

He grinned at her. "Call me Neil."

Angelica did not rise to the invitation.

Kintang nodded in temporary defeat. There were more important matters at hand than breaking down Angelica's defenses. "Rum on the rocks."

Angelica nodded, turned to a cart to fix the drink. When she handed Kintang his glass of rum, the big man brushed his fingers against her wrist. Did she jump? Kintang stared deep into her green eyes until she lowered them and turned to leave Kintang and Sun Chen alone.

Their wrought-iron chairs were positioned next to a marble fishpond. Broad lilies floated on the surface, beneath which the golden shapes of koi darted back and forth, the Japanese goldfish often rising to the surface to accept the morsels of food that Sun Chen idly tossed. For a long while Sun Chen said nothing, studying his fish. Kintang sipped his rum, waiting.

At last Sun Chen pressed his palms together as though praying. He fixed Kintang with a hard stare. "The time has come," Sun Chen said, "to speak of Lisa Han."

Neil Kintang was too professional to let his employer see the flash of excitement that raced through him. But Victor Sun Chen was too perceptive not to be aware of it.

"I thought that would please you," Sun Chen said with a chuckle.

"A full assignment?"

Sun Chen nodded solemnly. Nearby, a koi splashed insistently at the surface of the pool, and Sun Chen obliged it with a scrap of bread. "A bit more than that, in fact."

"David Wellington," Kintang said without emotion.

Sun Chen nodded. "You always impress me, Neil."

Kintang gave a slight bow.

"Lisa Han will be joining him in San Francisco on Friday," Sun Chen said. "Not much warning, I fear."

"I can move quickly," Kintang offered.

Sun Chen held up a hand. "Of course. But after all this time I think it would be more . . . elegant if Lisa and David could be taken down together."

"I understand," Kintang said softly. He finished his drink.

"Anything else?"

"A detail," Sun Chen said almost offhandedly. "Lisa should die last. That is important to me."

Kintang nodded. "Would you like her to watch?"

Sun Chen brightened perceptibly. "As you will," the Taiwanese said, with customary magnanimity.

"I'll give her something to look at."

Angelica emerged from the house to announce that luncheon was being served on the terrace.

As they rose to adjourn for their meal, Sun Chen whispered to Kintang: "Do not feel obliged to be swift, but neither should you underestimate them. Wellington has survived one attempt already."

"It wasn't mine," Kintang said simply.

Sun Chen looked almost contrite. "An error of impatience."

"That kind of error is virtually always fatal." Kintang's eyes were cold.

"David Wellington is becoming impatient," Sun Chen said, and explained to Kintang the business Hilary had described.

"Have *I* ever disappointed you?" Kintang asked unexpectedly.

"Of course not." Sun Chen clapped a hand to Kintang's broad shoulder. "Now, shall we dine?"

"Will Angelica be joining us?"

Sun Chen studied Kintang, a leer creasing his face. "A difficult assignment even for you, Neil."

"It's the difficulty I enjoy most."

"Then she shall be with us. The rest is up to you."

"That's all I ever ask," Neil Kintang said.

Marianne Ingwer stood outside Beijing's Forbidden City, from whose opulence the Ming and Qing emperors had ruled China for more than five centuries. Marianne was waiting for Dhao Zhu, who would be taking her to dinner at elegant Fang Shan, a restaurant —and a turn of events—that both pleased and surprised Marianne. She had arrived at their rendezvous spot two hours early, stealing the time for herself. Ever since she arrived in Beijing she'd promised herself a walk through the Forbidden City. No brief stroll, she quickly realized, could begin to take in even a fraction of its wonders. The palaces and buildings contained more than 9,000 rooms; each one, it seemed, was filled with fabulous paintings, fabrics, works of art.

But not even the wonders of the Forbidden City could completely distract her. True to Peng's dark prediction, Dhao Zhu, after Peng's hurried introduction, had kept her waiting for most of a day. When he finally did inaugurate their conversation, he was brusque and virtually dismissive. More than once he appeared ready to cancel their business altogether. It had taken every skill Marianne possessed to retain Zhu's interest, and when they resumed their conversation on Monday Zhu was still firmly opposed to Wellington's control of the technology.

Dhao Zhu himself was thirty-six, muscular, standing nearly as tall as Marianne. At first he struck her as being as completely humorless as his sparsely furnished office. But Marianne continued to probe, looking for enthusiasms, areas of interest that she could exploit. The carefully tailored Hong Kong suits and silk ties that Zhu wore gave Marianne a clue—it turned out that the bureaucrat fancied himself a sophisticate, a gourmet. After one of this morning's heated bouts focused upon Wellington's proprietary rights, Marianne started her campaign of exploitation in earnest. "And your favorite restaurant?" she asked, "in Beijing? The one that succeeds most fully on every level?"

Marianne had at first been startled by his ability to make a clean break between vehement business disagreement and interludes of casual conversation. It was an ability that she hoped would serve her well. "Fang Shan," the Chinese said finally. "An idiosyncratic choice for one in my position, but one that I would be happy to defend."

"Would you?" Marianne said, her eyes as wide as she could make them without giving herself away. "I'm not familiar with it. You must tell me what it's like."

Dhao Zhu's pride in his hard-won cosmopolitanism showed suddenly in his face. As Marianne watched, he grew bold. "Why not join me there?" he asked. "I have influence enough to secure reservations for this evening."

"I'd love to." Five minutes later they were locked once more in debate. She thought, though, that the heat of their disagreement had lessened somewhat.

Marianne left the Forbidden City shortly before she was due to meet Dhao Zhu. She had dressed carefully in a bright silk Scaasi print, cinched at the waist with an oversize Hermes scarf, and caught a glimpse of pleasure on Zhu's face when he spotted her and hurried to her side.

"Fang Shan is in Beihei Park," Zhu said after they exchanged pleasantries. "A few blocks north of here. Shall we walk?"

"Of course."

Beihei Lake was surrounded by one of the most beautiful parks in all of China. Marianne and Dhao Zhu entered the park through its southeast gate. Zhu indicated the stone wall that curved to their left.

"Tuang Cheng," he said, "Round Town. Once the home of Kublai Khan stood there."

They walked slowly across the graceful marble Bridge of Eternal Peace that connected Round Town with Qiong Hua Island. Marianne and Zhu passed beneath archways and onto the island. Nearby stood the gateways that led to the Temple of Everlasting Peace, beyond which rose the stunning rounded White Dagoba. The Dagoba was a glazed brick temple, Tibetan in style and structure.

"Another world," said Zhu softly, with something like reverence in his voice. "This was all sealed away following the Cultural Revolution. It was reopened barely a decade ago."

"To hide all of this," Marianne said in amazement. "To pretend it did not exist."

Zhu shook his head. "We thought that to embrace the future we must abandon the past. Now we know that the past must serve to remind us."

"Of what?" But Zhu did not answer her.

They strolled slowly along the "Covered Way," protected by its delicately painted beams and ceiling. By the time they arrived at the restaurant, Marianne felt as though a subtle temporal transition had been made, to another place, another time.

Fang Shan's cooks, Zhu told Marianne as they entered the restaurant, had been taught their craft by the master cooks of the Dowager Empress herself, and Marianne had no trouble feeling that she had stepped back to the days of imperial China. The restaurant spread through a series of courtyards and gardens, each surrounded by a low wall, giving diners solitude and tranquility. The service at Fang Shan was exquisite and unobtrusive, the food elegantly prepared, delicate and delicious. Marianne was sorry when she found herself steering the conversation back toward business—it would have been easy to pass the evening in Dhao Zhu's pleasant company, pretending that she was a merchant come to call on a representative of the Dowager Empress.

Zhu was talking. "We cannot permit ourselves to forget our past," he said, waving a hand at the imperial setting in which they dined.

"Nor should you," Marianne countered, looking for an opening. "This is wonderful!"

Zhu shook his head. "It is . . . *contained*," he said after some consideration. "It is here, but it no longer rules us."

Marianne savored a spoonful of her soup, "Stewed Three Whites," made of mushrooms, fish, and bamboo shoots. She placed the spoon beside her plate and looked directly at Dhao Zhu. "Doesn't it?" she said.

He gave her a smile. "You read me well, Marianne. I'm attracted to all of this . . . decadence." He savored the word. "Imperial rule itself is gone because the heart of the Empire *decayed*. Yet we retain this."

"It's worth retaining," Marianne said as a waiter removed the soup.

Zhu shrugged. "Now we are evolving again from a rule whose center had grown old and ill. I work in a building whose height would once have been considered an affront to Heaven. The work I do there is heretical to everything the last revolution stood for. And there are those in our government who hate that heresy."

The waiter returned, placing before Marianne a plate bearing chicken sauteed with green peppers, accompanied by snow peas. "And you must placate them," she said to Zhu.

"I must balance," he replied. "Between two worlds. The demands the Marxists make—and they still hold more power than the West believes—and the benefits that capitalism can bring to the people."

"David Wellington can bring your people many benefits," Marianne said carefully.

"Too many David Wellingtons, too many *deals*, can

bring all this tumbling down. I would remind you, Marianne, that for more than ten years all of this was sealed away, as though it never existed."

"But your people have had a taste of capitalism, now," Marianne pointed out. "Your own form of it, unlike any the world has seen. And David Wellington can help you make that form stronger—"

"And himself, and the West."

"Of course!" Marianne's eyes flared. "It flows both ways, and both are the better for it."

He held up a hand. "I don't disagree. But there are those who do. And they disagree violently."

"The medical benefits alone—"

Zhu shook his head. "Are not enough. There has to be something more. Something in addition to what, for all its medical wonders, is still a Western product."

"Something more," Marianne said. She nibbled a sesame biscuit stuffed lightly with minced, herbed pork. "I agree completely, as does Wellington."

Zhu leaned forward, interested. "And what do you propose?"

Marianne gave him the brightest smile. "The actual proposal will come from David," she said, stalling. "But we are in agreement that capitalism's responsibility is changing, and not just here in China. What we want to offer you and your people is an undertaking that will uplift and improve your people's lives, as well as their health."

"Not to mention your pocketbooks," said Zhu tartly.

"And China's as well," said Marianne. "There is a great deal of money to be made from this—and also a great deal of progress."

For a long moment Dhao Zhu studied Marianne Ingwer. "All right," he said at last. "Let's get to it. Let's *really* talk business."

* * *

Kintang took his time packing, carefully folding his clothing and placing it precisely in his Vuitton bag. Carrying no weapons, Kintang had plenty of contacts in San Francisco who could provide him with whatever he might need. Those contacts had already provided him with the information that David Wellington had arrived and taken up residence in his pied-à-terre. A floor plan of Wellington's house was awaiting him in California. He stepped to the walnut dresser and began to gather his toiletries.

Occasionally as Kintang worked, Angelica Nevins whimpered from the bed. She lay nude on the rumpled satin sheets, her firm long legs spread shamelessly wide, full breasts capped by nipples still stiff from arousal. Kintang felt himself stir as he looked over at her. The English secretary had remained aloof during most of the luncheon at Sun Chen's, but Kintang had watched her closely and seen more than once a look of mingled fear and curiosity pass across her features. She wanted him, he was sure, but she was also more than a little frightened. When Sun Chen instructed Angelica to spend the afternoon assisting Neil, Kintang knew that he had her.

The first time he fucked Angelica, Kintang held himself back, deceiving her a little. He was gentle and attentive to her responses and needs, lifting her to a powerful orgasm after which she curled against him, her fingers lightly touching his cheek. For a full minute, Kintang did not disturb her repose but breathed deeply, gathering his strength, focusing his concentration. When he took her the second time, so quickly after the first, Angelica sought to cry out, but Kintang covered her mouth with a big hand. He threw himself against her and into her with all the fury he possessed, leaving her limp and wide-eyed.

He'd taken her twice since then, each time more powerfully than before. Kintang could feel it building in him. The strength, the discipline, the edge that would carry him through his responsibilities. He zipped shut his shaving kit and closed the Vuitton bag. Stepping to the bed, he slapped Angelica's cheeks. Her eyes were glazed and only slowly came into register. Kintang grinned at her. His flight did not leave for another four hours, and it would be several days before he had such pleasure again. That pleasure would come from killing.

12

MONICA WELLINGTON THOUGHT New York had never looked lovelier. The pace of the city invigorated her in ways she had not felt in . . . *in a year and a half.* She completed the thought: *Since James died.* Springtime Manhattan had put on its finest features for her, bright fashions in immaculate store windows, flags fluttering in soft breezes, vendors grinning as they hawked their wares. From her suite at the Plaza, Monica could look down and see flowers blooming in Central Park and lovers walking hand-in-hand among the blossoms.

She stole some time Sunday afternoon to stroll through the park and passed an hour at the American Museum of Natural History. She and James had been lavish in their patronage of the great museum, yet on Sunday Monica did not introduce herself, nor seek any of the special privileges to which her patronage entitled her. She was content simply to amble anonymously through the endlessly fascinating halls, only occasionally grieving for the man whose name was etched on more than one plaque attached to an exhibit or display. Afterwards she took a cab back to the hotel, ordered dinner delivered to her room, and retired early. Monday morning she would begin her meetings with representatives of Ethan Drug.

She was meeting, in fact, with Hal McDaid, the company's president. McDaid had offered to start their talks over breakfast, but Monica demurred, requesting that a car come for her at ten. Monica had not expected McDaid himself. But as she rode beside

185

him in the sleek silver Mercedes, she was glad that he had come. By the time they reached Ethan's handsome suite of offices at One Astor Plaza on lower Broadway, Monica was even more pleased that McDaid knew nothing of her involvement with Hilary Bishop.

"Welcome to Bunker Number One," McDaid joked as he ushered her into his large office. The office walls were paneled in light Circassian walnut, the wood's dark veins making irregular patterns. Two handsome matched Paul Young flyrods were displayed on an inner wall. Monica stepped close to them.

"Do you fish often?" she asked.

"Not anymore." McDaid grinned. Tall, with ruddy cheeks and red hair showing hints of gray at the temples, the forty-year-old head of Ethan Drug had a sense of humor about his company's precarious position. "I meant it when I called this place 'Bunker Number One.' We're trying to avoid too much of a siege mentality around here, but in some ways it's unavoidable." He offered her a seat in one of the handsome leather-upholstered chairs that clustered around a low table. "To be honest, that's one of the reasons I was so intrigued when you called."

Monica could be honest herself. "Looking for a white knight?" she asked bluntly, "or just a reduction in the balance you owe Wellington?"

If McDaid took offense he did not show it. "Depends on what you're offering," he replied, flashing his contagious grin once more. "We're almost at the point where we'll take what we can get."

Monica granted McDaid a smile of her own. "Well, let's take a look at exactly where you are. Then maybe we'll have a better idea of how I can help."

Monica and Hal spent half an hour reviewing the history of Ethan Drug, McDaid more than once expressing his surprise at the depth of Monica's knowledge of the company. Monica was careful not to reveal the original motivation for her study, and before the conversation was finished had nearly forgotten them herself. Hilary's scheme for Ethan's holdings faded as Hal McDaid spoke. McDaid was candid, brutally so, about his company's current prospects, but he was also proud of what he and the others who had joined him in the buyout had accomplished.

"Most of us are kids of the sixties," he explained. "I'm a Vietnam vet, and so are a few others. My national sales manager is an old hippie, and ten percent of top management has Peace Corps experience. You know the type, inasmuch as there is any *one* type—fighters for Causes . . . people who believe they can make a 'Difference.'"

Monica nodded.

Hal McDaid sat back in his chair. "Maybe what we planned wasn't good business, but our hearts were in it. Look: we knew that Ethan was a heavily inner-city company when we bought it. We knew that we faced an uphill climb, a *steep* one." He sighed heavily. "But we also thought we saw a window of opportunity to turn things around, to make a profit. And to make a difference."

"What sort of difference?" Monica asked.

"Easier to let you see for yourself." McDaid rose from his chair and extended a hand. "Let's take a ride."

McDaid handled the Mercedes easily in the heavy midtown traffic, but it was quickly clear that he was headed for no elegant midtown addresses. In less than thirty minutes, Monica found herself riding through areas of New York City that previously she had only imagined. Monica recognized the Bowery address— Hilary had singled out this spot as one of Ethan's prime New York real estate holdings, targeted for early razing and rebuilding. Renewal and development were already pressing close.

For all that the setting was grim and filthy, the

Ethan drugstore was immaculately maintained. "Even the windows are clean," she remarked to Hal as they approached his store.

He nodded happily. "Costs us a fortune in squeegees, though." Hal held the door for Monica and they entered the store. She stepped inside.

The interior of the drugstore was as handsome as its facade, counters and shelves neatly labeled and sensibly organized. Monica immediately noticed a large, bright red and yellow Pandrex display, and wondered for a moment how carefully McDaid had stage-managed this tour. But she cut the thought off, determined to give him the benefit of the doubt. The display was no different from tens of thousands of others in pharmacies and convenience stores across the country.

A young female pharmacist in starched white lab coat dealt efficiently with an impressive stack of prescriptions. The counter staff was made up of teenaged, attractive girls, neatly dressed and adorned with Ethan nametags, unfailingly courteous, unflaggingly cheerful. Monica could tell that their attitude was not simply a show put on in response to the certainly unannounced arrival of Ethan's president. These people enjoyed their jobs, they *liked* working for Ethan Drug. The customers as well seemed at home in the store, calling to many of the employees by name.

"Well?" asked Hal after half an hour.

Monica measured her words. "Impressive, quite impressive. But so is Ethan's red ink."

Hal McDaid once more showed Monica his grin. "No arguments here. It's amazing, isn't it, that a company with such good intentions can run up such a whopping debt?"

Is he just being disingenuous? Monica wondered. There was no trace of the gallows to Hal's self-deprecating humor. Rather, the president of Ethan Drug seemed to be putting the best possible face on his company's dire situation. "Ready for some more?" he asked once they were back in the Mercedes.

"Lead on," said Monica. It was quite a tour that Hal McDaid gave her, one that she would not soon forget.

In stark Bedford-Stuyvesant, Monica watched as an Ethan-sponsored blood-pressure clinic was held. The Bed-Stuy store was crowded, but Monica did not need Hal to point out to her how many of the patrons made small purchases as well as taking advantage of the free readings. An articulate young man in pharmacist's whites explained to the crowd the dietary and lifestyle measures that could reduce the risks of high blood pressure.

In Newark, in an Ethan store in the midst of a block that would not have looked out of place during the blitz, Monica was startled to find three well-known players from the NFL lecturing a group of teenagers on the dangers of narcotics.

"Friends of yours?" Monica asked Hal, gesturing toward the football stars.

"As a matter of fact, they are," Hal admitted. He was silent for a moment. "They grew up nearby. They wanted to help give something back, just like us, so we provided them with the opportunity."

"Not to mention a lot of free publicity for Ethan."

"That, too," Hal said. They spent another moment listening to the lecture. "Ready to head back to the city?"

Monica nodded. She reserved any further comment until Hal was guiding the Mercedes back toward Manhattan. "You said you and your people had a plan for making all of this profitable?"

"That's right," Hal said, keeping his eyes on the traffic ahead of him. The afternoon was growing late.

"Want to tell me what it is?"

"Was," Hal said curtly. It was the first time Monica had heard bitterness in his voice.

"Go ahead," she urged softly.

He drew a slow breath, exhaled, then spoke carefully. "Look. We knew going into this that we didn't have the resources to compete with the big shopping mall chains catering to the suburb set."

"Even though your mall locations are by far the most profitable of your stores."

McDaid chuckled. "I keep forgetting how well you know us. But okay, sure. Those stores are our flagships, but we don't have the wherewithal to expand aggressively in that market."

"But the inner-city locations are eating you alive, Hal."

"For now." He sighed. "Our timeline got screwed, but our thinking was sound. The government's going to be caught by the financial short hairs, and the first areas to suffer are going to be the inner cities. They—and the state governments and city governments, too—are going to have to find a way to continue delivering basic health services. Our plan was to have as much of an infrastructure in place as possible, and let the government contracts flow *our* way. The people continue to receive the medicines they need, the taxpayer gets some relief because we can deliver the goods a *lot* cheaper than the Feds can, and—"

"Ethan turns a nice profit while still keeping your promise to do something that matters."

"That was the plan," Hal said. He steered the Mercedes along Broadway. "And we've got everything in place. The government's just moved a lot slower than we projected. We've put what pressure we can to get some relief legislation, but it's still moving too slowly."

"You think the whole company could run on this strategy?"

"Maybe, maybe not. Long range, it wouldn't really matter."

"What do you mean?" Monica asked.

"It's already starting. People are taking it upon

themselves to improve their sections. Industries are beginning to look harder at parts of this city that were written off a decade and more ago. As the renewal comes closer, the value of our property shoots up."

So he knows, too, Monica thought. She became bold. "Then why not just sell the property?"

"Short-term thinking," Hal responded. "We'd rather hold on and strike deals with the developers who need the land. Take a piece of the action, keep our store open, and follow the disenfranchised market as the money chases it away."

Hal gave the Mercedes's keys to the attendant at the parking garage near his offices, but steered Monica away from Gramercy Park. "Let's have a drink," he said. "How about the Algonquin?"

"Fine."

They walked up 44th to the awning that reached out before the hotel. The uniformed doorman ushered them inside with a friendly smile, and Hal and Monica stepped left off the lobby and into the intimate Blue Bar where they took a small table. Monica ordered a Booth's martini, Hal the same. After their drinks came he fiddled with the salted nuts in a bowl on the table.

Monica sipped her perfectly prepared drink, then asked, "What's on your mind?"

Hal looked up and met her eyes. "Your plans."

Monica watched him, but did not speak.

"I'll be frank, Monica," Hal said. "I need to know if you're here to call in our debts. I'd like a couple of days if you are." His grin seemed sincere. "Although I doubt it, there may be a few sources of money I haven't looked at yet."

"There may indeed," Monica Wellington said in a soft voice.

"What do you mean?"

Monica waited a moment before she answered. "Maybe I can help, too," she said.

* * *

David Wellington felt a surge of adrenalin when he heard Monica's voice over the telephone. "You're in New York?" he asked, glancing at his slim Rolex chronometer. It would be nearly midnight there.

"Just got back to the Plaza," Monica said. "But more importantly, how are things in San Francisco? Have there been any more—"

"Nothing, nor any signs of anything. I just talked with Lisa. She thinks it's *too* quiet."

"So do I."

"You could be right, but I'm not going to lose any sleep over it." David thought of his San Francisco valet. "Gregory's wearing a shoulder holster," he said with a chuckle. "I couldn't talk him out of it."

"Don't try," said Monica. "And cover yourself."

"I'll be all right," David insisted. "I promise." He changed the subject. "How were things with Ethan?"

"Very interesting." She gave him a quick account of her day.

"You're going back to Baltimore tomorrow?"

"No. Not until late Wednesday afternoon. In fact, I'm meeting with Ethan's Board first thing in the morning."

David whistled softly. "Know what you're doing?"

"Of course I do, David."

"Then do it," he said sharply before hanging up.

Victor Sun Chen had a deep pain in his gut, an ache that radiated outward from his stomach. He knew the cause of the pain, and there was no doubt at all that his diagnosis was correct. Sun Chen ached to see Lisa Han once more.

Kintang had been in San Francisco for two days, and already had David Wellington under close surveillance. The American was keeping near to home, according to Kintang's report. *I have frightened Wellington behind his walls,* Sun Chen thought eagerly. Lisa Han would join David Wellington on Friday, and by Saturday night Kintang's work would be done. *And a long duel over,* Sun Chen thought.

He prowled around his bedroom, stopping to finger a delicate quince blossom adorning a long branch that rose gracefully from its glazed porcelain vase. *She was a little flower.*

There were so many other little flowers. A new one, indeed, was waiting for him in another part of the house. He could not recall her name. It did not matter—he would not be visiting her this evening. It had become clear that before the night was out he would be bound for San Francisco.

Sun Chen had passed a long afternoon reviewing his many memories of Lisa Han. So few were of the months she had spent sharing his home and bed. He knew that she had been pleasurable—those memories could be electronically recalled any time he wished. But unlike most of the other girls, who found their way from Sun Chen's bed to the fine beds of other wealthy men, or those even less imaginative, who found their destinies on their backs in more squalid beds, Lisa Han had *made* her own way.

Imagination, Sun Chen thought. When he learned that Lisa had gotten to America, hadn't he been pleased as well as angered? One of his pupils had actually learned about ambition as well as sex! His fury had been directed at Candace Caillou, and he punished her hard for her complicity, leaving scars and extracting dues that were with the Frenchwoman to this day. As for Lisa, he had not directly touched her.

More than once he had wounded her financially, and he routinely ran operations aimed at blocking Lisa's ambitions, but until now, he had not threatened her life. Imagination was in such short supply. Twice over the years Lisa had actually outmaneuvered Sun Chen, and he had found it in himself to be magnanimous. None of her deals before Wellington directly threatened him, but it had never been less than clear that Lisa guided the growth of her company in such a way that a confrontation with Sun Chen would be inevitable. His only disappointment was that she had forced the issue so quickly.

But she had, and now it was all coming to a close. Sun Chen pressed his palms together and drew a deep, calming breath. *One can grow accustomed to the irritation that accompanies a thorn in the side—it can become akin to a pleasure.* He wanted to look into her eyes before she died. Lisa Han was, after all, Victor Sun Chen's creation.

The pain in his stomach began to subside as Sun Chen stepped to the telephone and ordered his 707 readied.

It was early Wednesday evening when Monica arrived in Baltimore, taking a cab from the airport to Hilary's Charles Street address and smiling to herself. She had spent a hell of a day in New York and she knew that an even more spectacular evening awaited her. She was looking forward to it.

Monica made it past "Electric Leda" and through the entranceway, tossing her Adolfo coat over one of the Corbu chairs before Hilary emerged from her bedroom. Hilary was wearing a silk teddy, and Monica noticed that her legs were marked with bruises and bite marks, her eyes puffy and reddened.

Hilary's voice, though, was in good form: "Where the hell have you *been?*" she demanded furiously. "I called the Plaza half a dozen times!"

Monica had instructed the desk to screen all of her calls and deter any from Hilary Bishop. "I could ask you the same thing."

Hilary stepped to the bar and poured herself a healthy knock of Jack Daniels. "I can tell you now," she said. "May as well—I was in David's territory. Taiwan." She shivered, pressed her hands against her flanks. "With Victor Sun Chen."

Monica started to move closer, but caught herself. "And?"

"Can't wait to tell you about it." Hilary arched her back languorously. "But later. I want to know why I couldn't get hold of you. And more important—what happened with Ethan?"

Monica stepped to a window and kept her back to Hilary. "Ask away," she invited.

"You didn't let on that I was involved, did you?"

"Hilary, your name never came up."

"I *knew* you could do it!"

"Your picture of Ethan was generally accurate," Monica went on. "They're broke, they're swimming upstream for all they're worth, and without help they can't keep going much longer."

"So we've got them!"

"Not exactly." Monica turned slowly to face Hilary.

"What does that mean—'not exactly'?"

"There's no 'we,' Hilary."

Hilary's excitement vanished. "You're not getting cold feet?"

Monica gave a slight, firm nod. "I won't be doing any business with you."

"Goddammit, Monica, don't do this to me. I'm going to have a hell of a time swinging this on my own, you know that. I'm—"

Monica spoke sharply, cutting Hilary off. "Pay attention! You're not going to be involved in any way, Hilary."

"What?"

"Ethan's not for sale."

"What the hell are you talking about?"

Monica showed her sweetest smile. *"Honey,"* she said with a laugh, "you go call Hal McDaid. Or read the *Journal* after we make the announcement. As of this afternoon, Ethan's a wholly owned subsidiary of Wellington Drugs." Monica collected her coat. "You'll be pleased to know that I'll be keeping the current management in place. I like their ideas—long-term." She headed for the door.

"Get out of here!" Hilary snarled.

Monica stopped and for the last time faced her old roommate. She hardly recognized her. "Hadn't you noticed, Hilary? I'm on my way."

Hilary's curses followed Monica to the elevator. They were music to her ears, an uninterrupted stream of obscenity every word of which reminded Monica again that she had won this contest. She would be leaving Baltimore immediately to spend a few days at Senator Wade's estate outside Arlington. It was time to start putting pressure on the government for legislation beneficial to Ethan. David had also asked her to review with Nancy a general outline of the deal he sought with China. A deal, Monica realized, that would be made or not within the next week.

Lying low did not agree with David. His spacious Victorian on Russian Hill was filled with books he'd long meant to read, but none of them could hold his attention. One large downstairs room had been equipped with a master craftsman's array of power and hand tools, a selection of fine woods and varnishes, but David found it difficult to focus his attention upon woodwork. By Wednesday, he was going stir-crazy.

Fortunately, there was a mountain of business to be dealt with. David filled as many of his hours as he could with work. He remained concerned about Rhonda MacLaren, and had requested that she contact him by satellite as soon as possible. The call from Beijing came late Wednesday. David eased back in his leather executive chair and held the telephone close to his ear. "Go ahead, Rhonda."

Her voice came clearly across the miles. "David, we're all growing curious as to when you're coming here," she said without preface.

David grinned. There was no mistaking the edge in

Rhonda's voice, nor had he expected that edge to be absent. He'd heard from Ernest Schliemann the night before: Rhonda was openly distrustful of the Chinese, and Ernest feared that her hostility would sour the deal before it was confirmed.

David took a breath. "First of the week," he said. "And I'm coming to set the conditions."

"You're still serious about going through with this?"

"Can you give me a reason why I shouldn't be?"

Rhonda was silent for a moment. "They're an impressive group here," she said at last, surprising David a little. "There's no telling what they'll make of our work."

"They'll make of it what we let them," David said firmly.

"If we let them."

"Going to try to block me, Rhonda?"

"I told you my conditions in New Mexico, David. You still have a few weeks left."

"It won't take that long, Rhonda. Not even close."

"You'd better be right."

Candace Caillou closed Lisa Han's carefully packed briefcase and carried it over to where she stood staring out her office's wide window at the gray rain that enveloped Kowloon. "The season is here," Lisa said quietly as she accepted the briefcase from Candace.

"Yes." She rested a hand upon Lisa's shoulder, and Lisa reached up and gave Candace's fingers a squeeze.

On Lisa's desk behind them, in an elaborately cut crystal vase, stood a dozen yellow roses. A simple card bearing careful calligraphy accompanied the roses:

To China!
Congratulations on your boldness.
We shall meet again. Soon.

The card bore no signature, nor did it require one.

Candace and Lisa stared out in silence for a long while into the rain that shrouded Hong Kong. At last Lisa turned and gave Candace a quick embrace before departing to catch the plane.

13

The first time I made this journey, Lisa Han thought, *I was escaping. Now?*

She did not know. Soon Sun Chen would make his move—his intentions were already announced. *Not that he will do the labor himself. He is so good at keeping his hands free from soil.* Lisa looked quickly about the first-class section of the aircraft. The faces of her fellow travelers were all opaque to her. *It could be anyone here.*

Lisa was seated next to a French businessman who had made an earnest attempt at picking her up. He had accepted her rebuff with Gallic good humor; upon realizing that he had no chance with the lovely Eurasian in the window seat, the Frenchman had promptly called for a pillow from the stewardess, put his seat back, and closed his eyes. As he snored softly. Lisa Han looked him over. *What sort of face does an assassin have?* she wondered.

She shook her head and turned back to the window, catching a shimmering glimpse of her own reflection. The tension showed in her face, she thought. She tried to remember how she had looked, years ago, when she was just a girl.

Lisa remembered sitting in the plane bound for San Francisco. She had not really cared where the plane was bound, so long as it was away from Taiwan. She wanted to be rid of all of it, the slums, the Academy, Sun Chen. *Everything.* Except Candace—the one good thing that had happened to her in her seventeen years.

The airline ticket was waiting for her at the Pan American counter, just as Candace had promised. Everyone at the airport was helpful, all of them clean and crisply dressed and professional, smiling as they showed Lisa where to go, what to do. They were all very nice, yet Lisa felt certain they knew about her, and she kept her gaze downcast until she was in her seat on the airliner. Her heart pounded wildly as she waited for the plane to taxi clear of the terminal, certain that their departure would be halted, that Sun Chen would burst onto the aircraft to take back what was his property.

By midpoint in the flight she was feeling better. She was seated next to a charming middle-aged woman who was from Topeka, Kansas. Lisa never forgot that, although she could no longer recall the woman's name. *Topeka.* It sounded so foreign to her, a magical word in a language and from a nation that she had studied, but did not really know. *Topeka.*

The woman had been a schoolteacher, and when Lisa told her she was going to be attending Berkeley she grew excited, and spent the rest of the flight talking earnestly about the challenges and rewards of a college education. Lisa took in every word, parting from the teacher with some regret upon their arrival in San Francisco. "You will do wonderfully well," the teacher had told her, her confidence almost contagious. "You're a bright girl and you'll go far."

Once customs was behind her, Lisa passed half an hour in a sudden state of bewilderment. Candace had told her to call, but Lisa did not wish to make so public a call from the airport. She clutched her bags and walked aimlessly about the terminal, fighting the tears she felt rising. She was on the edge of losing herself in despair when she overheard a man speaking to a cab driver: "Know any cheap motels?"

The cab driver was more than obliging. "Dozens of them. What's your price range?"

Lisa moved to the next cab in line. "A . . . an inexpensive motel, please."

She registered at the Sta-Awhile with only a little difficulty as a result of her lack of identification. Her passport overcame some objections, and she used a twenty-dollar bill to open the door the rest of the way. The room was shabby but clean, and best of all, it had a phone right next to the bed. The motel switchboard operator—Lisa recognized the voice of the woman who'd had to be bribed into renting a room—wanted no part of any long-distance calls. Lisa tried to explain that the charges would be reversed, but the woman only laughed and cut her off. Lisa marched back to the office. This time it took forty dollars. Lisa was learning.

Her conversation with Candace was brief, static making it hard for them to understand each other. Candace gave her a name and address on the Berkeley campus. "You will have to take some tests, but I have arranged things so that once you pass them you will be granted provisional student status."

"What does that mean?"

She heard Candace's familiar, rich chuckle. "It means you are to become an American college girl, Lisa. Here. Go to the school tomorrow. Find yourself an inexpensive place to live and let me know the address, but you must not call after that. Ever. You understand?"

"Yes, but—"

"No. Let me know where you are living. I will be in touch from then on, when it is safe."

The tests were not difficult and Lisa passed them easily. While Li Juan Academy had been preparing her for Victor Sun Chen's pleasure, the school had also provided a sound preparatory curriculum. Lisa found a room in what some of her classmates considered a disreputable area. *If they knew where I grew up,* she thought, *they would know that this could be considered luxury.* Besides, it was less expensive than living on campus, and Lisa enjoyed the solitude.

Although she kept to herself during her first few weeks at Berkeley, Lisa gradually emerged from her shell. No one knew her past, and she felt free to invent one, drawing liberally upon the romantic novels she had read in Taiwan. "My parents were missionaries," she told people in tones that let them know that she did not like talking about the subject. She was surprised to discover that she made friends easily, and she enjoyed the free and easy attitude California girls expressed. Lisa wore jeans to class, and added snippets of American slang to her vocabulary. She chewed gum and popped bubbles, twisted an ankle in a fall from a skateboard, learned to love McDonald's and pizza.

And fell in love.

She hadn't been paying attention. Lisa was in the spring semester of her senior year, and what time she did not spend studying she spent wondering where the time had gone. She rarely thought of Victor Sun Chen, and Candace never mentioned his name in her frequent letters. Those letters often included money, which Candace insisted Lisa accept. She did so, vowing to herself that the funds were loans, not charity. Two or three times a year Candace called Lisa, and they chatted for hours. It was difficult for Lisa Han to obey Candace's dictum forbidding her to make any calls or write any letters, and nearly impossible after Lisa fell in love. She had so many things she needed to say, so many questions she wished to ask. She had never missed Candace more, never been so miserable.

Nor so exultant. His name was Lee Richards, a senior, and he was the most wonderful person Lisa had ever met. They sat side by side in a crowded lecture hall, studying Shakespeare. Lisa's grades had propelled her into the top percentile of business majors, and her course selections were mandated by that department, but Lisa juggled her schedule to allow one indulgence each semester. She'd saved the Shakespeare course for the very last, and she was savoring every moment of it. In the fall she fully expected to attend Harvard University's graduate business program, where there would be no time for Shakespeare.

The class was deep in the intricacies of *Macbeth* when Lee Richards passed his first note to Lisa Han. *Coffee after class?*

Lisa stared at the note for a long time. She had noticed Lee, and wondered if he paid any attention to her. When she had looked at him earlier she felt certain that he was already committed, no doubt to some statuesque blond Californian. Lee was well over six feet tall, wore his hair more closely cropped than most of his classmates and carried himself with poise. Lisa looked up from the note and glanced at Lee, only to find that he was staring at her with blue eyes so deep that she began to blush. He raised his eyebrows as though hoping for a whispered answer to his invitation. Lisa jerked herself free from his gaze and locked her eyes upon the lecturer at the front of the hall.

Lisa had gone out before, but always in a group, never truly paired with anyone. A sophomore had once made a clumsy pass, but Lisa had let him down gently. Sitting in class next to Lee Richards she realized that she had protected herself well. She had not been with a man, had not even kissed a man deeply, since . . . *since Victor.*

A flush of shame flowed through her. She knew too well why she had not allowed herself to go out on dates, why she projected an aura of cool aloofness. She feared that any man who got too close would discover her past and all of the dirty secrets that lay hidden there. All around her were boys and girls, *innocents,* who could never suspect the ways in which Lisa had been used, the things that Victor had done to her.

Lisa picked up her pencil and when she did so she knocked Lee's note to the floor. It fluttered down slowly and she bent to reach for it. Lee leaned low at the same time. "Well?" he whispered. Lisa left the note on the floor and sat upright.

When class ended the other students hurried from the lecture hall in a clatter of laughter and energy. Lisa sat still, held by his blue eyes. She forced herself to break their mesmerizing hold, willing herself to look around the now quiet hall at the ranked desks, the lecturer's platform with podium and blackboard. She wished that she could will herself away from here completely. "Well, Lisa?" Lee Richards said again.

Slowly she turned toward him. "I really can't," she heard herself say.

His eyes smiled at her. "Why not?"

Lisa had no answer for him, and did not fumble for one, instead gathering her books.

"It's just a cup of coffee," he said. "What are you so scared of?"

Lisa stood up, held her books in the crook of her right arm. Lee stood facing her. *He's beautiful,* she thought. *Full of himself. And of illusions.*

It must have shown in her face. "You don't have to look so sad," Lee said suddenly. "I'll get over it." He spun and walked quickly toward the door.

Lee was nearly at the door when Lisa called "Wait!" She hurried after him.

The cup of coffee turned into a lovely day together enjoying the unfolding beauty of spring. Lisa and Lee cut the rest of their classes, left their books behind and walked for miles, talking. He was pre-med, taking Shakespeare for reasons identical to Lisa's: "I didn't want to get out of school without at least taking a stab at Shakespeare—although I've paid more attention to you than to the teacher." Lisa let that pass. She was determined not to encourage him, and tried to keep their conversation on more general topics. They talked of novels they'd both read, they watched a child flying a kite, they gave themselves headaches eating ice cream too fast. Lisa and Lee were walking near the spire of Sather Tower when the carillon it contained rang forth, announcing that it was six in the evening. Lisa waited for the bell tower to fall silent before she said to Lee, "I really must be going."

"I'll walk you," he said with a grin.

She shook her head. "No. Thank you, but no. I have to get back to the books."

"We could study together."

Lisa grew firm. "Lee. Please. Lee, don't do this." She looked around at other couples walking hand in hand. She felt a wave of regret, but knew that she was doing the right thing. "Thank you for this afternoon. It was fun, really. But I have to *go.*"

"It was the bells, right? Six o'clock and you turn into a pumpkin? Hey, wait—"

But Lisa was running, and she left Lee behind before he could recover from his surprise.

Lisa collected her books and hurried home, lest she encounter Lee coming after his own texts. She locked the door of her small apartment behind her. Candace had been more than generous, and Lisa had moved this year to more spacious quarters. Still not elegant, but a nice apartment in a residential neighborhood. She had a comfortable bedroom with a wide double bed, a compact and efficient kitchen, a sitting room, and a full bath. Lisa switched on the lights and stretched out on her bed. *I shouldn't have gone with him at all,* she told herself repeatedly.

She must have dozed, for the next thing she heard was a sharp knock at the door of her apartment. She looked at the clock on the small table beside her bed. It was after eight. Lisa rubbed sleep from her eyes and walked to the door. "Who is it?"

It sounded like the person on the other side said,

205

"Handsome prince," and, curious, Lisa opened the door without thinking.

Lee Richards stood in the doorway, beaming at her, hands behind his back. He didn't give Lisa the chance to speak. "You ran off so quickly I knew it had to be the chimes telling you to get home. So I looked for a glass slipper. This yours, Cinderella?" he asked, and pulled from behind his back a tattered, grimy running shoe, men's size 12 at the very least. Lisa stared at the shoe, its sole flapping loose from its upper, any lettering or logo long gone. She looked from the shoe to Lee, and his face was so sweetly expectant that she swallowed her worries and said, "Come in, prince."

Lee stayed until ten, talking, and when he left he kissed Lisa chastely on the lips and took with him her heart.

By the end of the week they were sharing every available moment. Lisa had lunch with Lee every day, usually a simple picnic on the grounds outside a classroom building. She avoided his questions about her past, using once more that story that her parents had been missionaries, and she avoided as well any thoughts that reminded her of Sun Chen and her shame. *That no longer figures. Lee need never know.*

As their first week together became their second, Lisa began to wonder when Lee would try to make love to her. They held hands, now, when they walked. He had put his arm around her shoulders when they attended a movie. More often than not they studied together, curled close on the sofa at Lisa's apartment. Their kisses deepened, but Lee seemed to sense Lisa's hesitancy, and did not make an issue of it. That consideration was one more thing that made Lisa love him. And by the time they'd been together two weeks she did not doubt that she loved him with all of her soul.

That love came to full flower unexpectedly. Lisa told herself later that once more she hadn't been

206

paying attention, but she had given herself to Lee willingly and without regret.

They nestled on the couch, Lee deep in a microbiology text, Lisa reviewing statistical abstracts and computer printouts for an economics paper. Their hands brushed together reaching for a Coke from the cooler beside the sofa, Lee's hip a pleasant pressure against Lisa's thigh. She ran her fingers lightly over his back, scratched the soft skin at his neck. Lee shifted position to lean more completely against Lisa, idly caressing her knee. The temperature in the apartment seemed to rise.

Then they were kissing and it was with a passion and a hunger that Lisa had never known. She pushed up Lee's shirt so that she could touch the hot damp flesh of his back. Lee held her hard, then his hands strayed to her breasts, fondling them through the thin jersey she wore. Lisa kissed his neck, his ears, heard him sigh deeply. "Come," she said softly, taking his hands and leading him into the bedroom. Lisa turned out the lights and the soft glow of moonlight pervaded the room.

They faced each other. For just a moment, almost more brief than Lisa could measure, she was afraid that he would see Sun Chen's mark on her. But there was no mark, and for Lee she became innocent once more, all his.

Naked, they lay down on the bed, its ancient springs creaking as it adjusted to their weight. Lisa giggled at the sound, and Lee laughed out loud. Their mouths met once more. Lee tasted sweet, with just a hint of Coca-Cola on his breath. Lisa pushed her tongue against his, ran her hands down his back, cupped his taut buttocks.

She urged him above her and opened herself to him. Lee kissed her neck, nuzzled her breasts. Lisa reached to hold his hard organ, delighted at the way its warmth throbbed against her palm. Lisa guided him against her heat, then arched her hips up as Lee entered and filled her. When he was fully inside Lisa he waited, holding himself still, pressed against her. A shudder rippled through the length of Lisa's body, and tore loose a long, guttural moan from her throat. They moved together, then, until more quickly than either expected, their passion overflowed and they melded into one.

Afterward, lying entwined, Lisa realized that for all of his precision and experimentation Victor Sun Chen had never shaken her so thoroughly as had the simple, gentle act of love she had just experienced. She knew what it was that had made her lovemaking with Lee different, and she gave voice to her new knowledge. "I love you," Lisa said softly, putting her lips close to Lee's ear.

"Lisa, I love *you*," Lee said. They slept.

Lisa woke early the next morning with Lee still snuggled next to her and slipped from the bed, taking care not to wake him. He was even more beautiful in repose, his strong features relaxed, the ghost of a smile on his lips. Lisa kissed his forehead, then pulled on a robe and hurried to the kitchen to begin breakfast. She wanted to surprise him.

The following weeks were, Lisa supposed, the most perfect of her life. All of the darkness of her past receded from her. When she thought of Victor Sun Chen, which was not often, she found that she could not remember what he looked like. His unwelcome image had been displaced by her overwhelming happiness. Lisa and Lee entered into a casual domestic arrangement, sharing most of their nights in Lisa's apartment. The arrangement felt right, absolutely correct. The apartment, which before Lee had been a prim, bookish retreat to house Lisa while she pursued her studies, now began to come alive. Lisa bought new curtains, bright yellow. Lee brought a lovely orchid and they waited expectantly for it to flower. They lighted candles at dinner, and found excuses to brush close to each other as they prepared breakfast. The slightest thing—a sunset, the sight of a couple wheeling a carriage, old movies—sent them into paroxysms of sentimental, romantic delight. They made eyes at each other during the Shakespeare class, and ran to embrace when they had been separated for more than an hour.

In early May, during a long Saturday walk through San Francisco, Lee startled Lisa by dropping to one knee, taking her hand, and saying, "Will you marry me, Lisa Han?"

It was the most flattering question she had ever been asked, but Lisa had no idea how to answer. She said as much.

"Answering's easy, Lisa. Just say, 'yes.' See? Try it."

Lisa smiled at him, but said nothing.

"You know it's right. Even our names go together," he said, repeating a silly joke they'd shared a thousand times during the spring: "Lee. Lee-Sah. Say *yes.*"

Lisa stared at him. Could she share his life? she wondered. *Yes.* There was no question of that. *Could I share my life with him? Would he still want me as his wife if he knew the truth about me?* She could not answer that, and so could not answer Lee's proposal. "I'm sorry," she said. Lee rose and walked away from her, lost quickly among the colorfully clad tourists and vendors of Fisherman's Wharf.

That evening he was silent during their meal. Lisa ate little; she was too filled with turmoil. *Would it make a difference to him?* she asked herself again and again. Once, she began to tell him the story of her life, but before she had gotten two words out she broke off in dread. It was easier to live with uncertainty.

But that was no solution, either, Lisa realized after the dinner dishes were cleared away. They retired to the couch for the evening's round of study, but Lee took up a position at the far end of the sofa, pretending to lose himself in the thick text he held on his lap and turning the pages with fury. When she asked a question or made a comment Lee answered with a grunt or a monosyllable. Soon, Lisa stopped trying to make conversation.

She opened her own book, but the print blurred before her, letters running together into a single black smudge. Lisa blinked away tears, hoping that Lee would not see them. She thought of her dear friend Candace Caillou, tried to recall her without the accompanying horror of Victor Sun Chen. She wished she could speak with Candace, could pour out all of her heart's concerns to her, could take from her the strength of good advice and deep affection. Lisa willed the telephone that rested on a small wooden stand across the room to ring but nothing came.

Then came a memory of a conversation she and Candace had shared during Lisa's sophomore year. She'd been feeling a vague senseless depression settling over her. The novelty of living in America had long since worn off. She was at home here, but she was also profoundly lonely. Lisa cried herself to sleep often, and left her apartment only to attend classes or shop for essentials. She spurned every invitation offered by classmates, preferring to be alone with her misery. In the midst of her black mood, as unexpectedly as ever, she got a call from Candace Caillou. It did not take much for Candace to sense Lisa's feelings, and she responded to them not with sympathy but with a stern, loving lecture.

"Listen to yourself, little Lisa—yes I know what I am saying—you are acting like a little girl, a child. You think you have had such a hard time of it, and your time has not been easy, it's true. But think of what you escaped. Others have had it far harder than you—and *never* escaped, and never will. It is true that Victor abused you, but also that you have escaped him. Now you are on your own, and that is never easy.

But it can be so wonderful! The things you have ahead of you—your studies, a career. Launching yourself." The sternness left Candace's voice. "And someday, Lisa, you will meet a young man who will love you for yourself—no matter who or what you have been. He need know only who you *are,* love you for that. And you will love him, and make a life and a family together."

Lee turned a page, his countenance still dour, his eyes locked onto his book. Lisa felt her heart swell with love, and said his name. He did not look up.

"Lee," she said again, more insistently.

Lee slowly raised his eyes and turned to her. "What?"

"Yes."

Comprehension broke over his face gradually, as if he did not trust himself to believe what she had said. "You mean it?"

"Yes," Lisa said again.

The semester moved toward its conclusion, and plans for an early summer wedding vied with her studies for Lisa's attention. Lee told her of his parents and two younger sisters in Oregon, who would be coming to California for the graduation ceremonies. He couldn't wait for her to meet them. "They're going to love you as much as I do."

"I hope so."

Perhaps it was the excitement with which Lee told her of his close family, perhaps the sense that a new life was beginning for her, perhaps even a wistfulness that she had no family of her own—Lisa could not stop thinking of Candace Caillou. *She is all the family I have,* Lisa thought, and waited anxiously for Candace to call. There was a letter from Candace not long after Lisa agreed to marry Lee Richards, but of course Candace had no way of knowing of Lisa's great new joy. Lisa lay in her bed at night, Lee warm beside her, and thought how wonderful it would be for Candace to be with her, to stand beside her as she was married. One night those thoughts drove her from her bed and to her writing table.

She heard Candace's words: "You must *never* try to contact me."

She remembered: Victor never looks at the mail; Candace sorts it for him.

Lisa took up pen and stationery. She sat at her desk throughout the night, pouring out her joy onto the page, telling Candace how much she loved her, how much she loved Lee, trying to thank the woman who had done so much to help her escape from Sun Chen and the destiny to which he had sought to banish her. The next morning before class Lisa mailed the letter air express to Candace Caillou.

Days went by and no call came. Graduation and marriage loomed, and Lisa spent much of her time making certain her apartment was neat and attractive. She worried over her appearance, and grew irritated when Lee laughed at her concerns. "They are going to *love* you," he said. But Lisa continued to worry.

Lee's parents were due to arrive on the Friday before graduation, and Lisa and Lee planned a special Thursday evening in Lisa's apartment. "The next time we have a night alone," Lee chuckled, "we will be man and wife." He stroked her cheek. "I feel as though we are already."

Lisa hurried home after her last Thursday appointment: a bit of discussion with a favorite professor regarding her future. The professor had wished her well, and presented her with a gold pen, a symbol of his respect for her achievement. Lisa thanked him effusively, but inside she was eager to be home. She had so much to do, and Lee had promised to deliver himself and a bottle of wine by seven.

At 6:45, the dinner prepared and warming, Lisa sat down to await Lee's arrival, her heart skittering nervously. What would she say to his parents? How would they react to her? Lisa noticed that her hands were trembling wildly. She drew deep breaths and tried to calm herself, but it did little good.

7:00 arrived at last, but there was no sign of Lee. It was not like him to be late. *He's worrying over the wine,* she told herself. *Silly.*

7:30.

8:00.

Lisa paced her apartment wildly. She called Steve Charest, Lee's roommate, but Steve had not seen Lee since morning. "I thought he'd be with you."

"He's supposed to be."

By nine she was phoning area hospitals and the police. No one matching Lee's description had been admitted to hospital, the police had no reports of any accidents involving young men.

Where was he?

By ten, Lisa was frantic. Every impulse told her to go and look for Lee, but she could not leave her apartment. The silent telephone seemed to mock her. Lisa left her number with the hospitals, the police, and continued to check with them every hour. At eleven, Steve Charest came to sit with her, offering soothing words that were empty of comfort. As midnight came and went, Lisa thought she was going mad.

At two in the morning there was a knock at the door. Lisa flew from the sofa, ready to hold Lee forever.

The detective who stood in Lisa's doorway was kind, and attempted to be as gentle as possible in relating the news he bore. There was no way to be gentle.

Lee Richards's mutilated body had been discovered in Tilden Park. With nearly surgical precision the murderer had removed Lee's lips. The detective coughed before telling Lisa that Lee had been castrated. Each of his fingers was broken. His face bore dozens of knife wounds. Evidently he had been tortured for some time before he died. The detective spoke in a low voice. "He had identification on him. But we need to have the body identified."

Steve Charest stood. "I'll go."

Lisa shook her head. She felt like a robot, as though her body and voice were under some control other than her own. "No. Lee was my fiancé."

They went together.

It was cool in the morgue. Lisa Han willed herself not to shiver, just as she willed herself not to cry out or display any emotion at all when Lee's body was revealed to her. His beautiful body had been butchered, more horribly than the detective had described. But there was no doubt, no chance that a ghastly mistake had been made.

"It is Lee," Lisa said, and reached to touch his skin a final time.

Lee's parents paid a call on Lisa the next afternoon. They were a gentle, obviously devoted couple in their sixties. Lisa offered them what small comfort she could, but they could not be consoled. She could tell that somehow, unspoken, Lee's parents felt that their son's death was connected to his relationship with Lisa. She said nothing to contradict their belief.

Lisa did not attend her graduation ceremonies. She lay in bed throughout the day on which she and Lee were to have been married. She lacked even the energy to weep. She tried to make sense of what had happened to Lee, but she could not.

Until the day a bouquet of roses arrived at her door, bearing a card of commiseration for her loss, signed by Victor Sun Chen.

The touch at her shoulder startled Lisa and she jumped in her seat. The interior of the airliner came into focus, she remembered where she was, where she was bound. Lisa turned to face the Frenchman who had touched her shoulder.

"I did not mean to frighten you," he said with a smile.

"It's all right," Lisa Han said.

His face showed concern. "You are crying."

"Am I?" said Lisa Han.

DAVID WELLINGTON WAITED impatiently. He parked his Aston-Martin Lagonda, his California car, at SFX half an hour before Lisa's plane was due, and passed a few moments at a newsstand. David picked up the latest edition of the *Examiner*, as well as the paperback of Miranda Glenn's latest book. Wellington Laboratories had received its share of knocks in her *Prescription: Death,* and David wanted to see who was catching the heat of her new focus upon the computer industry. He paid for his purchases and took a seat near the gate where Lisa's flight would debark. David loosened his striped Guy Laroche necktie, and opened the paperback.

But not even Miranda Glenn's strong, angry prose and well-documented charges could hold his attention. David could still taste the warmth of Lisa's lips, smell the cool fragrance of her skin. So much had transpired since he had parted from her on Macau's jetfoil pier. He was eager to show Lisa a bit of San Francisco, and if all went well they would soon be bound for Beijing. He closed his eyes and pictured her face.

Lost in thoughts of Lisa, David did not notice the giant of a man who sat nearby, watching him.

Neil Kintang kept his eyes on David Wellington, but he had other things on his mind. He'd been in San Francisco long enough to collect the tools he would need for his job, and had set up the conditions that would allow him to use those tools. Everything had gone smoothly. And yesterday he'd received news that changed everything.

Victor Sun Chen was in San Francisco.

The Taiwanese had arrived late Wednesday night and taken up residence in a suite at the Mark Hopkins. Sun Chen called Kintang early Thursday and, livid, Kintang had raced to join him over breakfast in the suite. Sun Chen was not interested in Kintang's irritation.

"I would like to see them, Neil," Sun Chen said. "Before they die."

Kintang pushed aside his barely touched plate of eggs, lox, and grilled tomatoes with fresh basil. "Victor, this is a dreadful mistake."

Sun Chen appeared not to hear him. "Surely you can understand my motives, Neil. Of all the girls over the years Lisa was the most—" His eyes seemed distant, unfocused. "Perhaps I should not have been so quick to cast her out."

"Victor, I must insist that you think about what you're doing. The dangers involved—"

Sun Chen brought his hand down hard on the linen tablecloth, rattling the cups and saucers. A bit of coffee splashed over the rim of Kintang's cup, making a dark stain on the tablecloth. Kintang watched the stain spread while Sun Chen spoke.

"I will not have you second-guess me, Neil. Not after the way you have indulged yourself. Your approach to pleasure is as peculiar as my own. Don't forget: I *saw* Angelica, I spoke with her."

"Completely different."

Sun Chen waved a hand in dismissal of Kintang's objections. "Elizabeth Jonklaas, then. Or from the matter at hand, Lisa's fiancé of all those years ago. Surely you could have dealt with them more . . . expeditiously than you did."

Kintang sighed heavily. His collar felt as though it had tightened around his neck. "Victor—"

"No!" Sun Chen's voice bit. "You are very good at

217

what you do, Neil, but you do it at my behest." Sun Chen's eyes burned. "We have had a long and satisfying relationship. But I have terminated relationships before. You will do as I say, Neil, or someone else will."

Kintang was bathed in the heat of Sun Chen's gaze, blistered by it. He sat very still. "She will be staying at the Huntington," he said at last, "and Wellington at his home in Russian Hill." His voice was flat and without emotion. "They will doubtless confer at his residence. I have materiel in place to take them both out at his home, with backup plans if necessary." He fell silent.

"Friday evening," Sun Chen said softly.

"I assume that you will not want to accompany me on the job itself?" Kintang asked, making no attempt to hide the edge in his voice.

"A glimpse, Neil. A word or two." Sun Chen attempted to make his voice soothing. "Nothing more than that."

It is enough, Neil Kintang thought, but said nothing.

Lisa Han withdrew a gold Cartier compact from her shoulderbag, and studied her face in its mirror. The compact had been a gift from Candace Caillou on the first anniversary of Lisa's hiring her. *I never regretted that, or anything involving Candace—save for one ill-conceived letter.* She snapped the compact shut and with it the flood of her memories.

The Frenchman in the next seat had not taken his eyes from her since witnessing her tears. He tried to engage her in conversation, to cheer her up, but Lisa showed him that she was capable of drying her eyes herself. The compact revealed that her dark eyes were clear once more. The seatbelt light flashed on and the plane began its descent into San Francisco.

"Is someone meeting you at the airport?" the Frenchman asked.

"Yes," said Lisa. *He means no harm,* she told herself, and even added a bit more information: "I have a business meeting."

He nodded. "I see. Nothing more than that?"

"Is that your concern?" Lisa asked frostily.

He recoiled as though slapped. "I do beg your pardon," he said hastily. "I simply felt that—" He searched for words. "Your tears. I was thinking that you have suffered a great hurt. San Francisco is a delightful city, you know, filled with amusing diversions. It occurred to me that an evening out might be helpful to you."

There was no warmth in Lisa's eyes. "So nice of you," she said, with an edge of sarcasm, "but I am one who is able to help herself."

"I see." He watched her for a minute more, then snapped open a newspaper and held it before him as though it were a curtain.

Lisa turned back to the window. The plane dipped lower, the sprawl of San Francisco becoming clear. *City of diversions,* Lisa thought, *and I will be sharing it with David Wellington.* She felt a sudden warmth, but caught it, sealed it into a hard capsule, and pushed it far away within herself, where no one would ever suspect its existence. *Diversions?* Lisa almost laughed aloud, but her laughter would have been a horrid sound, filled with death and memories of death.

The jet touched down.

Kintang watched David Wellington fidget through the final ten minutes. Kintang's anger was fading, superseded by pure professionalism. He was measuring Wellington for weaknesses that would make his job easier.

Wellington could not sit still, checked his watch constantly. Kintang smiled: he recognized the symptoms. Emotional involvement made it easier for him. When the time came, David would doubtless be more concerned with protecting Lisa than himself. And in that concern Neil Kintang would find his window of opportunity, and kill David Wellington while Lisa Han watched.

Unless, of course, Sun Chen's obsession ruins everything.

Kintang pushed the thought away, and with it the temptation to do the job quickly, perhaps even here at SFX, before Sun Chen indulged in his folly. Once Lisa and David were dead, Sun Chen would come to see the absurdity of it.

Kintang could wait.

David stood up and moved close to the gate as Lisa's plane taxied to the terminal. He felt a little foolish, *like a schoolkid,* he thought, *seeing his girl for the first time in weeks.* And he felt a certain adrenal exultance. Things were starting to move: everything was coming together. Important business remained to be done with the People's Republic, and David could not allow himself a moment to forget that there were deadly serious matters evolving around them, beyond their control. *But together we are up to whatever comes our way,* he thought.

Passengers began to emerge from the umbilical cord that connected the aircraft to the terminal. David scanned the faces, searching for Lisa's. The flight had been booked to near capacity; he could not see her.

And then he did and it was as if for the first time.

Lisa was radiant. Her black hair gleamed; she wore it pulled back, a clip holding it at the nape of her neck. Arching eyebrows and high cheekbones framed eyes that, as she came closer to him, struck David as even more beautiful than he recalled. David noticed the tension that drew Lisa's face tight, and resolved that this afternoon and evening at least, he would show her some distraction. Lisa had not seen him yet and David held back, wanting to surprise her, to watch her in secret for a minute more. She was wearing white silk, a severely cut Chanel suit over an open-necked blouse, a cluster of pearls riding at her throat. Lisa carried no luggage other than an oversized shoulder-bag on a long thin strap. She walked quickly. David stepped into her field of vision.

Did she brighten when she saw him? David could not tell—whatever momentary animation flashed over her features was gone before it could be recorded. "Hello, David," she said evenly, extending a hand for him to shake.

David caught Lisa's hand firmly in his own, locked eyes with her, pulled her to him before she could resist, lowered his mouth hard against Lisa's lips, his free hand going behind the small of her back, pulling her into him. Lisa's muscles tensed as she flinched and tried to break free, but David was stronger. Then her mouth flowered open beneath his and he felt the pressure of her fingers against his neck. She stroked his cheek as the kiss broke.

"Hello, Lisa."

Before she could answer him, a stranger stepped close. He spoke to Lisa with a slight French accent. "Enjoy your business here," he said. "It is a good city for it." Smiling broadly, he stepped away from David and Lisa and vanished into the crowd.

"Who—" David began, but Lisa was suddenly laughing too hard to answer him. Unexpectedly, tears sparkled in her eyes. David cupped her face and brushed the tears away with his thumbs. "Who was that?"

Lisa shook her head and shrugged. "A nice man who flew next to me," she said, and looked thoughtful. "I don't even know his name." She pressed her lips together in what might have been a frown. Lisa looked up at David and touched his face once more. Her fingertips were cool. "What a wonderful welcome," she said, "but we are blocking the flow of traffic."

Disembarking passengers moved around the couple, more than a few of them glancing at David and Lisa with bashful, happy smiles. "Come on," David said. "Let's get your luggage." They walked slowly side by side, David's fingers closed around hers. Free from the crowds of passengers, David tugged Lisa into the shelter of a small alcove. He bent to kiss her again, but Lisa stopped him to stare at the discolored weal beneath his eye. "David, you said it wasn't bad—"

"It's nothing," he said, and winked. "You should see the other guy."

Lisa's eyes flashed angrily at David. "You lied to me."

"Your guard was already up," David replied. "I didn't want you worried."

Lisa closed her eyes tight. The muscles at the corners of her mouth quivered. David stroked her cheek and she recoiled as though struck. "Don't!"

"Lisa—"

Her eyes were open now, and they were filled with pain. "We don't have time for that, David."

"Don't tell me you didn't feel it," David said.

"You make too much of it," Lisa cautioned.

"After that kiss I would say that I can make of it what I will." David moved his hands to her shoulders, holding her tight.

"You kissed me, David."

"It wasn't all one-sided."

Lisa was silent for a moment. "No," she said at last, "but it should have been."

"What do you mean?"

Lisa showed an almost wistful smile. "I mean that you're a wonderful man. Any woman would find you enormously appealing." She blushed a little. "But, David, it's a mistake." Her eyes showed David that she was serious.

David looked down: Lisa's hands were at his waist. "You're still holding me," he said.

Lisa smiled and David felt his heart skip. "You're

good to hold onto. I need that, now. But, David, no more than that. All right?"

"No," David said. "It's not. But I suppose it will have to be."

"It will," Lisa assured him. She took her hands from his waist, but leaned forward, pressing her face quickly against David's shoulder. "Thanks."

"Anytime," he said, and even managed a chuckle. They walked on without touching. "Why don't I get the car?" he suggested when they saw that the baggage conveyors were not yet running. Lisa nodded agreement.

David hurried through the parking lot to the Lagonda. He could still taste the full fever of desire that had surged from Lisa when he kissed her. But, as in Macau, she had withdrawn again. *She is hiding something,* he thought as he brought the Aston-Martin to life. *What are her secrets?*

San Francisco was never easy for Lisa—the city and the bay on whose shore it stood triggered too many memories. New factors made this drive even more difficult. Sharing the Lagonda with David was an agony, the interior of the sleek automobile pressing in on Lisa, reminding her of how close he sat. She tried to lose herself in the view of the many graceful hills and the architecture that adorned them, but it was no good. David guided the Aston-Martin effortlessly through the traffic, and he spoke only occasionally. When he did, Lisa made herself answer him, but her words sounded uncertain. Lisa's one attempt to talk business was a disaster; she completely lost her train of thought and compounded her embarrassment by rambling on aimlessly.

"You've had a long flight," David said sympathetically. "Business can wait, at least a little while. I've made dinner reservations at Alexis."

"Fine," said Lisa distractedly.

David seemed to understand her difficulty. He

placed a hand over hers and held it there. "Why not freshen up at the Huntington? We can talk over dinner."

Lisa nodded.

"You're sure you're up to tonight?" David asked as they walked into the Huntington's elegant, understated lobby. "Maybe you should sleep instead. We'll have an early breakfast and get down to it."

"No," said Lisa firmly. "We don't have the time. I'm fine." As she scrawled her name for the desk clerk, she wondered if she was telling David the truth. *Be honest with yourself—there is so very much at stake.*

When David offered to ride up to her suite with her, Lisa declined. "The bellman can handle the bags," she said, and made herself smile. "I'll meet you in the lobby at six-thirty."

David stared at Lisa for a moment long enough to worry her. Then: "Six-thirty, then." His words were clipped, and without a goodby he turned and left the lobby. Lisa rode to her suite in silence, tipped the bellman generously, and locked the door behind her. She drew the suite's thick curtains, sealing out San Francisco and all its memories.

Lisa busied herself for a few minutes putting her things away. Selecting a simple Emanuel Ungaro silk dress for the evening, she laid it out neatly on the bed. That done, she stripped off the suit that she'd worn during her long flight from Hong Kong. In the bathroom, she pinned her dark hair high on her head, and adjusted the temperature and spray of the shower.

Lisa took steam deep into her lungs, absorbing the heat, feeling her own temperature rise. She did not move for long, warming moments, making her mind a blank, her breathing a steady, meditative pattern. *Nothingness,* she thought, and then chased even that from her mind. Her consciousness shut down, her heartbeat slowed, her muscles gradually surrendered their tension.

An inner clock signaled her when it was time to emerge. Lisa brought into herself a deep, cleansing breath, then cast it out rapidly, eyes fluttering open and focusing. Lisa briskly scrubbed herself, then stepped from the shower. She rubbed herself dry with thick towels, then wrapped a fresh one around her trim body. Seated at the dressing table, Lisa took a moment to put in order the few cosmetics she would wear, then let down her lustrous hair. She held the carved ivory handle of her brush firmly, dragging it through her hair in long, even strokes, her scalp tingling from the touch of the stiff bristles. She tilted her head back, pulling the brush with more force through her hair.

Lisa grew more aware of her body. She was fully awake and alert, now. Her nipples brushed against the plush terrycloth towel. The mirror revealed the quickening pulse at her throat, the dilation of her pupils. Moving slightly on the cushioned bench, Lisa pressed her thighs together. She thought of David Wellington, of the way he had held her at the airport, of what it would feel like to have his hands touch her more intimately, those lips bring her more fully to arousal. Lisa's grip tightened around the handle of the brush, her breathing growing ragged.

She made herself begin to apply her makeup, and only slowly did the heightened awareness dwindle, then pass away. Done with the cosmetics, she tied her hair loosely at her neck, dropped the towel and walked over to the bed. For a moment she watched herself in the mirror, staring at her nude body as though it were a stranger's, at the firm breasts, rich swell of hips, dark tangle of hair between her thighs. She wished then that she could go to David, as she was and no more than that. She wanted to feel him on her, in her. *Body against body—if it were that simple I would have made love to him by now*.

For a moment longer she stared at the woman in the

mirror, then she turned to the bed and quickly pulled on silk underthings, donned the dress, stepped into her Bally pumps, and picked up the matching bag. It was nearly time to go down and meet David. Lisa drew a breath, ready now. Reflected in the mirror was a crisp, efficient businesswoman. The real Lisa Han.

15

"MONICA GAVE ME the idea, at least indirectly," David said over dinner at Alexis. "It's the sort of thing she's involved in at Ethan."

"It goes well for her, then?" Lisa asked.

David nodded. Lisa had seemed far away all evening, and he tried to reach her with his enthusiasm. "She's damned excited about it, and so am I. I wouldn't be at all surprised to see us make a real go of Ethan. The team there has got some innovative ideas, but so does Monica, and you know me."

Lisa nodded. David kept his eyes on her as she glanced around the restaurant at the almost overpowering Byzantine mosaics and Russian icons that helped create Alexis's illusion of Czarist magnificence. As though reminded that she was in a restaurant, Lisa at last cast her eyes down at her plate. She'd barely tasted the delicately grilled lamb chops and tender asparagus spears. She cut a bite now, but put down her fork.

David, on the other hand, worked his way heartily through every course, tossing off ideas and plans between bites. "From what you've said, Lisa, and what Marianne has reported, I have to think that both Zhu and Rhonda will buy my plan—each for their own reasons." He showed Lisa a grin. "At any rate, it's what we've got."

"Yes," Lisa said. "Marianne will be pleased. And I suspect Zhu will be satisfied."

The waiter removed their plates and brought coffee.

David sipped his, staring at Lisa. "We need to talk," he said.

"I thought we were."

"You keep drawing back," David said bluntly. "And I think I deserve to know why."

Lisa's smile was patient. "I think you deserve the very best brokerage of your deal with China that is available. I have provided that."

"I agree. But this has nothing to do with business and you know it."

Lisa held up a hand. "If it is not related to our business, David, then little purpose will be served by discussion."

David caught himself, signaled for the check, and did not speak to her as they left the restaurant.

For a while this evening Lisa had been able to forget the demons that pursued her. As in Macau—had it been only weeks before?—she found David Wellington to be stimulating company, but she'd been careful not to let him see that. How could she? She could see poor Lee's shredded features, and the bruises that lingered on David's face reminded Lisa of the danger she had placed him in.

Lisa was touched by David's efforts to engage her, but the dangers they faced had so very little to do with what they were trying to accomplish in China.

Lisa moved close to David as they stepped from Alexis as though next to him she thought she could find protection. But she could not, and realized it when a voice came unexpectedly from behind them:

"Lisa Han."

Lisa froze in place. After all the years she still knew that voice. David looked curiously at her, but Lisa could not meet his eyes.

"Lisa," Victor Sun Chen said.

David's fingers tightened around Lisa's hand, but only fleetingly. He released his grip and turned. "Sun Chen."

Lisa could not find her breath. Her stomach was tight, her heart beating fiercely, yet she slowly pivoted and made herself stand tall beside David Wellington, before Victor Sun Chen.

Others, who knew him less well, would have found Sun Chen trim, muscular, immaculate in a dark Saint Laurent suit. But Lisa saw deeper—the lines around his eyes, gray at his temples, a hollowness to his cheeks even as he dared to smile at her. *I will not be afraid,* she thought.

Sun Chen extended a hand to David Wellington, but David ignored the gesture. "What do you want?" David demanded. Lisa noticed that he had stepped forward as though to shield her from Sun Chen. She could not have that, and moved even with David once more.

"A word," the Taiwanese said softly. "Nothing more than that." He looked at Lisa. "For old time's sake?"

She drew herself up before him, and did not even have time to wonder where her courage came from. David started to speak, but Lisa cut him off. "Victor," she said coolly, "years ago I ran away from you, and I have never regretted that. Now I would only say, 'get out of my way.'" As she held her gaze steady against Sun Chen's his eyes widened, and she could see in them as well that he had aged.

Sun Chen's voice, though, held all of its old timbre when he spoke: "You forget. You ran only after I had banished you." He shrugged broadly. "And perhaps I was in error there, my little *whore.*"

David sprang toward Sun Chen before Lisa could stop him, his fingers clutching the Taiwanese's lapels, jerking him forward violently. David's right hand shot up at blinding speed to slap Sun Chen hard across the face. His hand was drawn back for another blow when from the shadows at the edge of the sidewalk there appeared a giant of a man who effortlessly lifted the American away from Sun Chen. As the giant bounced David against the wall of the building, Lisa heard the air go out of him, yet she stood transfixed, immobilized. Sun Chen's rescuer pounded a huge fist into David's stomach, then slammed another against his face. Lisa saw David's nose spurt blood.

"Neil!" Sun Chen barked. The giant stepped back and turned to face Sun Chen, his dark eyes sparkling with anger. "Enough, Neil," Sun Chen said more softly. "I am sure Mr. Wellington will cause us no more difficulty."

David leaned against the building, breathing raggedly. Lisa stepped to his side.

Sun Chen was talking, the huge man he had called Neil standing behind him. "I simply wanted to see you, Lisa. Sentimentality, I suppose."

"Bastard," she hissed.

"No more than you, my dear." Sun Chen took a step closer to them. He spoke to David. "I hope you are not too badly hurt, Mr. Wellington. My friend, you see, has something of a history of causing pain to Lisa's boys. Lee Richards, I believe his name was, Lisa?"

Then the two men left as silently as they had come.

Lisa shut out everything, hardly aware that David, groaning, had taken her by the arm and was guiding her swiftly past a small knot of onlookers. He all but pushed her into the passenger seat of the Lagonda and did not speak until he had brought the powerful Aston-Martin to life and steered it out into traffic. Lisa noticed the way David's eyes flicked to the side and rearview mirrors.

Then all of the fear that she had swallowed when Sun Chen faced them came back to her. For a moment she thought she would be sick. She bit that back, and caught and contained the fear as well. Emotion, as always, was her enemy. When she was certain she could speak calmly she said, "I am sorry, David, to have involved you in this."

David's hands were tight on the Lagonda's steering wheel, maneuvering the car gracefully through the winding streets that led to Russian Hill. "What is it you haven't told me?" he asked.

"Too much," she said.

"Don't evade me," David snapped. "What was that about back there? What is it Sun Chen has on you?"

"Old times," Lisa said. She did not want to weep in front of David. "Perhaps you should take me back to the Huntington."

"Like hell!" David's laughter was harsh and guttural. "I'll be damned if I'll take my eyes off of you now that I know Sun Chen's in town."

"David—"

"No arguments," he said. He steered the car into the compact parking area beside his home. "You're staying here tonight." Lisa started to object, but David would have none of it. "Don't insult me, Lisa. You know how many people he's killed. And I know that he's made a mistake now, gotten sloppy." He shut off the engine and turned to stare hard at Lisa. "But you've got to be completely honest with me. Let's go inside."

Lisa followed David wordlessly, convinced as they walked the short distance from the car to the front door that someone was watching them, waiting in the shadows, ready to spring. David ushered her into the house, stopping to exchange hushed words with the valet. Gregory nodded solemnly, and David returned to Lisa. He studied her for a moment.

"Gregory's going to seal everything up tight," he said. "He'll prepare the guest room for you." A smile crossed David's face. "I'm afraid we're a little short on women's sleepwear here. You'll have to make do with one of my flannel shirts."

Lisa nodded. "That will be fine."

David's smile vanished. "But we've got a lot of

talking to do before you retire." He gestured in the direction of the study.

Neil made no attempt to hide his anger as they rode back to the Mark Hopkins. "You've fucked the hit," he snapped. "You gave them my name! You know that, don't you?"

Sun Chen waved a hand. "I'm sure you'll find a way to redeem the situation, Neil."

"God damn you," Kintang said. "You've never interfered with my work before—"

"No?"

"Not like this. They'll have their guard so far up—"

"That only Neil Kintang himself could overcome it. Don't tell me you're afraid of a little challenge."

"Challenge? Jesus Christ! You've always talked of this as though it were some sort of game, but you've gone too far now." The limousine approached the hotel. "I ought to deal myself out, right now."

"Ah, but you won't, Neil. Will you?" Sun Chen smiled ferally. "Of course you won't. Because you know how easily I could replace you."

"Not with anybody who'd give you what I do."

"The *elegance* of your work? The *panache?* Please." Sun Chen leaned close, his breath hot against Kintang's face. "I've seen her. Now I want her dead. *Now.*"

Kintang said nothing for a moment. Then: "Three million. Flat fee, payable upon completion."

"Done," said Sun Chen without hesitation. "Now complete the bargain." He climbed from the limousine and walked quickly into the hotel. After a moment, Kintang got out of the Lincoln and hurried away from the Mark Hopkins on foot through the gathering fog.

Every instinct told him to back away from this one now. But even as his instinct spoke, Kintang knew that he could not listen. It was more than the money, although three million dollars would buy him retirement—at least from the services he rendered Victor Sun Chen. Already his mind was racing through setups and playouts.

Wellington's guard would be up, but he would not be expecting Kintang to move immediately. And that, he realized, was exactly what he must do.

They faced each other in the tastefully appointed study. David sat alone on the long navy Kittinger sofa, Lisa facing him from an elegantly overstuffed armchair. Before retiring, Gregory had poured each of them a Hennessy VSOP in a Baccarat snifter and he'd left the bottle on the low table beside the sofa. David waved his snifter beneath his nose, but did not take his eyes from Lisa Han.

"I've had enough of this," he said with no emotion in his voice. "My people have been killed, my factories destroyed, and it's been Sun Chen all along. I want to know what there is between the two of you."

Lisa sat perfectly erect, immobile for a moment. Then she raised her own snifter in what might have been a toast, but became a simple sip of the fine champagne cognac. She held the Hennessy in her mouth and drew air in sharply through her nose, filling her head with the cognac's exhilarating bouquet. Fortified, she fixed David with a solemn stare.

"To explain that," Lisa said finally, "I must tell you of myself. And that is a long story."

"I have time."

He did not move during her recitation, struck silent not only by the tale Lisa related, but also by the coolness and composure with which she told it. She showed no trace of emotion as she recounted her summer in Sun Chen's service. If there was pain in her recollection of her young love for Lee Richards, Lisa had it deep inside her. David could not help but be impressed with her display of discipline, but at the same time it frightened him. *There are gales inside her waiting to be freed,* he thought as she came to a close. *And when they are it will be one hell of a storm.*

Lisa stopped talking, and rose to refill her snifter. David stood and sought to step close, but she retreated from him, shaking her head. "What is it you want to offer?" she demanded almost harshly. "Comfort? Consolation for poor Lisa Han?"

"Nothing like that," David lied.

"Then what?"

David had nothing to say.

"I am Lisa Han. And now you know what that means, David. Why I draw back." She stood tall. "But I have learned to live with what I am, what *he* made me."

"And what is that?" David asked.

She stared at him for a long moment, then drank the last of her Hennessy in a single swallow. "A whore, David, as he called me," she said, her voice rough. "A *whore.*" She fled the room.

Lisa closed the guest-room door softly behind her, though her every impulse was to slam it. Her head spinning, she was dizzy with a tumult of emotions. Sun Chen here! His boldness astounded her, and she knew that it could mean only one thing. *This is what I have brought David—his death is what I have brokered.*

She was suddenly exhausted from the effort of holding her emotions in constant check. Lisa hung the Ungaro carefully in the handsome cedar wardrobe that faced the pencil-post bed. She stepped into the bathroom, nude, and washed her face, fearful of looking into the mirror, of the terror she might see reflected.

Folded neatly across the bright blue quilt was a kelly green flannel shirt, the improvised nightwear David had promised. The flannel was soft from wear, and Lisa pressed the fabric gently against her cheek before drawing the shirt on. She buttoned it slowly, enjoying the warming feel of the material upon her bare skin.

And then she could not help herself, but thought of what it would be like to curl in such a shirt against David Wellington, to snuggle and play, to *love*.

As with Lee?

Her emotions broke free. Lisa's control collapsed and she fell onto the wide bed, burying her face in the pillows as she wept.

David had another Hennessy after Lisa abandoned him, and decided against a third only after thoughtful consideration. Lisa's story haunted his thoughts, and he felt inside himself a fuller fury toward Sun Chen than ever before. He would kill the bastard with his own hands if he could.

David put down his empty snifter to stare at his broad hands. By God, he *would* use them, if only to shake some sense into Lisa. It was time—past time!— that she stopped being terrified of the Taiwanese. David took the stairs two at a time, heading for the guest room.

He paused at the door and heard Lisa weeping in the privacy of her room. David opened the door and stepped inside.

She lay on the bright quilt that covered the bed, her face hidden in the deep pillows. Muffled sobs filled the room. David padded slowly forward, reached out and gently placed a hand on Lisa's quivering shoulder. She jumped, startled at his touch, then raised her face from the pillows. Her perfect features were contorted by pain, tear tracks shone on her cheeks, her dark eyes were wet. David cupped her face in his strong hands and with his thumbs brushed the tears from her cheeks.

"Lisa," he said, "it's all right."

She shook her head. "No, it isn't, David. This has gone on too long, Sun Chen and me. It is a dance . . . a ghastly dance that brings pain and death to everyone near me." She placed her small hands on his thick wrists, squeezing gently.

"Not this time," David said firmly.

Her laughter was awful, a horrid sound. "No? He could have killed you tonight, David, and I could do nothing to stop him."

"I didn't die," David said.

She unexpectedly brushed his hands away. "Not yet—" she started to say.

But David had had enough. His hands moved to her shoulders and he shook her. "Goddammit, I've told you before," he said, "Sun Chen doesn't win this time. *No!*"

"David—"

His eyes were hot with anger and determination. "Haven't you listened to anything I've said? Hasn't any of it gotten through?" David sighed, searching for words. "Isn't it time you stopped letting him dominate your life?" A cruel expression crossed his face. "Lisa, isn't it time you paid him back?"

"The risk—"

"Risk?" David snorted with laughter. "What we're putting together in China is a *risk,* Lisa. Risk—real risk—has to be important. And Sun Chen isn't. No, don't argue with me! Listen, Lisa. He's dangerous, sure, but dangerous the way a poison snake or a rabid dog is dangerous. Vermin. That's what he is." David made his voice more gentle as he moved to sit beside Lisa on the bed. "And back home, we learn early what you do with a mad dog, with a snake."

Lisa's voice was small. "What?"

"Why, Lisa, you put them out of our misery," he said simply. "You deal with them. And it's time for you to deal with this."

He could tell what an effort it was for Lisa to speak. "And if I can't?" she asked.

David shook his head. "Then I was wrong about you." He reached out to stroke her cheek, and felt her press against his touch. "And I'm never wrong."

The dam that Lisa had erected against her emotions broke down completely, and she was in his arms then, weeping, letting it all flood out. Wrapping his arms around Lisa as she wept, David spoke soft soothing words into her ears. As his hands moved in gentle, ever-changing patterns across her back, up and over her shoulders, David could feel the tension being loosed from her, and he pressed his fingers against her spine, helping her work the knots of tension free. He lost track of time, holding her, helping her, comforting her until the tremors that shook her began to subside.

At last she looked up at him. Her lips were full and moist, but David caught himself before lowering his mouth to hers.

She sensed his hesitation, and smiled. "Make love to me."

David's mouth met Lisa's, opened against hers, their tongues engaging in a sudden fierce duel. He kissed her with mounting hunger, his hands now ceaseless as they stroked her back. She arched herself against him, her own hands busily unbuttoning David's shirt. He shrugged it from his shoulders, and shivered slightly as her fingernails raked his bare chest. The kiss broke and Lisa sat back, bracing herself with her hands on the quilt.

Slowly, teasingly, David unbuttoned the flannel shirt he had loaned her. He pushed the shirt open to reveal Lisa's body, catching his breath when he saw her. Lisa was perfectly formed, firm breasts riding proud over her taut, flat belly. David stroked her nipples, and felt them grow stiff against his fingers. His hands roved lower, to where Lisa's hips flared gracefully to flow into long legs. Her pubic hair made a dark nest between her thighs, and David placed his right hand there. He could feel her heat and when he stroked her she moaned softly.

Lisa unfastened David's pants. He stood and stepped out of them while Lisa turned down the quilt.

On the bed they kissed again, more deeply. Lisa wrapped her fingers around David's growing hardness and he felt himself swell against her touch, a groan of pleasure escaping.

David lowered his lips to Lisa's breasts, kissing her nipples, biting them gently as Lisa arched her back. She crooned his name as David flicked his tongue over the hard tips of her breasts, then licked their undersides. He traced his way lower with his tongue until he found the hot moist center of her. David lavished attention on Lisa's delicious warmth, ministering to her as her hips rose and fell, tidelike in ancient rhythms that were suddenly new. Lisa moaned and opened herself more fully to David.

At last David took his mouth from Lisa, and moved up to gaze into her dark eyes. Lisa placed her hands on David's face, drew him to her for a kiss. David moved between her long legs, drawing a breath as Lisa reached down to guide him into her. She rose up to welcome his entry, calling his name once more as she locked herself around him and they set a pace that joined them fully, completely.

David steadied himself with his hands on her hips, moving with her, feeling the flood of sensations that came near to overwhelming him. Lisa was hot and tight around him, clutching at him with inner muscles. Her hands cupped his buttocks as though to draw him more fully into her. He kissed her eyes, buried his face against the salty flesh of her neck, felt her heavy pulse with his lips.

Lisa grew more insistent, the roll of her hips against him becoming stronger and more demanding as she climbed toward release. David felt that release within her, struggling to break over her, but each time she came close, Lisa stiffened, drew back, containing her passion as though afraid of it.

David slowed himself, moved deep within her and held there. "Lisa," he whispered to her. "It's all right. Nothing can hurt you here."

"David—" she said, her voice thick with need.

David pulled back until nearly withdrawn from her, then lowered himself to fill her once more. "I love you, you know," he said softly.

She cried out and bucked her hips furiously against him, her heels beating against his legs, her fingernails digging deep into his back as wave after wave broke over her. David felt his own control waver, then give way as he flowed fully and forever into her.

16

THE MIST COULDN'T obscure the readings his snooper-scope took, but it sealed out everything else. Kintang was grateful for the fog, which wrapped itself around the homes of Russian Hill as it had wrapped itself around the whole city, sealing it in, insulating it. As he was insulated, he thought, from his better judgment, if nothing more. *Three million dollars buys a lot of insulation.*

The play of lights in the house told him that David and Lisa were in the guest room. He wondered if he would catch them *in flagrante. Wouldn't that be something to tell Sun Chen, wouldn't that pay my tab neatly.*

The guest-room lights had been out for half an hour.

Kintang switched off the scope and left it on the seat of his sedan. It was time.

Lisa looked down at David as he rose up within her and flooded her with his warmth. It was the second time they had made love, and the sensations were even more intense. She rode up and down on David as he pulsed inside her, emptying himself. She cried out once, and then again, before lowering herself to rest upon David's chest. Kissing the salty flesh of his neck, she shuddered when David's fingers traced their way up her spine. "Love," she said softly. In moments, she was asleep.

The thing of it was that the hit had been set up so beautifully. Long hours of unnoticed surveillance before Sun Chen arrived provided Kintang with a sense of the house's rhythms and dangers. The valet was the only other person in the house, but he was armed. An afternoon at the library over old *Architectural Digests* gave Kintang the floor plan and layout. A grand in the right place bought Kintang the props he used to get a closer look at Wellington's security system. Dressed unobtrusively as a power company employee, he'd been thoroughly ignored as he tapped the house's electric and phone lines. He worked at a juncture two houses down from Wellington's. It had all gone smoothly, and Kintang was never closer than a hundred feet to Wellington's house. No one even knew he was there.

The flip of a switch on a remote transmitter would cut the house off and silence its alarm system. Kintang would enter through the back, near the valet's quarters. *Deal with him and deal with them,* he told himself, *and out quickly.* He rested his finger on the switch.

The kitchen and its well-stocked refrigerator, Gregory Hartzel thought, stood high on the list of the job's real perks. It was just after two, and the house was quiet. Hungry, Gregory sat up and swung his legs from the bed, grinning slightly. Many times, David had joined him in the kitchen for a middle of the night snack, but Gregory did not expect to see his employer tonight. It had been clear from David's manner that Lisa Han was someone special, and that pleased Gregory. He was even more pleased that David was through with Hilary Bishop, who had never failed to treat Gregory with an infuriating, peremptory bitchiness. The Oriental woman was quite different.

He walked quietly through the dark hallway connecting his room with the kitchen. He could find his way blindfolded, and nearly always made the trip without turning on the lights. Safe passage earned the tasty rewards revealed by the refrigerator's bulb. There was a platter of spiced shrimp on Gregory's mind, and an icy Anchor Steam. He'd carry them back to his room, maybe check the late movies on TV.

Gregory swung open the refrigerator, but there was no light at all. At a hint of movement he dropped fast into an instinctive defensive crouch, but he was no match for the thick arm that locked itself immovably around his neck. Gregory's pistol was in his room, and he realized he would never again have the chance to make such a mistake. He reached, clawing, to dislodge his attacker, but it was like trying to move an oak tree.

The arm tightened suddenly and even as he died, Gregory Hartzel kicked out furiously, overturning the breakfast cart he'd set up just before retiring. The cart flipped with a crash of breaking glass and skittering silverware. Enough noise, Gregory hoped desperately, to warn David and give him at least a fighting chance.

David lay on the edge of delicious sleep when the clatter came from downstairs. Instantly alert, David reached over to switch on the lamp beside the bed. Nothing. He held his breath, listening. The house was too quiet; Gregory couldn't have slept through such a racket. David pushed back the covers. He silently palmed open a drawer in the bedside table and withdrew the snubnosed Taurus Model 85 that rested there.

Lisa came awake. "What—"

"Quiet." He drew on a pair of slacks, eased his feet into his shoes. He handed Lisa a small flashlight, but told her not to switch it on. "Get dressed and keep down." He stroked her cheek gently and left the bed.

Lisa moved swiftly to follow his instructions. *Good girl,* David thought as he padded to the bedroom door. He caught himself as he reached for the doorknob. If there was someone in the house, if Gregory was not a factor, position was going to count for everything. David backed slowly away from the door.

Lisa was dressed, and he led her through the bathroom and into the adjoining dressing room. A door led to the hallway at the head of the back stairs, and David stood before it for a long moment. Still no sound. *Where is Gregory?* David tightened his hand around the grip, and eased open the door.

Kintang left Gregory on the kitchen floor, racing for the stairs as quickly as he could without being heard. He felt as though a chill sweat had broken out over him, and he wiped his palm against his flank before drawing the silenced Smith & Wesson he'd carried as backup for his blade. It had not been Kintang's plan to use a pistol at all, but then it had not been his plan to confront David and Lisa. This one was suddenly, royally fucked. He stopped one step below the top and caught his breath before moving to the landing, easing toward the door to the guest room.

He nearly made it.

David did not breathe as he stepped into the hall, holding the pistol before him. Squinting, he saw Kintang bend at the other door. "Right there," David said. "You're covered." Expecting the intruder to pivot on him, David's finger tightened on the trigger.

But Kintang froze in place and for a moment no one moved.

"Enough." David Wellington said. "Put the pistol down or you're dead."

Kintang looked at Wellington's shadowy form, knowing from his voice that Wellington would shoot. As Kintang lowered the pistol to the parquet floor he flexed his left forearm and felt the Gerber throwing knife fall into his fingers. "The gun's down," he said.

"Stand up. Slowly."

Kintang came erect, easing the knife into position.

"All right, Lisa," Wellington said. Kintang tautened his wrist for the flip and was launching the knife when Lisa Han stepped from the dressing room, switched on a flashlight and shone it directly into his eyes.

The knife flew toward David Wellington, but he had already moved.

Something red-hot seared David's side, and the air emptied out of his lungs in an explosive grunt. The blade had bitten shallowly, grating off a rib even as David squeezed off two shots. He was certain he'd hit Kintang at least once, but the giant charged, roaring. David didn't have time for a third shot, and had barely braced himself before being hit with what felt like the force of a fast-moving truck. The Taurus spun from his hands. David made himself limp, flowing with the attack, letting the momentum lift him up.

Kintang's rush carried them down the hall and over the lip of the stairs. David tucked his head as they tumbled. They fell over each other, David writhing frantically to ensure that he remained on top. He was fighting before they came to rest at the foot of the stairs, trying to force his thumbs into Kintang's eyes. Kintang brought his fists up and effortlessly broke David's hold, pounding huge fists into his face. David kicked down hard and heard the crunch of cartilage as Kintang's knee shattered. The big man barely groaned, but began levering himself off the floor. David knew that if he allowed himself to become pinned, he was gone. At the last moment, he rolled away from Kintang, crashing into one of the low settees at the base of the stairs.

Kintang was fast, scuttling toward David, heedless of his ruined knee. David backed away, furiously searching for weapons. His fingers tightened around the leg of a chair, and he sent it sliding toward Kintang, but Kintang was unstoppable.

A door to David's workshop was on the far side of

the living room, and David made for it. There were tools there, weapons.

If he was fast enough.

Grabbing Kintang's pistol, Lisa raced for the stairs. She heard furniture crashing below, and stopped in a crouch on the landing, playing the flashlight beam over the area. The light revealed David just as he stumbled backward through a doorway off the living room. Lisa saw Kintang lumbering after David, and she aimed, fired, and knew even before the recoil that she had missed. Kintang did not even look back.

The bitch has the pistol.

The thought barely registered. Lisa Han would have to wait. Wellington, too, unless he could nail him in the next moment. Kintang's left leg was nearly useless, and his ears still rang from the fall down the stairs. One of Wellington's shots had grazed Kintang's shoulder. If he could catch Wellington now, fine. Otherwise, Kintang was out of here and away before Wellington or the bitch made enough noise to wake the neighborhood. Kintang launched himself through the doorway after David.

Running his hands across the pegboard, David's fingers closed around the polished handle of a sharp wood chisel, and he lifted it from its hook, spinning as he heard Kintang career into the workshop. Like a remorseless, inexorable robot, Kintang came at him. David drew a painful breath and planted himself firmly, knowing he'd be lucky to get even a single chance.

Then Kintang was on him and David brought up the long chisel in a hard fluid stroke, every energy he owned behind the stabbing motion. The sharp point entered Kintang just behind his chin. He felt a single searing flash of pain and saw a final awful image of

Victor Sun Chen, the man who had killed him. Then the chisel passed through his palate and pierced his brain, shutting out that and all other images forever.

Kintang quivered once and fell to the floor, dead.

David saw Lisa standing over the man who had killed Lee Richards, who had done so much of Sun Chen's foul work, who had tried so hard to kill them. She looked at David and her heart beat more fiercely, but Lisa controlled her excitement. She had something to do.

She walked slowly to Kintang's slumped form and aimed the pistol carefully at his head. Before David could stop her she fired two shots into Kintang's sightless eyes.

17

DAVID STEPPED TO Lisa's side and took the Smith & Wesson from her. She released the gun and came into his arms. He held her, then slumped a little and let her support him as they walked from his workshop, grinding his teeth together against the pain that seemed to flow from every inch of his body. He forced himself to think clearly.

"There's a phone in the Lagonda." It hurt to talk. "I'll call for help."

"I'll go," Lisa said.

"Not a chance that I let go of you," David said, tightening his grip around her waist. He held his finger in position against the Smith & Wesson's trigger, praying that Kintang had worked alone.

David caught his breath sharply when they entered the kitchen, the narrow beam of the flashlight revealing the body of Gregory Hartzel. David knelt beside Gregory, but there was nothing he could do. David pressed his fingertips against Gregory's temple. "You saved our lives," he whispered. "I hope that you knew that." He gently closed Gregory's eyes, then made his way to his feet again.

In the Lagonda, half surprised that no one had emerged from the fog to finish Kintang's work, David punched Michael Stewart's number. Head of Wellington's San Francisco office, Stewart was a man David could count on. Stewart answered sleepily, but came to immediate attention when he heard the tone in David's voice.

"I'm going to need the police, but not yet," David told him. "Charter a jet that can get me to Beijing, fastest possible clearance. Pull any strings you have to."

"Right."

"Get some people from security to my house as quickly as you can." David gave Stewart a quick account of Kintang's attack. "Make sure they're armed, tell them to be damned careful. I'll meet you at the office."

"Anything else?"

"Yes," David said, giving Lisa's hand a squeeze, "the most important thing of all. I want to know where Victor Sun Chen is. Find out."

By dawn everything was coming together.

David sat still in his office as Hugh Webster stitched his knife wound. A respected Bay Area physician, Hugh had worked with Wellington Labs for years, and David knew that he could count on his discretion.

Hugh checked his sutures, then examined the traces of the knife wound David had taken on the streets of Washington. "Running with a rough crowd these days?" he asked in obvious disapproval. He'd given David a lecture on his responsibility to report any wounds, even as he was opening his bag and setting to work.

"Not by choice," David said through tightly drawn lips.

"No point, I guess, in me telling you you're lucky to be alive."

David thought of Gregory Hartzel, and of how small a part luck had played last night. "None at all."

Hugh Webster rustled in his bag and withdrew a hypodermic and a small vial.

"What's that?"

"A painkiller," the doctor said as he filled the hypo.

"Sorry, Hugh," David replied. "Can't use it."

"Don't try to tell me you're not in pain!"

"Truth is, Hugh, I hurt like hell."

"Then—"

David shook his head. "Can't fog up my thinking now." He felt almost giddy, and wondered if a light shock was settling over him. David fought it away.

"Same kind of work?" Hugh asked, his disapproval growing.

"Lot more fun," said David. He stood, somewhat shakily at first, then more steadily. "Thanks for coming tonight."

The physician stared at him for a moment, then put the hypodermic back in his bag. "How about your companion?"

There was no way David could stop the grin that spread achingly across his bruised face as he ushered Hugh toward the door. "She's just fine," he said. "You've got no idea."

David closed the door behind the doctor, and slumped against it for a moment. He rallied his strength, knowing that he and Lisa could sleep on the 707 chartered for noon departure. Candace Caillou had arranged flight clearance with the Chinese. The other elements of David's plan were already beginning to converge on the Mark Hopkins. All David needed to do was remain alert through the morning.

He pushed away from the door and walked to the dressing room and bath that adjoined his office. Lisa was stepping from the shower, and he felt a surge of hunger as he saw her nude form. Lisa recognized the look, and showed David an incredulous expression of her own.

"You're hurt," Lisa said. "You can't."

"Can't I?" David stepped close.

"No, David—"

But then she was holding out her arms to him, welcoming David into her warm embrace. His clothes fell away and they made love standing, gently because of David's wounds, but no less exultantly for that. All of the horrors of the previous night melted away as they flowed together. Lisa's teeth nipped at David's shoulder as he came deep inside her. He had never felt more fully alive, more certain of who he was and what he must do. He held Lisa close for a long while, then released her and set to work making himself ready for the morning. By the time they were dressed, the sun was fully up.

Sun Chen was finishing breakfast in his room when the knock came at the door. *Kintang,* he thought, and placed his fork on the linen-covered table. He had slept well the night before, and had not dreamed. It was as though seeing Lisa was the finish of all this— and Kintang's work just a detail. But Sun Chen had awakened early and begun to wonder where Kintang was.

A second knock.

"Come."

The door swung open and Lisa Han entered the room, followed by David Wellington. Sun Chen was speechless.

"Hello, Victor," Lisa said coldly.

Sun Chen coiled himself, as though to spring from his seat, but Wellington produced a silenced pistol from beneath his jacket. "Sorry, Sun Chen," he said in a voice that chilled the Chinese, "but you'll have to sit still."

"I won't—"

David Wellington's arm became straight, his eyes narrow. The pistol was pointed directly at Sun Chen's forehead. *"Still,* I told you!"

Sun Chen did not move a muscle.

"That's better." David relaxed a bit, although the pistol's aim did not waver. "Recognize this?" he asked. "It was Kintang's."

Sun Chen's spine was straight. "Neil is dead?"

"Yes," said Lisa.

"He killed another of my people, Sun Chen," David said, moving closer to the Taiwanese. "On your orders. How many is that?"

Lisa was beside David, her voice as filled with loathing as his. "*I* helped kill him, Victor, the way I would have helped Lee. But you gave Lee no chance, did you?"

Sun Chen placed his palms flat on the tablecloth. He faced them, his eyes wide, his expression implacable. "My error was giving you a chance, Lisa," he said, and nodded also to David. "I would say that I didn't know what came over me. But—" He presented them with a smile. "Seeing you now, that would be a lie."

Lisa spat on him.

"What are you saying?" she demanded. "That it was some kind of sick *love* that brought you here? That was why you wanted to see me again? You're wrong."

"Am I?" Sun Chen said. He exhaled slowly.

"Yes," said Lisa, reaching swiftly into her bag. She withdrew a small aerosol and discharged it inches from Sun Chen's face. In the same motion she covered her own face with a handkerchief and stepped back.

Sun Chen felt the spray strike his skin as he inhaled. He cut the breath short, but not in time. The mist was inside him and already he could feel something happening. He tried to speak, but the connections were severed and his body would not obey him.

David Wellington was studying his watch. After what seemed an eternity, the American nodded and lowered his handkerchief. "All done," he said, and put the pistol away. Lisa Han's eyes were cold, and remained riveted to Sun Chen.

"The pig should die," she said.

"He will," said David, "on our terms." He stepped to the door and signaled to three men in nondescript business suits who entered the suite. Sun Chen felt their hands on him as he was roughly lifted from his chair.

"I know you can hear me," David said sharply. "The spray cuts your motor functions but not your senses. You'll be all right in six hours or so." After a pause, the American added, "Or as all right as you'll ever be again."

The men lowered Sun Chen to the floor while David continued. "You'll be smuggled out of the hotel and taken to one of my facilities. No one will ever hear from you again, Victor. When you die—and you will, eventually—no one will know." David issued a short bark of laughter.

"You're going to die in a laboratory, Sun Chen. Under observation. Shall I tell you what Lisa and I are taking to the Chinese this afternoon? What this has all been about? It's called omnigene, and it can cure any disease you care to name."

Sun Chen could not close off his hearing, could not shut his eyes. David Wellington looked inhuman, as though possessed by some supernal righteous fury that would not be stopped.

"My people are going to see to it that you get some of those diseases, Victor. We're going to make you sick. We're going to grow tumors in you and then we're going to cure you with omnigene. Again and again. Eventually, of course, your body will give out. But not before you've contributed at least something worthwhile to the world you so badly served."

For a moment it looked as though David, too, would spit upon Sun Chen. But all the American said was, "Get this filth out of here."

One of the suited men opened a large trunk and Sun Chen was lowered into it. Lisa stepped forward before the lid was closed.

"All those years ago, Victor—I never said good-bye." She dropped to a knee beside the trunk. "No different, now," she said, smiling as she lowered the lid and sealed Victor Sun Chen into darkness.

The chartered 707 was equipped with every luxury, and David and Lisa slept in each other's arms most of the way to China. By the time a limousine deposited them before the CITIC building, they were refreshed.

Marianne Ingwer awaited them in CITIC's lobby, and David shook her hand warmly. "Got them all warmed up for us?" he asked with a grin made painful by his facial bruises.

"I think so," said Marianne. "Your scientists are in a conference room with Zhu, Xiang Peng too."

"Then let's get to it."

Candace Caillou met them as they emerged from the elevator. David watched as Lisa and Candace embraced, then accepted a hug of his own from Candace.

"You took good care of Lisa," Candace said to him. She studied his wounds. "Better care, I think, than of yourself."

David nodded. "I hope to take care of her for a very long time."

Lisa linked her arm through David's. "He is the one who needs caring for," she said. "But I think he's serious."

"He'd better be," Candace laughed, wagging a finger at David Wellington. Then her face clouded. "And Victor?"

"That's over," Lisa Han said with a profound finality.

David waited just a second, then straightened his Cerutti suit. "Let's do some business," he said.

In the conference room, David was introduced to Dhao Zhu. They looked deeply into each other's eyes, as though testing strength. Neither wavered. At last, Zhu turned and gestured David toward a seat. David took the time to speak brief greetings with his scientists, waving away their curiosity about his appearance.

"Am I about to be surprised?" Rhonda MacLaren whispered to David as they moved to their seats.

"Rhonda," David replied, "I think you're going to be shocked."

When everyone was seated, Lisa spoke. "Zhu and Peng have reviewed all the details with Marianne. The Chinese are eager to have Wellington Laboratories do business here, and introduce omnigene. But they feel that Wellington must give more incentive before the deal can be struck." She looked to Zhu. "Is that correct?"

Zhu spread his hands wide. "We wish simply to make the best bargain for our people that we can."

"That's an attitude I appreciate," said David, his voice rich and full, "and my father would have shared it. Isn't that right, Peng?"

"James Wellington was a businessman as well as a humanitarian," the elderly scientist agreed.

"He was a pretty modest man, too," David said, "but omnigene meant a lot to him, and I'd like him to have a memorial. Here, in China."

"What sort of memorial?" asked Zhu, leaning forward, his forearms resting on the surface of the conference table.

"A living one," said David Wellington. He stood up and looked at the gathered businessmen and scientists. "I've got two proposals.

"First: Wellington will guarantee lifetime employment to each Chinese hired."

"You offer that to all of your employees, worldwide," Zhu objected.

"True—but few of the other nations make us hire as many people as you're going to. Right?"

Zhu stared solemnly for a moment, then nodded and allowed an almost sheepish smile to break across his features. "And your second proposal?"

"Wellington Laboratories is ready to fund the establishment of a university for the study of advanced medicines. Right here in Beijing. Everything about it will be state-of-the-art. But the best thing about it will be the chancellor I propose."

"Who is?" Zhu asked.

"Rhonda MacLaren," David Wellington said, looking directly at her. "Under the conditions I'll insist upon in the charter, she will set the university's policy, hire the best people, order the newest equipment. The school will even provide paid leave to go to Stockholm when she wins the Nobel."

Rhonda's features relaxed into a warm smile, and she gave David a nod that said, "Well done."

David returned his attention to Zhu. "Two hundred full scholarships to promising Chinese students. A university that will in a generation be one of the world's great centers for biomedical research. The school where omnigene was discovered!" he announced with a smile. "Funded with *one half* of my profits from omnigene in China."

"In the entire Pacific region," Zhu said quickly.

"Done," said David without hesitation. He extended a hand.

Zhu was not yet ready to shake. "It would persuade those who object," he said, and Peng nodded from his nearby seat, grinning like a child. "You have no other conditions?" Zhu asked.

"Only one," said David. "It's to be called the James Wellington Institute of Research."

After a moment, Zhu shook his hand. "Welcome to China, David Wellington."

"Glad to be here," said David, glancing at Marianne. "Lisa has provided Marianne with a more detailed prospectus, which I'm certain all of you would like to go over." He bowed slightly at the group. "You'll forgive me, but I must ask to be excused. I'm exhausted."

"Of course," said Zhu. The others shook David's hand before he left the conference room with Lisa and

Candace. They barely spoke as the elevator descended.

"We have a suite reserved?" David asked Candace in the lobby.

"Yes. I'll have the car fetched." She walked purposefully toward the doors.

Lisa snuggled against David, paying no attention to the crowds of people swirling around them. "Exhausted?"

"I just hope the hotel has a good bed," David whispered close to her ear.

"But you slept fifteen hours on the plane!"

"I know," said David Wellington. He kissed Lisa deeply, then kept his arm around her as they left the building and emerged into a new world that was all theirs.